REPRESSION

REPRESSION

L.A. FIELDS

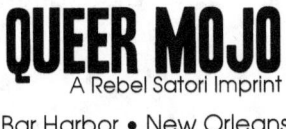
A Rebel Satori Imprint
Bar Harbor • New Orleans

Published in the United States of America by
REBEL SATORI PRESS
P.O. Box 363
Hulls Cove, ME 04644
www.rebelsatori.com

This is a work of fiction. Names, characters, places, and incidents are the product of the author's imagination and are used fictitiously and any resemblance to actual persons, living or dead, business establishments, events, or locales is entirely coincidental. The publisher does not have any control over and does not assume any responsibility for author or third-party websites or their content.

Book design by Sven Davisson

Library of Congress Cataloging-in-Publication Data

Fields, L. A.
  Repression / L. A. Fields.
    pages cm
  ISBN 978-1-60864-113-0 (pbk. : alk. paper) -- ISBN 978-1-60864-114-7 (ebook)
  1. Gay teenagers--Fiction. 2. Life change events--Fiction. 3. Drinking of alcoholic beverages--Fiction. 4. Florida--Fiction. I. Title.
  PS3606.I365R47 2015
  813'.6--dc23
                    2015016922

Alcohol is the anesthesia by which we endure the operation of life.

—*George Bernard Shaw*

Prologue: A Muttering Retreat

A delirious and academic mind was driving through a midnight Florida. Frank stopped before he actually crossed the state line, reluctant to just breeze past it as if this place had only been a vacation. When he retired to the Sunshine State he was so sure he'd have the privilege of dying there, warm no matter where he was, or what season, or what time of day, and soon after that: his ashes drifting gently, eternally in a tropical sea.

But it was not to be. It could have been worse—Frank wouldn't want to live out the rest of his life in a Florida *prison* after all, and certainly not for the so-called crime he'd committed. He's heard that prisoners don't take kindly to child molesters. But who's to say what molestation is anyway, and at what age a child? It all depends on the context, really. As with literature, so it was with life.

It had almost gotten too late to leave before someone called the cops, but it still felt too soon to say goodbye forever, and so Frank stopped. He bought himself a motel room for the night at a tacky little place in Jasper, Florida. It was so hideous, but Frank would miss the lurid painted stucco once he was gone; flamingo pink, Haitian yellow, and Caribbean-cruise-pamphlet blue. He would miss the casual use of stone embedded with fossilized coquina shells, and he would miss the terracotta roofs with their gap-tooth appearance from where the last hurricane snatched a few tiles away.

Frank unpacked only a few things for the night. He had another long twelve-hour day of driving ahead of him before he reached St. Louis, and he didn't plan to even undress for sleep. All he wanted out of his Volvo were a toothbrush, a heating pad for his back, and his prized bottle of Scotch. He had been saving it for a special occasion ever since it was given to him for his retirement, but he'd thought he had a lot longer to wait for the right moment.

As he poured out his fine liquor into a bathroom cup gone foggy with scratches, it occurred to him that he might have shared a drink with Marley. Sure the kid was way too young for the legal drinking age, but it might have been nice to give him a sip for his sweet sixteen. It could have been one more of the boy's firsts that Frank would have shared in.

Oh well, Frank thought. *At least I dared to eat a peach.*

He remembered the way Marley put it once (such a smart kid, and such a sponge for literature, the kind of bookworm Frank has always wanted to teach, but never managed to find in a classroom), he said it was all so Humbert Humbert, so von Aschenbach, so Oscar Wilde at Frank's house. Frank chuckled a little to think of it, or maybe because he was on his second helping of Scotch. Either way, Frank thought that it would be nice to leave his library to Marley someday. Probably he was the only person in the world who would treasure those books as much as Frank did.

Frank shook his glass and wished for ice, not just because of the sweltering night, but because of the music it would make, a nocturne in his nightcap. He couldn't say that he regretted nothing, but he could say that he would do it all over again if given the same choice. So what he had to leave town? So what his cranky old neighbors thought he was a pedophile? So what he was going to die where he was born, in some frigid hospital in Missouri? He ate a peach, he dared, he bent his damn coffee spoons, he was drinking too much, but what did it matter in the end? He was fifty-seven already with a bad heart. What harm could it all really do him *now*?

It was good to have known that boy, mentally, biblically, all of it. It was good to have known a smart, strange, eager kid like that, and it was pure in its way. Awkward, unpracticed sex with a scrawny virgin? Sure, it had its temporary appeal, same as it always did, but what held more of a thrill for Frank in the end? The salt and sweat of a handful of sex acts, or Marley's young hand wiping the dust of years off a library that had been put out to pasture? Wasn't it really the awakening of everything enduring in Frank's life, his love of books and teaching, that caused this last mistake to be so worth the making?

Frank taught that boy how to debate; Marley would never find himself out of depth in any English class. They were Socratic together, Classical. Marley had a natural talent for persuasion. After all, he managed to convince Frank to chuck away several decades of careful student-instructor boundaries with just a couple weeks of unabashed, childish flirting. Though of course retirement had blurred the lines a bit too, and Marley had never been *his* student, thank God.

Frank met the middle of his bottle before finally feeling loose enough for a stroll. He wanted to smell the mildew of an inexpertly kept pool one more time, and listen to the plastic rustle of the palm fronds. He should have been remembering all that he hated about Florida so it wouldn't be so hard to go. Why not think about the way rattan furniture irritated his skin? Why not think of fire ants? Why not think, *Well at least I'll never mop sweat from my bald spot again, good riddance!* But he couldn't bring himself to hate the place. It wasn't the worst bereavement of his life, but that was only because he had experienced it so late. Live long enough and lose everything, that's what his grandfather used to say. Frank was already two years older than Pops ever got, so he'd learned to endure loss a long time ago.

Frank passed out feeling as liquid as the humid air that night, and the next day he called his sister and told her not to expect him for another day or so. He wanted to have one last hurrah in the state he'd worked so hard for, polish off his bottle and set it adrift in the pool with a message inside that said, *Eat a peach, squeeze an orange, have some fruit.*

He didn't stay more than a week, but when he left, the sad little hacienda seemed sorry to see him go. Even the palm trees waved goodbye as if the wouldn't-quite-call-it-regret was mutual.

Part One: Reunion

Chapter One: The Unheard-of Work

Two years later, Marley Kurtz wakes with a stab of panic. It's the same feeling someone else might experience if they woke up from an unauthorized snooze to find out they are hideously late for work. Marley isn't late—he allows himself an ample two hours every morning to get ready for his job—but this happens every time his alarm goes off. The sudden, painful jolt, the realization that it is time to get up, get dressed, and go outside. Today is especially bad because he has a lot of responsibility today; a writer is coming into the bookstore for a signing, and Marley wants to get his autograph.

He rolls up into a sitting position around the uncomfortable constriction in his chest. On his left, his boyfriend blinks up at him in the light from the alarm clock. Marley thinks, not for the first time, that Jesse never truly sleeps, that he just lies down and closes his eyes and waits for the sun to come back on.

"Are you excited?" Jesse asks quietly, the husk in his voice the only real indication that he might have been resting.

"Sure, I guess you could call it that," Marley says back. *What is excitement if not a form of optimistic terror, right?*

Marley touches Jesse on the chest as he gets out of bed, unhappy to leave. It's not the warmth of the sheets (it's plenty warm in August in Florida anyway) and it isn't the companionship (though Jesse's pretty all right), it's just that it's always a struggle to leave the safety of their cozy little flophouse room to walk twenty minutes down the road for work. The way the semi-trucks suck at him as they barrel past, the way shady homeless people suddenly appear in the murky dawn like an image in a Magic Eye picture... Marley has yet to arrive at work without his blood pressure shaking his eyesight in time to every heavy, fearful thump of his heart. Most days Marley can keep that feeling at a manageable thunder, but today isn't the same routine. Today is going to be an ordeal.

Marley gets dressed in the dark. He doesn't have a creative wardrobe, and as long as he gets his shirt on right-side-out, it's all the same to him. He puts on an over-shirt despite the mud-slap of the muggy morning air. He huddles in the open flaps of the thin flannel all the way to the store, hunched and hiding in his long hair. He isn't comfortable until he finally gets inside, turns on the lights, and locks the door; when alone, he finally feels unobserved enough to pull back his hair and tie his shirtsleeves around his waist. It's okay to have his scarred arm out before the store opens. Marley doesn't mind the sight of his scars at all.

He has a little more setting up to do. Marley has already stacked the front shelf of the store with Gregory Haywood's most recent book, the one Haywood's coming in to promote. There's a cardboard cut-out with the author's photo and some critical acclaim that he has to drag out of the back and stock with books as well. Marley's read this new one—he's been reading Haywood's books since he was in middle school—but the latest book is not the one Marley is hoping to get autographed.

Haywood's first book, *Wish I Were At Home,* still remains Marley's favorite. It's this excellent sadsack novel set in rural Kansas, about some poor queer who falls in disastrous love with a vicious rodeo competitor. It's full of roughly spat out sex scenes and miserable prose, and in the end the cowboy breaks his neck while bull-riding, and the main character is left wondering whether he's better or worse off than before. Marley's read it over six times.

Haywood's other novels have been good too, but they're more adult, more polished, which Marley doesn't actually care for. The first book was about raw youth, raw hide, and raw hatred. It bothered him for days after reading it, made him feel guilty for the parts he liked, made him ache for all the unresolved characters in it. Interviews with Haywood reveal that he finds this juvenile effort embarrassing, but Marley loves that embarrassment, that inescapable sense of confession, as if Haywood couldn't help but tell the truth because he hadn't learned how to lie yet. That unwise sort of honesty is what endeared Marley to him in the first place.

The next novel was about a gay man and a lesbian who marry each other in a misguided attempt to have a 'real' family. They grit through fucking each other a couple of times and spend their son's life having discreet same-sex affairs and developing a mature, familial love for one another that lasts into old age. It's called *Never*, and went pretty heavy on the Peter Pan and Wendy imagery, but it's sort of sweet, in its own way.

From then on however the books get more educated and more boring. *Under the Topsoil* is about a professor going through a midlife crisis. He likes to garden and starts fucking his heterosexually married neighbor and nothing really comes of the plot but it's all very tastefully written. *Cheat and Charmor* is about a WWI soldier's unrequited love for his fellow fighter. It was way too historical for Marley, way too painstakingly researched and overworked, and of course 'unrequited' means that nobody even got laid. So not worth the effort. And the last one before this latest book, *Skyclad*, was even more disappointing. It was about a porn star with inner turmoil. Who cares? At least the soldiers spent their time pining over each other, but this character was too narcissistic for love or even infatuation.

Marley might have stopped reading stuff by Haywood if the next book hadn't sounded like a vast improvement: *Upbeat* was all about a singer/songwriter duo, childhood friends, who fall in love slowly, realistically. It's a three-book series, and today Haywood is here to promote the second installment, *Backbeat*.

Marley has his copy of *Backbeat* all ready, in case there's a rule about only signing the new book, but he's much more excited to get Haywood's signature on *Wish I Were At Home*. He's bouncing behind the counter with nervousness as his boss arrives for work and the first few customers wander in. He's got his shirt back on and is digging his fingernails into the fish-belly flesh of his wrist, trying to get himself under control.

When Haywood himself finally arrives at Purple Prose, it is clear that he has never been before. Marley can tell by the way he stares around at the wild décor: the whole place is done up to look like a fluffy-cloud sky, the shelves all color-coded to the rainbow. First timers always either gawk, giggle, or sneer. Haywood is gawking, which makes Marley like him even more. The gigglers are usually mocking the place, and the people who roll their eyes should think about going somewhere else if they're too cool for a little whimsy.

Marley must stay behind the counter, but there is a respectable crowd milling around and he joins them in polite applause when they spot the man. Haywood looks like the guy in his author photo's average-looking older brother; same hair, eyes, and smile, but not as glossy or confident, and not quite so young. Marley checks the book blurb to see when Haywood graduated from college, and then does some math to guess he's about 38 or 39. Not bad.

"Wow, I guess he's a big deal," says a sarcastic voice from over Marley's shoulder. Tristan works here part-time when his foster mother can use the help. Rita owns the place and set this whole deal up, and sometimes she demands gently that Tristan do some honest work for the family's alternative bookstore. But even without requests from Rita, Tristan mostly bums around in the store trying to make the older guys uncomfortable, like, antagonizing them with his youth. He says it's funny to watch them sweat. Marley doesn't think it's very nice, and often reminds Tristan that he'll be old too someday, if he's lucky. These days Tristan just laughs at Marley too.

"Well, when you write your seventh book, maybe you'll draw a bigger crowd," Marley says touchily. He's still a little star-struck by Haywood, even if the guy is just regular like everyone else. Some of the lines in his books are just so striking, so beautiful. Haywood has a special penchant for making the closing line of every book the prettiest thing you ever saw. It's a trick to keep readers in it until the very end and coming back for more, probably. It totally works on Marley.

Tristan snorts and punches Marley in the arm just a tad harder than he should. Marley ignores him; if Tristan thinks a little pain will bother him after all that Marley has done to himself, the boy is severely mistaken. Marley simply turns his attention to Haywood, to listen to whatever intro he has to say for himself.

"Thanks to everyone for coming out," Haywood says in a blustery joker's voice, probably because he's nervous. He's already got sweat stains growing on his shirt, even though it's icy cold in the store to counteract the wet summer weather that's dragging its ass up and down Florida's gulf coast.

"I, uh," Haywood goes on. "I had high hopes for this series, and I'm quite pleased with how it's turning out, and with the attention it's getting." He looks out over the store, over his modest crowd. He's behind a table on the right hand wall of the store, placed there so the line forming for his signature can easily morph into the line for the register. At the end of scanning the room, Haywood pauses on Marley, probably because he's so far away from the rest of the group. But then it's like he forgets what he's talking about for a second.

He stares at Marley.

Everyone else stares at Marley.

Marley blushes and starts restacking some books for no damn reason at all. He hears Haywood start back up again, thanking his agent and his friends and his mom and basically everyone except Jesus. Marley can't really hear what Haywood's saying until he feels every last pair of eyes leave his face. It's like panic deafness, like the blood from his ferocious blush has filled his ears and muffled the world outside.

God, crap, I must look like an idiot today, Marley thinks. He's wearing his long sleeves with his long hair and he must look like some kind of weird, stupid kid. It sucks when people notice him like this, but whatever, *whatever*, Marley insists to himself. Life goes on, unfortunately.

Haywood starts signing books, and Marley starts ringing people up without looking at them. He wanted to get his book signed, but now he's too chicken-shit to leave his post and walk over there. He has already resigned himself to going home and replacing the book on his shelf unchanged, but when the crowd finally disperses, Marley is confronted by the author himself. Greg Haywood is standing at the end of his own crowd, in line with nothing but a wide, Professor Lockhart sort of smile.

"Hey," he says, sounding quite a bit less nervous than when he first walked in.

"Oh, hi," Marley says. He lifts up his hands and hesitates, then dives for the book he's been keeping under the counter. It's actually more worn than it would have been if Marley had owned it the whole time, but he got it out of the used section here. Not that Marley minds a book with some damage; it gives the thing character. But his own books, the ones he buys new, never look like this one. He is too careful with them.

"Would you sign this, maybe?" Marley asks Haywood. "It's my favorite. I've read all of your books." Marley can't help thinking, *I'm your number one fan!* He's read too many books.

Haywood makes a noise when he sees it like someone coming across a fugly yearbook photo of themselves, sort of embarrassed and nostalgic at the same time. Haywood picks it up and flips through a couple of pages, shaking his head fondly.

Haywood holds out his hand. "Give me a pen," he says with a smiling sigh.

Marley pulls one out of his own pocket, a pen he keeps in case he thinks of something pressing, so he can write it on his hand instead of driving himself crazy thinking he'll forget it all day. It's warm from sitting so close to his body heat. Marley hopes Haywood doesn't mind.

Haywood asks, "Who should I make it out to?" And Marley tells him, "Marley with an L-E-Y." And Haywood hands back both the book and the pen and says, "I'm Greg."

"Yeah, of course," Marley tells him. Greg smiles in a faux-modest kind of way as Marley opens the cover and finds that it's signed, *To the cutest boy in the room*, which flatters him even though he neglects to look around the room first. He looks up and Haywood is the only person he can see. The man keeps smiling at him, almost like he's licking his chops. He leans over the counter.

"I only meant that *you* can call me Greg," he clarifies. "Would you like to go out to dinner some time?"

Marley chews his lip for a second, wondering whose life he is in now. "Um, like on a date?" Greg nods, his eyes steady, watching Marley. "Oh. I've never been on a date before..." Marley says kind of wistfully before remembering why he won't be going on one now either. "Oh, I mean that I have a boyfriend."

Greg grins. "How'd you get a boyfriend if you've never been on a date?"

"How do you think?" Marley asks back, blushing again and looking down at the counter. Greg guffaws at him good-naturedly.

"Wow, he's funny too," Greg stage-whispers to himself. "How about I take you out to dinner just to get to know you? Not a date, I swear; not-allowed-in-the-scout's honor."

Marley laughs, even though the joke is awkward.

"Well..." Marley says. He looks around like maybe someone will tell him the proper response, but all he sees is Tristan across the room, watching him skeptically, one eyebrow up, leaning a chair against the books that Marley painstakingly straightens every day. Tristan has gotten to be such a judgey, hateful dick ever since he and Marley's sister glued themselves together; they act like royalty, walking among the common folks of a foreign country, aghast that these low people have no appreciation for how grand they are, but feeling all the more superior because everyone else is so ignorant. Tristan's stupid face makes Marley accept this offer for not-a-date. Can't he have fun too? Can't he be normal?

Tristan sat his ass in the reading section at the back of the store, totally uninterested in whatever poser show-boating this writer prick was doing. Tristan read one of the guy's books, the first in this trilogy, and thought it was okay. Could have used more sex, but otherwise who cares? It certainly wasn't a big enough deal to come out for the sequel though, which is why only about seven of this guy's friends showed up, and everyone else in the store is left confused and inconvenienced.

Oh well. Tristan has gotten rather critical of everyone else lately. It happened when he and Marley's sister Lindsay got close last year, they just started feeding each other's prejudices; their deepest suspicions about everyone else's failings were confirmed by one another's perfection.

Lindsay is far superior to her brother. Tristan was once friendly with Marley, back when his self-esteem was in the toilet too, and he even thought he had a crush on Marley at first (so pathetic). But between the way Marley likes to treat his sister and the way he treats himself? Dude... fuck him. Tristan can do so much better.

And here's this situation now, with the writer man going up to Marley, a chicken hawk picking off the weakest thing in the room. Tristan pulls some of the artful holes in his pants a little wider and watches the silent tragedy in front of him: Writer Man sort of slithering up, Marley getting flustered. Writer Man getting his own book handed to him and pretending to be shocked and humbled, Marley nearly peeing himself over the attention. Writer Man chats him up for a while, and Marley looks around to see if anyone's watching this clown parade. Tristan can't even hide his contempt at a distance. Marley gets a defiant booboo lip and Tristan leaves to puke.

It's time to place a call to Lindsay. They got cell phones through Rita (who was tired of her landline bills) and can call each other constantly now without fee or fear of consequence. Rita told them when she handed over the phones that they'd get sick of each other at this rate; they drive to school together, spend all day meeting in the hallways (Lindsay just started her sophomore year, Tristan is newly a junior), they have the same lunch period, and then drive home again. Then they usually choose Tristan and Rita's place to hang out in, rather than the Kurtz hen house. With the divorce finally complete between her parents, and Marley on his so-called own, Lindsay is in a house with just her mother and little sister, and it can get awfully catty. Little Rebecca's getting big enough to talk back these days, and the former Mrs. Kurtz is overzealous in her new role as primary caregiver. It's killing Lindsay's beautiful soul.

"Hey, Butch," Tristan says when she picks up.

"Hey, Sundance," Lindsay says back. They can get totally creative with the phone greetings. Tweedle-Dee and Tweedle-Dum. Bonnie and Clyde. Cagney and Lacey. It turns into a challenge sometimes for whoever picks up to name the counterpart. Lindsay once tripped him up with Chip and Dale. He got her last week with Leopold and Loeb, but it's not really a competition. They just love each other like that.

"Your brother's over here making a high-flung fool of himself, flirting with one of the old guys." Lindsay knows all about the old guys; Tristan has taught her to mess with the straight ones, pull some Lolita shit in the grocery store and just drive everyone to distraction. They both think it's hilarious. Lindsay gets free stuff from them all the time, exploiting what might otherwise make her uncomfortable.

"He's flirting with him for real?" she asks. "What about Jesse?"

"Marley may not realize what he's doing, he's so dense," Tristan says. "It's gross, I couldn't even look at it anymore."

"No, you shouldn't have to," Lindsay coos soothingly at him. "You should come see me instead."

"I'm already on my way," Tristan tells her, and it's true. He walked out of the store and has been strolling to her house all the while. They keep yapping on the phone until they're standing right in front of each other, then they just hang up and keep talking without a single pause.

They pass her mother on the couch en route to Lindsay's room. She still gives them a sour look, just because she can't get past a boy being in her daughter's room—with the door shut no less! But she'd probably give the same look to Jesus Christ, so it's not like it's personal, it's just a Penis Thing.

Lindsay still lives in Marley's old room, but since she too has lost her affection for him, she's finally obliterated every trace of him and made this place her own. Her clothes are decorating everything in an intricate spectrum from clean to dirty. She has a big piece of some kind of butcher paper on the wall where she blots her lipstick, and it looks like Oscar Wilde's grave now, covered in kisses.

"So Marley's sniffing around the old folks' home again?" she asks, sitting down at her vanity table.

"Who cares?" Tristan says as he flops down on her bed. "He's gonna be such a train wreck all his life."

"Totally," Lindsay agrees. She looks like she is about to dish something really delightful when her phone twitches towards her. She checks the screen to see who is calling her and makes a mysterious face. Tristan can't tell if it's a smirk or a grimace.

"Who is that?" Tristan asks, wondering who else would know Lindsay's number and what the hell they want.

"It's just um... this guy from my math class. We're supposed to be study partners. The teacher made us exchange info."

"So what is that text, a math problem?" Tristan leans over to try and see.

Lindsay hands him the phone. "I think he likes me," she says.

The text says: *hope its ok i think ur cute.*

"Well, fuck, how can you tell? He's so subtle and everything."

"I know, right?" Lindsay says. She twists a bit of her hair around, getting her words in order to tell Tristan something. He knows the move, and he waits patiently. It's actually something her brother does too, since he has long greasy hippie hair. Lindsay's hair is a mature brown with golden subtleties in it. Tristan helped her dye it back from a blonde phase she went through, before she knew him. It looks like a beautiful dessert sunset now, lighter at the bottom and growing deeper in color towards the top.

"I'm thinking maybe I'll look into this guy, see if he's okay," Lindsay tells him. "I'll need you to help me vet him, of course."

"Of course," Tristan says. He thinks he must sound sad or something, because Lindsay picks up his hand with the phone in it and looks him right in the eye.

"I still remember our pact," she tells him. And naturally he does too. It's like the rock of his whole life.

When they met a yearish ago, they both felt so abandoned. Tristan's father had just died, leaving him an orphan, and Lindsay's family was falling apart like a November jack-o-lantern. They couldn't count on anyone they knew; everyone was either insincere or else incapable of keeping their promises. Lindsay and Tristan, they weren't hiding anything that first night at Rita's, they couldn't possibly. And they promised each other that, since they couldn't rely on anyone else, they'd trust each other one hundred percent. None of this high school crap where people are friends one day and enemies the next. No losing touch over the summer. No blowing off one another for some starter boyfriend. They made a promise and they were serious about it.

Tristan clasps her hand and deposits the phone in her palm. He knows he can count on her.

He doesn't like the idea of this dweeb sniffing around Lindsay though. She's solid, sure, but who knows how long this child could bother them? She probably wouldn't put up with someone so lame, but how long will Tristan have to tolerate a third wheel before she figures out this kid isn't worth her time? Why not just assume he's nothing and get on with their business?

But Lindsay deserves a little play. For the past year, her whole freshman year in high school, everyone assumed that she and Tristan were dating, and nevermind that everyone also knew he was gay (and harassed him for it). However at this point Tristan's had enough of guys, all of them, from his time in the boys' home and beyond. But Lindsay, she's optimistic, and she's still new. She's thinking she might like a boyfriend, since it's only the men in her family who have let her down so far, but not everyone will value her like Tristan does. Probably no one could even get close.

"What are you texting back?" he asks her. That's supportive, right? Anything for her.

"I'm gonna say, *Of course it's okay*, but with proper grammar."

Tristan grins, and Lindsay smirks as she types, then tosses her phone aside like it's unimportant. Tristan wins again.

They spend the rest of the afternoon ignoring the buzzing phone, talking shit about the people at school, especially the new crop of freshmen. Those kids seem to be pretty evenly split between terrified mice and arrogant dicks. This boy who's chatting up Lindsay, he is probably one of the mousy ones. This cutesy bullshit, sending her flirty messages... Tristan already hates him. He's kind of concerned that Lindsay doesn't have the same reaction.

But he doesn't bring it up again. He gets kicked out at dinner time (the houses used to host each other's kid, but after a year they just shoo everyone home already) and walks back to Rita's. She doesn't even wonder where he's been, just asks how Lindsay's doing.

"She's fine," Tristan says, picking up a lid on the stove to find chili, which is totally acceptable.

Rita's sneakers squeak across the kitchen's linoleum as she sets the table. Tristan turns from the stove to watch her retie her ponytail; wisps of hair had come loose in the heat from the stove and stuck themselves to her round, rosy face. Tristan watches the way she fixes her hair and considers that Rita used to be a teenage girl. He figures he could maybe ask her about this... thing.

"Lindsay's got some kid in her math class hitting on her," Tristan tells Rita, not liking to say it. The words force their way out of Tristan's mouth like a barf.

"Oh?" Rita asks casually.

"It's just, you know, dumb, isn't it? I mean like what's the point of trying to date when everyone's just in high school and it's not even going to last."

"I think it's healthy to date a little in high school. It's good practice, lets you learn how to socialize with the opposite sex. Or the same sex," she concedes to Tristan. "Romantically. It's good to learn how to talk to people."

"Whatever," Tristan grumbles. "She's too good for him."

Rita snorts. "Well maybe you should ask her out then, if you think you know so much about her. Dinner's in five minutes, go wash your hands please."

Tristan frowns his way to the bathroom. Maybe that's it—he's a little possessive. Not really jealous in the way an ex-boyfriend would be jealous, but maybe the way a brother would feel if his baby sis started dating. Not Lindsay's shitty, self-centered brother perhaps, but a real one, one who knew the meaning of the word.

Tristan thinks about maybe calling her again, but it's like suddenly he can't trust his motives. He decides to just leave her alone, something he's never felt he had to do before. Is this how it would feel all the time if she got a boyfriend? Could he stand it?

He thought he'd told Lindsay enough cautionary tales about the guys he'd been with to convince her of the non-viability of dating. She's never dated anyone; she doesn't know what she's getting herself mucked up with.

"You've never dated anyone either though," Tristan tells the bathroom mirror, out loud, like he just couldn't keep the cap on it any longer. And he's right; he never dated any of the guys he fucked around with. But what's the difference?

It's bothering him all through dinner, and Rita can tell. Divorced and self-employed at the book store, she has nothing but time to devote to her foster son. She's even working on trying to adopt him. She thinks it'll be a surprise, but Tristan can tell by the way she hides papers when he walks into the room, and the way she looks at him like she's already calling him 'son' in her head. It's sweet, but Tristan doesn't want to get too caught up in it. Not until it's official, at least.

"You're disturbed by her talking to other boys, aren't you?" Rita asks.

"Yes." *Disturbed* is definitely the right word. It's very unsettling.

"It'll be all right, Tristan. You can't be everything to her," Rita says, apparently not aware that this is precisely what he's afraid of.

Listening to Greg's story is starting to make Mitch's skin crawl.

They used to be such tight friends, back in college, wondering what kind of coincidence put the only two queers on the floor in the same room. But the older he gets and the more attention his writing garners him, Greg is becoming an insufferable, entitled prick. And he's putting on this creepy lecher routine that Mitch has never seen before. Why would someone force such an unattractive image? It's like he thinks he can't be a writer and a decent, regular person at the same time. It just wouldn't be glamorous enough.

"Ooh, you should have seen this kid, Mitchell. Somebody's unattended son, yum!" Mitch tries not to roll his eyes, catches his own reflection in Greg's TV, and tries to distract himself by thinking about a haircut. Maybe it's time for him to grow up too; he's had this long hair and Vandyke forever. He's almost forty now, and it may be time to just give it up already.

"Here, Mitch," Greg says, all chatty like they're gabbing over coffee. Where did that tone come from? It's so artificial, and it's so far from the way they originally bonded, by being awkward together. "Look, I snapped of picture of him with my phone."

"Smooth," Mitch mumbles. He looks at the picture, clearly a candid shot, taken from some shadowy corner probably, while this boy stood behind a cash register. He's not like what Mitch was imagining, picturing one of those cocky young dudes, the kind you hated yourself for liking in high school. But this boy looks like a sweetheart—spindly and slight, long hair in his face but not cut in some slicing fuck-off stylish fashion, just lank around a private little smile.

"How old do you think he is?" Mitch asks.

"I don't know. He looks young though," Greg says proudly. He grins as he takes back his phone. "He says he's got a boyfriend," Greg goes on, making a jerk-off motion as if it couldn't possibly be a mature relationship, like he would know. Greg hasn't maintained anything serious longer than a few hectic weeks. Greg will make a lot of noise about his new man, and then when the guy disappears it's like it was all just a fling to him, another one in a long line that trails out behind his constructed world-weary persona. Mitch figures he's the closest friend Greg has, but even he doesn't know if this serial monogamy is anything more than a performance for Greg. Does he ever really mean it when he gets involved with someone? Is all the drama a defense mechanism, or is every date a big show right from the start?

"So, I'm thinking I'll take him somewhere casual, because I can't see him getting dressed up and being comfortable at the same time."

"People will think he's your son," Mitch warns tiredly.

"Hush, jealous! Then if that goes well, I'll bring him to my birthday party. You're still coming right, Mitch?"

"Sure," Mitch forces out. "No one's going to feel like babysitting though."

"Knock it off!" Greg play shoves Mitch in his shoulder.

Really? Mitch thinks. It's getting exhausting just to sit here with his mouth shut. He would desperately love to say something cutting.

"Besides," Greg says. "You might really like him. And maybe he has cute friends!"

"Or maybe his boyfriend does!" Mitch exclaims mockingly as he gets up quickly to go to the bathroom before his tongue gets away from him.

Mitch runs a bunch of water in the sink and washes his face and hands as slowly as possible. He doesn't really want to hang out with this kid, but he'll show up at Greg's party regardless. It was going to be awkward anyway, ever since Mitch and Shawn broke up. Mitch thought after a series of shallow, brittle relationships that it might help to date someone who was already a friend. False; all it did was make the friendship shallow and brittle too. By the time Mitch finally called it off a few months ago, the whole group dynamic had changed, with some people hearing the discomfort from Shawn's side, some from Mitch's, and a little line down the middle of their crew of about seven or eight friends (depending on who has a boyfriend). Maybe that is what's contributing to Mitch's exhaustion with these people. Or maybe it really is time to just shift circles. It's hard to see the forest you're standing in.

Mitch leaves the bathroom and keeps his eyes low. This is his chance to leave. "Hey, Greg, I think I'll take off," he announces.

"Wait," Greg says, hurrying to stop him. "I found something I wanted to show you." Greg goes to the fridge and snatches something out from under a magnet. "I was going to decorate for the party with old pictures of everyone, and I found this."

The photo is nearly twenty years old, and it's of the two of them the day they moved into the dorms: skinny, sweaty, and so, *so* uncomfortable, standing still for a few pictures to appease their moms and get them to leave. And then after the parents were gone, Mitch remembers himself and Greg each putting up sexy posters of half-naked men, and instantly becoming friends. Hanging out was easy back then, effortless. They were both so simple and so new it was like being the same person, the same soft lump of clay. Growing up would make them so different. Complexity would tear them apart.

"That's sweet," Mitch says. Greg cuffs him on the back of the neck and they man-hug before Mitch leaves. It's this kind of moment that keeps him coming around, that reminds him of all their shared history, of all the memories he could never replace.

Mitch drives home to his lonely bachelor pad through the heavy August air. His students always look forward to summer with such enthusiasm, even though they are the most barometrically unpleasant months of the whole year. Mitch can remember every seventh period he's ever had to contain on that final day of middle school, knowing they've been bored by his history class all year and are anxious to make what feels like their longest period go as quickly as possible.

Mitch enjoys being able to smile at the students indulgently, at last, and tell them to just keep the noise down. No more lessons, no more rules, other than to be discreet with this stolen time. They leave appreciating him so much, like he hadn't been a stickler all year long, or if he was it was just because the bosses were making him. He teaches the eighth grade, and he likes to take a moment before every summer to savor these kids before they all change drastically. After a year in high school, he won't recognize half of them. They'll be depressed or vicious, having too much fun or not enough. Fourteen seems like the last year of pure youth, childish and unselfconscious. But maybe Mitch is just too old to really remember.

The new crop of kids comes in dejected at the end of every summer, and Mitch doesn't even work to disguise his glee on the first day, much to their snarling displeasure. Summers for him aren't all pool parties and sleeping in like they are for most of the kids. Mitch starts feeling oppressed by the heat and the boredom; during the year he's too harassed by grading and tutoring to care that he only goes home to a pale gray tabby named Anastasia.

"Hi, Tasi," Mitch greets his kitty when he gets home. She has a tiny, sickly-sounding mewl that completely belies how robust and sassy she is. She follows him into the kitchen hoping for treats. There's a picture of her on his fridge, but that's as far as it goes. There are no cat pictures in his classroom where someone else might have a snapshot of their family, Mitch isn't that pathetic yet. There's a picture of Tasi over at Greg's house, but that's... that's just one more thing about Greg he could live without. It's framed on the wall in his entryway and everything. Greg thinks it's funny. He just loves telling people that Mitch loves a hairy pussy. Ha, ha.

But then, Greg is the person who got him the cat, as a kitten, as a gift for his 35th birthday. It was sort of a backhanded thing, "So you won't be so lonely!" And this was nearly four years now, so it's become a real pattern, this behavior from Greg. But this thing with the kid at his signing seems new and unpleasant. It was all jokes before, but now it's real. That boy might have recently been one of Mitch's students for all he knows, though Mitch didn't recognize him. Maybe one of the kids in the advanced classes, since Mitch teaches regular, or else a student at one of the other schools... what does it really matter? It's still inappropriate.

Greg is nearly forty years old too, but he'd like to ignore it as long as he's still technically in his thirties. He's turning thirty-nine next month, and there isn't a lot of time left to delude himself. A flame burns brightest before it burns out, isn't that the idea? And maybe that explains Greg's nonsense more than anything else. He's pretending everything is fine, and he's doing it a little too hard. Maybe they'll all calm down once they're over the hill. Maybe it'll be a relief when the pressures and pleasures of youth (such as they were and weren't) are finally behind them.

Chapter Two: The Marvelous Body

Later that evening, a large purple van is heading south on I-75, traveling towards sunny southwest Florida. Contained within are three musicians who collectively style themselves The Homo Superiors.

Riding through Georgia gives Missy an unsettling feeling, probably because last year she almost died in this state. Her appendix ruptured in some nowhere asshole town after a couple days of agony. She hadn't known what the pain was, at first thinking it was something she ate, or maybe someone she'd done, like maybe she might be pregnant again... But the day it burst, it *felt* like something bursting. Though still in pain and weak, she'd felt strangely better for about a day because the pressure was finally gone. She thought: maybe it was an ectopic accident, or maybe something a little more standard, like trapped gas. But when she stayed pale and sweaty and sleepless over another night, her bandmates finally insisted she go to an emergency room; Darian thought it might have been her gallbladder, and Aaron thought for sure she was dying, his face was so full of torment, guilt, and fear. He loves her so much she feels sorry for him sometimes.

The sky is dusky, epic and beautiful, but Missy can barely look at it. The air feels nice from the open window of the van, but she has too many memories burbling up on her: puking in the waiting room at the hospital so violently she wondered if her body wasn't trying to expel her diseased appendix (a thing which Missy pictured like a cracked up peach pit, the shards stabbing her just above her right hip); losing consciousness before surgery with a burning fire in her IV arm; waking up to the pockmarked ceiling, feeling more alone than she'd ever felt in her whole life; leaving the hospital against doctor's advisement because they'd given a fake name and had no insurance. Missy shudders. She hates this fucking state.

Missy unbuckles her seatbelt. The metal is warm-hot from resting against her stomach, a stretch of skin more full of scars than the whole rest of her body. There's a web of silvery stretch marks from her pregnancy, the deep dent of the scar from her surgery. She does all of her living in her guts, it seems. Darian, he's her lead guitarist, he definitely lives through his hands; he writes with them, creates with them, even manages to talk with them when he gets excited. Aaron's life is all over his face, his puppy love, his judgments of everyone else's behavior; he falls face first into all of it. Missy is more bodily than either one of them. She shoots from the hip, she bleeds from her most vital organs. She and Darian, they're both song-writers, but his lyrics are clever, cerebral, and his songs are technically superior. Missy's, the few that she's written on her darker and more drunken nights, are simple, guttural; her songs are the ones that make people cry.

Aaron moves a soda out of the center console to accommodate Missy as she sighs, undoes her seatbelt, and crawls into the back. She clambers over dirty clothes and a dirtier mattress, which she shoves aside to get to the cavity where a spare tire should be, but where they actually keep all their open containers of alcohol in case they get pulled over. Darian is sleeping on the mattress, but he just rolls over after being disturbed and falls right back into his dreams. Even with his lovely blonde hair matted down and dark with grease, two days of stubble on his strong jaw, and the stupid, slack expression of exhaustion, he still looks gorgeous to Missy. All the pretty ones are always gay. It's the greatest curse of her life.

Missy ruffles Darian's hair lightly, affectionately, a little wistfully, before taking a half-full bottle of vodka back to the passenger seat. It's her bottle; everyone in the van has a different poison, which means they never have to worry about their stash being raided. Aaron drinks gin like an old woman, and absolutely *has* to mix it with juice if he doesn't want to get sick. Darian drinks Southern Comfort almost exclusively, the homo. Missy loves vodka with all her Irish soul. Her last name, Marquez, comes from a step-father in the woodpile. But her pale skin, coppery hair, and Catholic guilt keep her true roots from ever being forgotten.

Missy can feel Aaron biting his lip as she comes back with the bottle. She bites hers so she doesn't snap at him; she hates the way he makes her feel like an alcoholic just because he's such a lightweight, because he doesn't have anything to drown out, like she does. Missy uncaps the bottle and takes a whiff. It smells so sterile, so antiseptic... Missy was worried her stay in the hospital would ruin the affection she feels for this smell, but the memories have only joined it. In spite of what Aaron thinks, alcohol isn't about forgetting for Missy, it's about remembering everything all at once, a multicolored blur of everything she's made of, so she doesn't just get bogged down in the bad shit.

Missy takes a swig. Sure, the smell still reminds her of alcohol swabs and IVs, but she also remembers the fall and winter she and Aaron spent in San Francisco nearly two years ago when she was fifteen, crisp Halloween-colored leaves falling through the chilly air as they drove up and down California, couch-surfing and trying to get paid for gigs. And she remembers the very first night she sang for a live audience, the first time she felt perfectly like herself, stripped of everyone else's influence, even as they all looked at her and saw only what they wanted to see; it wasn't about them anyway. The audience is just furniture that can breathe.

Vodka still smells like ozone to her, like a day after it rains, like the fog that comes rolling off of dry ice. She has tried to write odes to it, but she can never quite say it right; this stuff makes her feel impenetrable. It's less about getting drunk and more about giving herself permission to feel as good as she believes she can be. She's had a lot of great times on vodka, a lot of brave moments, and definitely she's had more good nights than the bad mornings could ever sour.

We can't drive through Georgia forever, she thinks, suddenly feeling tougher. In a few hours it'll be Darian's turn to drive; this van hardly ever stops rolling unless they're performing. The trio will be in Florida by morning, and they will keep heading south, to Darian's hometown of Sarasota, and his legendary mother, the patient patron of their struggling band. Neither Missy nor Aaron have met her yet, and Missy is actually

20

pretty excited to see her. She's another redhead as well, a sister.

After that... well. Missy is actually not super excited about Florida either. She had planned to avoid it her whole life, just because she used to know a boy from the Sunshine State, and it depresses her to remember him. She walked away from a lot when she was fifteen; from her mother, her daughter, and her best friend. The mother she didn't miss, and the daughter was only a small infant lump, but Marley... that one still twinges. If it were just she and Aaron still, they would probably avoid this whole area of the country, keep to states in the Northwest where there is a higher tolerance for young ne'er-do-wells like themselves. But they met Darian over a year ago, and Missy can't regret that, even if he does like the rattier states, and even if he is taking her now to a place of pain. Fuck, she'd rather go back home to Vermont, or even see goddamn Loweville, Colorado again. She and Aaron might not even be right with the law in that town, and there's a little girl who looks like Missy running around with some other family's name, and *still* that might be preferable to this.

Missy takes another swig and sighs heavily. Her breath comes out in a flammable plume, like the gas before the pilot light clicks on. Headed where she is, Missy feels like lighting a match, but really there's no call to be so dramatic.

She's survived a lot of pain already, so what's a little more?

After Tristan goes home, Lindsay spends the rest of her evening dreamily messing with her phone.

Head on her pillow next to the radio, she sends a text. Taking a nice bubble bath with a bottle of soda, she receives a text. Before she realizes it, she's wasted half the day talking to this guy. Jordan Southwick. He's not so bad, really. He's not at all like Tristan though, that's for sure.

Right on the surface, the comparison between the two boys is stark.

A day spent talking to Jordan has gone away like an evaporating mist. Lindsay's day disappeared slowly, but then in an instant it was totally gone; so gradual and so sudden. A day spent going back-and-forth with Tristan accounts for every single second—Lindsay is always exhausted after talking to him, they're just so intense around each other. None of this "how are you, what's up, what're you doing" chitchat. They go right into love and hate and their deepest fears. There's just no help for it; they're soulmates.

Tristan is like blood, like family only better, because they chose each other. But whereas Lindsay is put at ease by having Tristan in her life, she thinks their love is starting to stress him out. Maybe it's because he has lost so much already, an only child and an orphan. Lindsay has too many relations around, both of her parents, an older brother, a younger sister. Sure Dad and Marley are out of the house, but it still feels pretty crowded around here. Lindsay just needed someone who wouldn't punk out on her, and that's Tristan. With him at her side, Lindsay feels a lot more confident about taking risks, and even trusting people, like talking to Jordan. Maybe she'll start dating him and it'll be nice, and maybe he'll turn out to be a jerk, but either way he can only add to Lindsay, he can't diminish her.

Lindsay is brushing her hair when her phone twitches and beeps with another text. Tristan helped her dye her hair back to brown from the blonde she had the year she met him—it's grown out long enough now that only the ends betray that mistake. They have a thin, yellow look as opposed to the rest of her natural color. Lindsay should cut it off already, but she's kind of partial to that bit of hair. She's thinking about keeping a lock of it, and maybe tying a little up for Tristan like her favor, but that's a very muted train of thought at the back of her mind. Lindsay puts down her brush and picks up her phone, thinking that it must be Jordan wishing her goodnight (she told him she was going to bed even though it's still early; just a kind way of ending the conversation for the moment), but it's Tristan. Her suspicions about him being a little too knotted up over her having a new friend are confirmed in three words: *What's his name?*

Lindsay makes a 'hmm' noise, wondering at the odd feeling of dread that's just come over her. She types in Jordan's name, sends, and waits. She waits for over ten minutes, never putting the phone down all the while, and then types to Tristan, *Are you ok?*

The response comes back fast this time, a simple, *No.*

Lindsay is alarmed. She tries to call Tristan for an actual conversation, but he's turned his phone off, and she is left to twist her earlobe and worry. She is so unused to having her worries bottled up inside of her that she picks up the phone at least four times to call Tristan before she remembers that she can't, that he's her problem for the first time in ever. Somehow she never expected this; their pact makes no mention of what happens when it isn't the world threatening their bond, it's something internal, a domestic threat within their own borders.

Lindsay needs to vent to somebody. She thinks about calling her brother, since Marley knows them both and could listen to her fears without having to be told the situation, but she's still so mad at him for being such a weakling. She can hardly remember the specifics now, something about him choosing his boyfriend over her, and a physical memory of the way her heart hurt when he betrayed her, but otherwise it's only a sureness that Marley cannot be relied on because he's too soft. Tristan never lets Lindsay forget, never lets her really forgive Marley; he reminds her that if she tries to care about him, she only gives him the power to hurt her again.

Does Tristan think Lindsay could *ever* betray him like Marley did her? Ditch him for some guy she hardly knows? Is that why he's so upset?

For the first time in a long while, Lindsay wishes she had more friends, someone else she could turn to for advice. She briefly considers talking to her mother, but the thought of the satisfied look on her face if she thought Lindsay and Tristan were on the rocks makes it impossible. Lindsay and Tristan had themselves convinced they didn't need anyone but each other... and maybe that's a bad idea? If it is, Lindsay certainly doesn't want her mother to know.

Lindsay gets up from her vanity, slips on her flip-flops, and decides to go get some air. She's still in her pajamas—pale pink with little ice cream cones all over—but she's not going far, just onto the back porch to pace around the pool. Her room, Marley's old room, is so small it's suffocating, and she always suspected a residue of her brother has lingered in there. It used to bring her peace to feel it, when Marley was sent to live with Aunt Bess just for being gay or whatever, but now Lindsay is starting to think there *is* something wrong with Marley, something totally unrelated to his sexuality, something wrong with his *head*. Lindsay feels like she's catching it sometimes, a panicky, trapped feeling close to what she feels when doing flips underwater, and needing air several seconds before she reaches the surface.

Lindsay passes her mother watching TV in the living room, some mindless sitcom. Valerie sighs audibly to see Lindsay headed outside with her phone; she knows Lindsay goes outside so as not to be overheard. This time, of course, Lindsay is just hoping Tristan will call her. It'll be a long night if she can't talk to him until school the next day.

Lindsay resigns herself to getting sweaty again, even though she just got dry after her bath. The dying ember of dusk in Florida is like a coal sauna, it's revoltingly humid out. And yet the heavy air is still less oppressive than her brother's old room. Lindsay must look crazy to the neighbors in her 'jammies and sandals, pacing around and chewing the nails of her phone hand, but oh well. It's not like they're any help either.

Lindsay does at least three laps around the pool before she thinks of calling Jordan. It's like, if he likes her so much, he can prove it by listening to her problems, can't he? She brings up the number and presses Send. He picks up really fast.

"I thought you were going to bed," he says. He sounds excited that she's calling him. Probably he should worry about this call being from a snooping parent, and never answer it with a sentence including the word 'bed,' but he doesn't come across as a suspicious sort of person.

"Well, I am. It takes longer for girls to go to bed." Lindsay doesn't really think that, but she's not interested in battling stereotypes right now, she just wants him to listen. "Listen," she tells him. "Do you have a best friend?"

"Um, yes?" Jordan says. "I guess Will is my best friend. He used to live a few blocks from me when we were kids, and—"

Lindsay cuts him off unkindly. "Do either of you have girlfriends?"

"I don't," Jordan mumbles. "Obviously."

Lindsay waits a beat, and doesn't conceal her annoyance well when she says, "And him?"

"Oh, no."

"So how do you think he'd feel if you suddenly got a girlfriend?" It occurs to Lindsay that Jordan will take this line of questioning entirely the wrong way, but what he thinks he knows isn't exactly her problem. "I mean, how close are you guys?"

"I don't think he'd care," Jordan says hopefully. "It's not like we're joined at the hip, you know? We have our own lives."

Lindsay rolls her eyes. Great; that means Jordan wouldn't know the first thing about the dynamic between her and Tristan.

"Okay, that's all I needed to know, bye," Lindsay says quickly and hangs up. Was that unfair to Jordan? Yeah, probably, but he can just join the freaking club.

"Am I your type?" Marley asks Jesse. Marley is sitting at their kitchen table after dinner, tapping his fingernails while Jesse washes the dishes, even though Jesse is also the one who cooked the chicken they just ate. The balance of chores is oddly divided in their relationship, as is the balance of power. Marley has noticed that Jesse likes to control and do for himself just about everything, and though it means that Marley himself remains perfectly handicapped when it comes to life's most basic tasks (cooking, fixing, anything involving pipes is beyond him), he doesn't mind it. Marley has his own uses.

Laundry is Marley's job, and so is most of the cleaning. These are mostly symptoms of his restless compulsion to straighten and organize. Folding and stacking their clothes big-to-small is soothing to him.

So is scrubbing the corners of the bathroom with a bleach-soaked toothbrush. He likes to watch the color go from dingy to white in neat little quadrants. Marley likes to dust, and sweep, and mop—nearly anything that can be done in a perfect, repetitive order has become his domain. Making food is too messy, too organic. Marley can barely stand to watch Jesse wash the dishes because he stacks them in the drying rack as they come to his hand—forks and spoons mixed all together, bowls behind plates, glasses wherever they can teeter. Marley used to dry for Jesse until he was chided for being so particular about stacking, so now the dishes just drip dry in the other part of the sink. Because of that incident too, Marley does his small share of the chores while Jesse is downstairs working in the garage, so as not to be made self-conscious about his methods.

"What?" Jesse asks. Either his task is too loud or he was off in a cloud somewhere. He isn't as present in his surroundings as Marley is, probably forgets where he is half the time while Marley remains painfully alert whenever he isn't under the covers with the lights out. Jesse can get pretty far away from himself, and that is something else Marley has noticed about him, and adapted to. While gathering the crumbs on the table into little piles, Marley simply repeats himself.

"Am I your type? Like if you didn't know me, do you think you'd be attracted to me?"

"I've known you for a while," Jesse says. Marley nods, even though Jesse is facing away from him at the other end of the kitchen, standing by a window that is headed towards but not quite arrived at being reflectively opaque. The sun is nearly finished setting.

Jesse means that he hasn't thought about his type in a while, since they've been together for so long. And they've been so quiet, so easy together. That's the only kind of relationship Marley can imagine himself in; a relationship that needed a lot of compromise or communication would wither under his meek ministrations. He and Jesse have been so natural, in fact, that Marley hasn't thought of it in some time either. Until today.

Greg Haywood asking him out kicked loose a lot of memories for

Marley, memories a lot older than Jesse. The appeal of Greg has a lot to do with Marley's first... not his first *boyfriend* exactly? And not really his first love either. Just his first. David Franklin.

Because Marley believes he *does* have a type, or did, before he got together with Jesse. Frank, as he was known to Marley, wasn't the fluke everyone thought he was just because their rather considerable age difference made people jump to conclusions. This flirtation with Greg is making Marley think that Jesse might be the fluke, since now it seems that Marley naturally prefers men of letters. The key term there being 'men' rather than boys. A lot of young guys come through the store, and Marley never looks at any of them and thinks, *Boy, if I wasn't in a relationship...* But Gregory Haywood smiles at him a few times? It's made him start imagining things.

Marley still thinks of Frank often, and fondly. Though it might be easy enough for Marley to find and contact Frank now that he's eighteen and out of his parents' house, as with most things he never finds a good enough reason to go out of his way, or to change his very careful routine. It's already enough of a stressor to just go about the same old activities he's had daily for more than a year—leaving the apartment is never easy to do, since the world outside is so unpredictable. Work, the grocery store, maybe babysitting for Jesse's boss, it's already on the absolute threshold of what Marley can deal with. How would he even start looking for Frank? Send a letter to his old address and hope that it would be forwarded? Perhaps search him out on the computer at work? If Marley found him, then what? A phone call? A visit? No, no, it would all be too strange. Marley is sure that Frank is doing well in St. Louis, and that is a comforting thought.

Now with Greg it's a different story. He's doing all the courting here, and Marley is intrigued by the idea of knowing a writer in real life. Marley's books are so much a part of him, and since several of his books are Greg's books, he feels like they must already have a lot in common. It's like meeting someone who likes to vacation in the same obscure little town you do. The bond would be powerful, immediate: an instant connection.

Marley still hasn't figured out how to broach the subject of his not-really-a-date with Jesse though. It seems pretty obvious even to Marley that he's testing the waters of another guy, but probably it's all innocent, right?

"What about me? Am I your type?" Jesse asks as he walks back to Marley drying his hands, which are as clean right now as they've been all day. He never loses that line of mechanical grease under each fingernail, but after soaking in hot dish water, the skin is at least cleansed. His pale fingers have turned red from the hot water. They transfer their heat to Marley as Jesse touches the back of his neck.

Marley shrugs. He figures Jesse isn't looking for a real answer, because he kisses Marley rather than waiting for one. It's a good thing too, because Marley doesn't want to delve for that answer, at least not on this side of his not-a-date. He'll have to bring it up with Jesse some other time, because as Jesse kisses him again, deeper, the moment is suddenly very inopportune.

"You know, I don't think you could be my type," Jesse says, with a pleasant look on his face, not really a smile, since it's not in his lips. He twitches the open edge of Marley's over-shirt, his way of asking for permission. Marley shrugs the shirt off, relieved they're clearly done talking for now—that was sort of a bad way to start this conversation, but Jesse brings it to a neat conclusion. "You're, like, one of a kind," he says.

"Nice," Marley says, grinning back at Jesse as they both mosey a few feet over to the bed.

The sex doesn't take long. They've gotten pretty good at it with practice, and they've tried enough to know which acts are part of their greatest hits collection, and which are only for special occasions. Today's a weekday, and so is tomorrow, so they both get off together very perfunctorily and then hop into a shared shower.

Marley tries to reintroduce the subject of Greg once they're in bed. Jesse's hair, though longer than it used to be at Marley's request, is still short enough for him to dry it by scrubbing his head with a towel, the way most people dry their dogs. Marley never sees Jesse brush or style his hair, but somehow he still wakes up with little blonde ringlets and half curls that last all day. Marley's hair usually stays damp until well after he wakes up, and now as he rolls over onto Jesse, it leaves little wet trails like just-cleaned paint brushes on the pillow and sheets. Jesse puts his hands in Marley's hair and starts combing it with his fingers. Now is definitely the moment, and Marley has chosen his phrasing very carefully.

"I met that writer at the store today, and he agreed to let me pick his brain some time." By making it sound like it was his own idea, Marley hopes to sneak around Greg's probable motivation, but it's no go.

Because Jesse asks, "Really? When are you going to do that?"

And Marley can find no other way to say, "He'll pick me up here on Saturday night. For dinner."

Jesse is quiet for a moment, looking placidly at Marley with his pale blue eyes, and then makes his little throat-clearing noise that he uses when he wants to laugh.

"You don't care, right?" Marley asks. "I mean, you know you have nothing to worry about."

"Okay," Jesse says simply, sliding out from under Marley and turning away for sleep.

Marley is up half the night wondering what the hell Jesse might have meant with that one word, while Jesse drops nearly instantly into blank, untroubled dreams.

Chapter Three: Our Former Disharmony

Missy sits in Miriam Jule's vintage-style kitchen, watching her bustle around in an apron and a string of pearls, pulling a pineapple upside down cake in and out of several appliances, all of which are candy-apple, nail-polish red.

Knowing Darian, Missy expected his mother to be beautiful, but she was not ready to find out that her six-foot Nordic prince of a friend was sprung from June Cleaver's tiny, brassy younger sister. The woman has on a cute little sundress, heeled sandals that match both her necklace and earrings. There are ruffles on her apron, and a makeup compact in one of the pockets.

She smiles at Missy like she's keeping a joke to herself when she asks, "So how exactly did you and my son meet?"

Missy smiles back, rolling her eyes and sighing as they both break into giggles.

"It's a long story." Missy cranes her neck to see out the window, just to make sure Aaron is out of earshot. He and Darian are outside throwing tools at the van's engine with Darian's soon-to-be-ex-step-father, all three of them scratching their heads, trying to find where the funny new keening noise they developed just after Gainesville is coming from. Missy knows from Darian that his mother is a bit of a Venus fly-trap, marrying men and divorcing them within five years, making a neat bit of alimony each time, and improving her house with honey-do lists while they're in residence. Apparently Darian's father was the only one she could never nail down, and the man isn't in either of their lives. Miriam is only a hair above forty, with a saucy smile and a wicked gleam in her eye. Missy wishes she had a mother like this. She wonders, *very* briefly, if she could have been a mother like this, if she had stayed in

Loweville with her baby.

"If it's that long a story," Miriam says, also glancing out the window to make sure the coast is clear, "then why don't we let this cake cool on its own and I'll make us a couple martinis?"

"God, you're fabulous," Missy says, following Miriam's swerve into the living room where there's a large booze cabinet.

"So you know that Aaron and I ran away together, don't you? And my... troubles?"

"Oh, sweetheart," Miriam says, laying a cool, soft manicured hand on Missy's bare arm. "No one could be more sympathetic than I am. You know I had Darian when I was very young, too young really, though I think I've done all right by him."

"I mean, he totally adores you."

"Yes, but that isn't always the mark of good parenting. I was hoping he'd stay in college, but he gave it a year before he told me he wanted to be a rock star, and what could I do but support him? Having children means setting your own desires aside, you know."

"Yeah, I know," Missy says, accepting a dirty martini and feeling very wise. "That's exactly why I left."

"Well, you were even younger than I was, weren't you?"

"Fifteen," Missy confirms with a salty smack of her lips after swallowing that first dear gulp of alcohol. *Hello, pal o' my heart.*

Miriam nods, lifting her own drink. She sips daintily, leaving just the barest lipstick stain, like a sweetheart kiss. Missy bets herself that this woman has never woken up with her makeup smeared around, that no one has ever seen her flushed and crocked, drunkenly stumbling into furniture, even with those stilted heels (unlike someone else in this room, who does that in her own bare feet sometimes). *Well,* Missy thinks, *all women can't be ladies.*

And as if more confirmation were needed to prove that she and Missy are of the same mind, Miriam says:

"We aren't all meant to be mothers, that's just the honest truth. And you were blessed with a daughter, weren't you?" Miriam touches her pearls and looks skyward as Missy garbles her yes around an olive.

"Nightmare! I put a lot more years on my parents than the passing of time ever did, I can tell you that."

"Huh," Missy says, kicking up the bottom of her glass. She knows she's in the gold medal category of difficult daughters, the grand prize: Unwed Teenage Mother.

She doesn't really credit her parents with 'putting up with her' since she hasn't seen either one of them in years. Sure all teenagers are handfuls in one way or another, and yes parents who raise their kids every day through hell and high water do deserve some appreciation. But just producing another variation of your genetic material doesn't win you some kind of sainthood, like Missy's mother seemed to think in her long-suffering, Catholic way. Missy's given birth to someone, but she's never been anyone's mother, and she knows that's true for a lot of women.

Her face must betray her inner semantic battlefield, because Miriam hands Missy the rest of her martini with a wink, and takes Missy's empty glass for her own. No wonder men keep marrying her; she's like a naughty Martha Stewart.

Missy sets her lips against the stenciling of Miriam's lipstick and notices that this drink is drastically stronger than the one she was just holding. Oho! Mother's little helper! Or wait, wasn't that pills? Or wait again, who cares?

"You know, I was seventeen when I got pregnant with Darian, but even a few months older or younger makes all the difference at that age. If I had been any younger, I never would have made it. It was all I could do to keep the two of us together even then."

Miriam comes back from her bar and uses her non-drink hand to comb a bit of Missy's hair and pet Missy's long single braid. She laughs cutely into her glass and says, "You know, before I found out he liked boys, I always hoped Darian would bring home a girl like you, and look! I've gotten my wish. Life's funny like that."

"Yeah, it's hilarious." Missy, feeling Miriam's fingernails drawing lightly across her head, is struck like a gong with the tragedy of her female line. It hums through her teeth almost, the knowledge that she is now motherless, that she left someone else motherless, and that the comfort of mom is something no one should have to live without. Missy lets out a sigh and grits her teeth. What's the use of being sad if she knows she isn't going to do a thing about it? Missy's never really considered trying to contact either her mother or her daughter. Her fingers don't even twitch towards the phone when she feels like this. She just slaps a lid on that pot of anger and guilt and lets it simmer on the back burner.

"Mmm!" Miriam says, patting Missy on the shoulder and returning to her seat. "We got away from ourselves. How did you find Darian?"

"Oh, right. Well, me and Aaron were in Arizona. We had left L.A. okay, and we were *trying* to get to Phoenix to join up with this band Aaron knew, 'cause we weren't doing our own thing back then or even covers, we just kind of filled in for people who needed bass or backup or whatever. So it's super vacant and bullshit out there because it's the desert. Like, we had to watch our gas between towns so we wouldn't run out, but a lot of good *that* did us when something in the engine burst or cracked or whatever when we were in the middle of *nowhere*."

"That sort of thing happens, as you can plainly see with our old van. Had you been driving all over the place?"

"Oh yeah, up and down California like a dozen times, but Aaron wanted us to... get away for a while."

Actually he wanted to get *Missy* away for a while. Even though she had never promised him anything; not fidelity, not forever, not even friendship, really. He kind of assumed a lot when she ran away with him in the first place, due in large part to Missy gently misleading him.

In the beginning they were fellow escapees. They rescued each other from the slow death of a small, conservative town. They went to California, they fell in with bohemians, they became street performers, playing for spare change. Aaron plucking a simple guitar, Missy singing songs she knew, attracting dollar bills from men mostly because she was so cute—her pale freckles, her Rapunzel braid, her sun dresses. She learned how to flirt safely with just one guy in a crowd, make him feel special and give generously. She even started hooking up with some of the younger guys. Not the suits, but the androgynous street kids.

Here and there a bartender, a bike messenger, a college student. Aaron watched her walk off with them, his face demolished in sadness. Sucked for him, but life's a grim reality. If Aaron doesn't like what she does or who she does it with, he can leave. Missy herself is always prepared to walk away from anyone.

After a few months of this strain, Aaron got the sneaky idea to start touring with their musical act. He just wanted her out of the city, thinking it would make her stick closer to him, as if the road weren't more conducive to anonymous sex and one night stands, which Missy actually prefers to the sort of on-again-off-again fucking around with local folks that she'd had in San Francisco. Instead of having to deal with the diplomacy of making rounds with the same old guys, she could find a new boy each night, and never tire of any one or have to deal with any unpleasant clinging. In the city she was buffet grazing, coming back to the same limited variety day after day, but these one night stands were like bonbons: small, sweet, and perfectly decadent. She never regretted a single one.

It was killing Aaron though. Missy was waiting for him to leave her, but he just never pulled the trigger. When they originally took off from Colorado, she *knew* they would be temporary. They were already ditched by their parents, their friends had paired off and forgotten them, it was only sensible to think that this too would end. But Aaron was in love, the poor idiot, and he remains in love still.

The night they met Darian, she thought Aaron had finally snapped. They were a few miles past an exit for some girl's name town, and who knows how many thankless miles from the next one in the wide, rocky Arizona desert. The map Missy was studying in the pinging light of the open car door said there was a turnpike or something up ahead of them, but it was such a dark wasteland out there that she didn't hold out hope for a town or a hotel or even a gas station. Missy made a mostly innocent crack about who do you have to fuck to get out of the desert (last time the answer was Aaron), and it broke him.

"God, how can you say that shit to me!" he yelled, the sound muffled. He had his head in his hands, his elbows on his nearly hairless knees, exposed because he was wearing shorts, an item of clothing that Missy has always hated to see on any non-kid, but especially hates to see on men. He was sitting on the back bumper of the car, a few feet from where Missy was lying across the back seat, but he felt very far from her and always had. He sounded like he was about to cry, but he just yelled louder to keep it down.

"It's like, I love you so much and you don't even want it! What kind of robot just doesn't care like that?"

And something about being stranded *again*, in the desert *again*, and having Aaron whining at her about her inability to love him? Missy finally broke too.

"I'm not a robot, you fucking child!" Missy pushed the map out of the car and crawled out after it. She shoved Aaron's shoulder back so that he'd be forced out of his pitiful slump and made to face her. "You've been acting like such a victim ever since Colorado and you have *no right*. Maybe your love is unwanted, okay? Maybe you should wonder why you have no self-respect instead of wondering what's wrong with *me*, like you don't *already fucking know!* You took me out of a nursery and you wonder why I don't want to be your girlfriend? Well take a *wild fucking guess!*"

Aaron, to his grudging credit, didn't crumble like she thought he would. He was up off the bumper like a shot, suddenly standing a foot from Missy, both of them swathed in the steam-drift from their hissing engine, having it out properly.

Aaron was all, "Don't pretend you haven't been using me for a year!" And Missy came back all, "Don't pretend you weren't happy to take advantage of the fact that I was abandoned and desperate!" And then Aaron said, "Well I was in the same situation, but I still shared everything I had with you!" And at that Missy finally let fly with the truth that, "Yeah, well, all I wanted was a fucking ride and you don't even have that anymore!"

A couple of cars had passed while they were having this fight, fingers in each other's faces, their screams expanding into the empty night and letting them feel how much sonic nothing was standing between them and the distant mountain range. After growing up in Appalachia and being condemned to the Rockies, Missy hates mountains; she could feel them looming out there in the darkness like spectators at a coliseum, waiting to see some blood.

Aaron was quiet for a moment, looking at his old station wagon with his lip quivering and his eyes magnified by tears, and that's when a big purple van slowed onto the shoulder. Missy backed away from it several arm's lengths (it looked like a great vehicle to get snatched into), but when Darian leaned out his window looking glorious, and explained that he had stopped maybe a mile east of them to take pictures of Sore Finger Road and heard their fighting on the wind, and said he wanted to make sure they were okay... the tension was punctured. Between Missy and Aaron, it was like deflating a hot air balloon, and for all three it was a pop of recognition. Maybe it was some kind of musician's vibration, or the shared sense of humor that erupted when they all paused long enough to realize how ridiculous this night was, and started laughing.

Whatever brought them together then has kept them together ever since. They abandoned the station wagon, packed into Darian's van, never made it to Phoenix, and instead found themselves playing back-up to Darian in Las Vegas. He filled in all their empty spaces: Aaron finally had a friend to complain to, Missy found a drinking buddy almost as slutty as herself, and Darian gained a band with some musical ability but absolutely zero opinions on creative control. Darian had his own plans and vision, and Missy and Aaron adopted them easily. Aaron quit guitar and took up bass, and while Missy had her voice to contribute, Darian was clearly their lead singer, so she picked up keyboard to round out their sound. They became a tight unit very quickly, sleeping on the same mattress half the time, bunking in the van.

"Being on the road," Missy explains to Miriam, "It's like a college dorm times a prison cell to the power of summer camp. It's like... instant bonding."

Hearing herself, Missy realizes she's in that magical alcohol-induced window where she's just lubed up enough to be creative, but not so tanked that she can't hold a pen. This is when she usually jots down lyrics, which she later takes to Darian to find them a tune. She's never written a song completely on her own, like Darian does. Missy can only contribute to a more beautiful whole.

Missy is standing at the liquor cabinet when the boys return looking defeated and sweaty.

"I don't know how much longer that van will last," Darian's step-dad says. "What year is it?"

"We bought it new, and what year was that, sweetheart?" Miriam asks her son.

Darian grimaces as thinks. "It was Phil who gave me the van, and he was with us in... '07 wasn't he? The year I dropped out?"

"Yes, but you didn't get the van until the next year, but we'd been using it already for a while... honestly I don't think it was Phil that bought it, I think it was Marty, which would make the thing... oh maybe seven or eight years old? Definitely no more than ten."

Aaron levels an uncomfortable glance at Missy, who is smiling in amusement. They've both realized that these are some of Darian's other step-fathers being talked about, and by the worried look on the newest guy's face, he realizes it too.

"Oh," he mumbles unhappily. "You must have put a lot of miles on it then."

"We certainly have," Miriam says heartily, wiggling her eyebrows conspiratorially at Missy. Darian is smiling indulgently, but at no one in particular. He must have a lot of practice pretending his mom's husbands are not a penny a dozen.

"Well, you'll take the credit card for your trip to the Keys, just in case," Miriam says, gesturing towards the husband to get out his wallet and hand it over.

"Ah, hon," he starts to say to her, but Miriam overrides him casually by still speaking to Darian, saying, "We can't have you stranded out in the swamp if something goes wrong, can we?"

"Wow, mom, that's really sweet of you guys," Darian says in a rush, snapping up the card and hustling out of the room. Missy is quick enough to follow him (or buzzed enough to not care if she's being rude) while Aaron is stuck trying talk his way out of the awkward air. They've been here less than a week, and it's comfortable, but getting less and less so every day as some form of marital tension builds up. Missy is suddenly thankful that they're leaving right away the next morning.

In the kitchen Darian smiles at Missy, and gets out his wallet.

"I almost hope whatever that noise is busts up soon, this won't be good for much longer," he says, flicking the card before tucking it away. "I bet she's already called the lawyer, she always starts really bilking them after she's decided to dump them."

"Your mom's a real man-eater, isn't she?" Missy asks.

"Well, where'd you think I got it from?"

Missy snorts. "You might not have gotten it from anywhere. Some of us are just naturals, you know. Prodigies."

Jesse is watching himself as much as he's watching Marley in the bathroom mirror right now, trying to figure out how a normal person would feel about this.

"Almost ready for your date?" Jesse asks. Marley is brushing his hair into a ponytail, and Jesse starts to bat it back and forth like a cat. He's plumbing his insides trying to find a visceral reaction, some jealousy or resentment, but he's coming up dry. The well may be deep, but it's empty.

Marley smiles at him. "It's not a date," he says for maybe the thirtieth time. "Greg knows I have a boyfriend."

"Yeah, but does he care?"

Marley shrugs and turns away from the mirror. "It's really cool of you not to be weird about this. I like this guy's books a lot."

Jesse nods. He knows this already. In fact he even looked through Marley's Haywood books and found himself unimpressed. Each book is probably about a hundred pages too long, the kind of writer that goes on and on about the scenery and shit. Jesse picked up the one about gardening or whatever and skimmed at least three pages of flower minutia and different kinds of growing methods before he rolled his eyes and put it back down. After a while it was like: we get it, you did a lot of research about flowers. No one cares.

But Marley sees something Jesse doesn't, clearly. He's put on his nice T-shirt and his clean sneakers. He cares what this douchebag thinks about him.

"Do you wanna meet him when he gets here?" Marley asks.

"I'll come down with you," he says, careful not to tell Marley what he's really thinking, which is, *I want this prick to meet* me.

He and Marley leave their loft-ish room, still undecorated after two years except by the stacking towers of Marley's books, and walk down the metal staircase and out into the garage. This is where Jesse would like to meet Greg, in a room where he's the expert. Greg walked up to Marley in a bookstore because as a writer, that's where he is confident. Let him come around all these machines, several of which could clip his talented little fingers right off, and still feel so smart.

Jesse started out at Kenny's Garage as sort of an apprentice, but he's gotten a couple of promotions since then. Not only does he live above the garage, where he can manage emergencies and provide low-level security for the tools and equipment and the semi-vulnerable junkyard of spare parts out back, but at this point Jesse can do everything he's seen Kenny do. He's like those piano prodigies who can play any tune after hearing it once. That's less to do with art and more to do with the medium, with the tool of the trade. If you understand a piano, and you understand music mathematically, you win. Jesse understands engines, one machine to another. He'll never invent anything, but he'll be able to fix it all.

This is probably why he doesn't feel jealous, the way so many other people might. He hasn't run through all the reasons point by point in his head, but Jesse knows generally that Marley isn't going anywhere. He's too timid to make changes, too embarrassed to reveal himself to anyone else, let alone to the keen, judgmental eyes of a professional writer. It simply won't go down like that. If Greg and Marley haven't figured it out yet, so much the worse for them.

Marley and Jesse loiter downstairs to wait, Marley swaying back and forth with the oscillating fan, trying not to get sweaty. Greg pulls up in a Mazda Miata, just in case there was anyone left on the planet who didn't know he was a fag from his books, or the way he walks, or how he talks, or the limp handshake he lays on Jesse. Marley introduces them, and Greg smirks the whole time, thinking he's being funny by treating Jesse like a father figure. "I'll have him back before curfew, harhar!" Jesse just smirks right back at him. Greg's never even met Marley's real father, so he doesn't know just how unfunny he's being. He's got nothing that could compete with Jesse.

Jesse waves as they drive away, thinking, *Good luck trying to fuck my boyfriend, 'cuz you're gonna need it.*

Jesse starts turning out the lights in the back of the house, slowly working his way to the garage doors, flipping switches, turning locks, the same routine every night. It's been the same thing every night more or less since he came to Florida with Marley. There was some drama last year with Marley trying to move back in with his family, but other than that Jesse isn't accustomed to spending his nights alone.

After closing down the doors and securing the ground floor, Jesse gets stuck on his way back to his room, just sort of standing in the middle of the floor, trying to think of something special to do with his sudden free time. He's still paused when the phone rings, and it brings him out of his cloudy spaces to answer it.

"Hey-o boy-o," Kenny says. "Is Marley around?"

"Um, no."

"Really? Where is he?"

"It's a long... I don't know Kenny, what d'you need?"

"We want him to come babysit," Kenny says, beginning to ramble. "We're taking Felicia to a gymnastics tournament, and we need him for a few hours. He's really not there? He's always been there before, we just assumed we could call at the last minute. I guess that wasn't a very good idea."

"I mean, I'm free if you're really in a bind."

"Oh! Let me uh... let me ask Marianne."

Jesse smiles and fluffs some of his strange new curls over his forehead as he leans waiting in the darkened garage. Marianne has really grown to dislike him, and Jesse's pretty sure that if it wasn't for his sweetheart of a boyfriend, she'd be lobbying her husband to fire Jesse. She'll like to hear that Marley is out on his own recognizance tonight.

"Jesse? Yeah it looks like we could use you, we'll pay you the same as Marley, but... have you ever watched kids before?"

"I grew up with my younger cousin," Jesse says, which is dead true. He was never left alone with Billy before the kid was fourteen, but Kenny didn't ask that.

"All right! If you could get here within half an hour that'd be great, but the sooner the better, okay?"

"I'm out the door." Jesse doesn't even return to his room first, his keys and wallet are already on him. Marley packs a freaking bag when he goes to babysit, even though he never stays the night. Mostly he takes his books, but he also brings pens and notebooks and chapstick and headphones and hard candies and all kinds of loose nonsense; he's like a lady with a purse.

Jesse hops up into his truck with the closest thing to cheer he's ever felt. Something about his truck brings a spring to his step. It doesn't look very nice, and in fact it looks a tad crunchier than it did when he first got it; this isn't a body shop, and Jesse isn't very vain, so he's let any cosmetic problems remain. But the engine has been babied and doctored at regular intervals, and whenever Jesse finds himself working on his own truck, that's the nearest he ever is to feeling sentimental. He has memories of his father's truck, of handing him tools and holding the flashlight, and discreetly collecting the tools again whenever Dan either passed out drunk or hurled them across the room in anger. They may not be the sweetest memories, but it was the only childhood Jesse had, and it still makes him smile sometimes.

Maybe it's his strange experience growing up that makes Jesse feel so removed from Kenny's children, or maybe it's because they're girls, but the two little ones just stare at him when Jesse walks in. Jesse can't even tell them apart, they both look like his mother's kewpie dolls to him. They've been known to rush into Marley's legs hard enough to knock him off balance, Jesse's seen it happen. But not tonight; Julia and Theresa are hiding behind their father, eyeing Jesse like he's a large dog.

"So where is Marley? Is it something to do with work?" Kenny asks.

"Nope," Jesse says, flopping down on the couch. Kenny keeps watching him, waiting for more information, so Jesse says, "He went out." But that isn't sufficient either, especially when he sees Marianne emerge from her bedroom, hostile in her curiosity. "He met a writer he likes at the book store and the guy invited him out to dinner."

Marianne exhibits a satisfied smirk, and Kenny gives Jesse a sympathy smile and tries to move the evening along by calling for his oldest daughter. She comes out in a sparkly, flesh-toned dance suit and is immediately infuriated that Jesse has seen her. She has yet to get over her misguided former crush on Jesse, and distracts everyone by yelling, "Oh my GOD someone could have said there was company, JESUS," and diving back into her room to put a robe on over her outfit. She looks very injured standing there in a fuzzy blue robe with her hair pulled tight and glittered, her face done up in nightmarish stage makeup.

Her parents become focused on getting her out the door after that, and on boosting her spirits back up for her show. To Jesse one parent yells out bedtime, the other says the emergency numbers are by the phone, and then the door slams behind them.

In the slapped silence that follows this exit, Jesse turns to his two young charges, standing huddled together in 'jammies in the dark of the hallway. Jesse waves at them, but it only makes them shrink further back. Marley probably reads them stories, or plays them music, or draws with them or something, maybe that's what he's always carting back and forth to this gig. But Jesse just shrugs at the girls, and they go back into their room to entertain themselves until bedtime. Marley isn't here.

It takes Marley a long time to loosen up after Greg picks him up.

The car ride was only gritted through by discussing the habits of traffic. Then there was some initial anxiety about ordering dinner when it occurred to Marley that he should have brought money and not just assumed he was being treated. It's just that he never goes anywhere and it isn't a habit for him to bring his wallet to work, so he's used to leaving with nothing but his house keys. Greg probably noticed how uncomfortable he was, because he told Marley, "Order whatever you want, it's on me." It's just a chain restaurant, so he's not exactly out with Gallahad, but Marley is appreciative anyway. He's afraid of carrying money around, it feels like asking to be robbed.

It's also easier to relax when it becomes clear that Marley isn't really expected to talk. As much as Greg made all this sound like he was interested in getting to know Marley, he spends most of their time together talking about himself. Maybe trying to impress Marley? But it's not really working. He yammers about all of the places he's traveled, not knowing that Marley doesn't like traveling and doesn't see the point in going somewhere when it's much less of a bother to read a book set in that place. Greg talks about the parties he's been to and the famous people he's met—Marley hates parties and doesn't know who any of these people are, or why it would be special to meet them. Marley's thoughts start to drift away from the person in front of him, leaving his eyes glazed and empty, but Greg doesn't notice. Likewise, Marley doesn't clue back in until Greg starts talking about books. That perks him up.

"I'm doing some editing work for a friend of mine right now," Greg says. He hides his mouth behind the back of his hand, leans across the table, and whispers, "His writing is terrible, but!" Greg leans back again, his voice at a normal volume. "He *is* paying me, so I can't really complain."

"Are you writing anything right now?" Marley asks. It's the first he's spoken in a while, maybe since the waitress left. Greg smiles knowingly. What does he think he knows?

"Actually, I am. I've started a story about you. Well," Greg amends quickly before it gets too weird, "at least about someone who looks like you."

"Really?" Marley asks.

"Yes. I hope that's okay. It's not really about you, not your name or anything, and it's already mutating into something of its own, the way they do."

Marley starts asking questions now, wondering where else Greg gets story ideas, how does he get started on something, what happens when he gets stuck. As Greg answers and goes on and on about his process, he gets more passionate, more animated. He's not trying to name-drop or impress anymore, he's real about this; specific and emphatic. His appeal starts to shine through again, that same artistic shimmer that Marley was pulled in by at the store. It's strange to reconcile the books Greg has written with the person he presents; Marley feels an intimate connection with many of his characters, many of his settings, and every time he remembers that all of it came from the guy sitting in front of him, he's awed and fascinated. *How in the hell?*

Dinner is over quickly, and once they're back in the car, Greg asks Marley if he'd like to drive around and see some of the local spots that inspired his stories. Marley says yes, and he tries to quell the lick of worry about allowing himself to be taken to undisclosed locations by someone he hardly knows. His mother used to drill it into his head how dangerous men could be. Or was she mostly talking to his sisters? Isn't Marley himself a man, technically?

They're already on the move as all this rolls through Marley's head however, and he won't interrupt a thing in motion. Fortunately, Greg really does want to show him where his stories touch the real world. He shows Marley the house he imagines the characters in *Never* living in, and Marley readjusts the details he created in his head, the details he couldn't imagine at the time he read the book, in high school. It's a pretty grand house with Corinthian columns holding up the front porch, sitting on a huge corner lot. Marley can't ever remember which kind of column is supposed to look like what, but he knows that in the book this house had Corinthian, and he assumes that the ornate leafy design at the top of each one is what corresponds.

Next is a house with a rampant garden, which inspired *Under The Topsoil*.

"This isn't my neighborhood," Greg says as they keep snaking deeper into this wealthy area. He doesn't drive as smoothly as Jesse does, doesn't let the wheel slide or the brakes ease down, doesn't seem to treat the experience of driving as mutual and collaborative, but he drives okay, if rather perfunctorily. Marley thinks most of the smoothness of being driven around by Greg might be from how new the car is, not from any skill at handling it. The radio has two round vents above it that make the whole dash look like a friendly owl. This car has an electronic jack with Greg's cell phone plugged into it, rather than a tape deck or even a CD player. Marley feels like he's time-traveled into the future as he takes it all in.

"I come here to take walks and just try to imagine the sort of people who live in these big houses," Greg goes on. "Where did they come from, how far did they travel to get here, stuff like that. I don't know anyone around here and I work really hard not to even speak to them. I prefer to make them up out of thin air; I'm always afraid I'll be disappointed by the reality. Do you ever feel that way?" he asks Marley.

"Yes," Marley says simply. Only constantly.

"By the time I'm done figuring their personalities out, I have a full story to write down. I get the best results when I work backwards from the individual and find the plot that would have made them. And then it sort of writes itself while holding me hostage."

Marley hums out a laugh instead of responding. He wants to mull that around for a while, the idea of the writer being taken hostage by his story as much as Marley is always being hijacked as a reader.

Greg leaves the fancy neighborhood soon after that, and drives them past several communities that get less and less ostentatious as they go, until eventually there are passing not homes, but clusters of apartment buildings. Most of them are only one- and two-story buildings; Florida really likes to spread out, not up, not when there's no view of the water.

Greg slows way down at a complex called The Gulls. "I live in here,"

Greg tells Marley. "I just redecorated my office as sort of a birthday present to myself. I'd love to show you where I write all my stuff. Would you like to come over for a while?"

Marley would not. He frowns and opens his mouth, trying to think of a way to put it nicely, but Greg claps him lightly on the shoulder first.

"Don't worry about it. Hey," Greg says, switching gears immediately. "You liked my first book the best, right?" Marley nods at him, relieved. "Okay, then I know where we're going next."

They drive straight through The Gulls and exit on the other side, right onto what looks like an old highway, a long stretch of undeveloped road bordered by low, tangled brush and ending in a cow field. Turning left, it's another blank length of road, trees on the one side, cows on the other, until they come to a horse stable where Greg pulls in and parks. He turns off the engine and leans his arms across the steering wheel so he can start pointing.

"In there's where they keep the horse I liked, her name was Sugar, but I changed it for the story."

"Yeah," Marley says. "To Cinnamon."

"Right," Greg says, his smile a little self-conscious, which Marley is happy to see on someone older and wiser than himself. It's nice that such an isolating feeling is so universal.

"I get cute with my names sometimes," Greg confesses. "I do anagrams, or sounds-alikes sometimes. I can't help it."

"Understandable," Marley says.

Greg turns a friendly face towards Marley. He looks younger when he's telling his secrets, his winning smile a little more natural, his eyes more engaged. Marley is really starting to like him.

"You know Troy? From the book?" Greg asks shyly.

Marley nods. Troy was the rodeo fuckhead that the nameless narrator of the book was infatuated with. He's a fascinating character, contradictory and cold. He was the rock of the novel.

"There was a guy who hung around here for a while, named Roy," says Greg, stopping to roll his eyes at himself. "I think he's in jail now, but he's the one I focused on. He was so cute, and such an idiot." Greg shakes his head wistfully. "But I had to get him out of my system. That's what the book was about."

"I could tell," Marley says. Greg raises his eyebrows, and Marley tries to explain. "I mean, I obviously didn't know all that, but I could tell compared to the other books that it was more... personal."

There's a moment of silence in the car while something builds, and finally Greg says, "Would it be okay if I kissed you? Maybe just on the cheek?"

Marley thinks about it for a second; he's at the height of his affection for Greg after an evening of being unsure, and his dominant thought is, *Why not?* He's got relatives more invasive than a kiss on the cheek, aunts and uncles who got him on the lips—without even asking first—clear into his teens. What could it hurt?

"Okay," Marley agrees. He turns his face towards Greg and tucks some loose hair behind his ear. Greg leans over the console between the seats and presses his lips over Marley's cheekbone.

Greg stays planted there for a second, kind of too long really, and it's awkward enough to make Marley nervously smile. When his face moves, Greg releases the suction, but he sets his lips down again a little lower, this time putting a hand on Marley's right shoulder, turning him closer. Marley puts his hand on Greg's elbow, trying to urge him away from such liberties, but at his touch, Greg moves again, this time kissing Marley on the lips.

"Um, okay," Marley says, moving as far away from Greg as he can while still remaining fastened in his seatbelt.

"Sorry. I guess I let myself get carried away."

"That's okay," Marley tells Greg, even though it's pretty much not.

"So!" Greg says loudly, returning to his area behind the wheel and starting the car again. "I suppose it's time to get you back to your boyfriend. It's nice of you both to put up with me. What's his name again?"

Marley would be willing to bet that Greg remembers perfectly well, but whatever. "His name is Jesse."

"He's good-looking, sort of rough though. He probably would have gotten along with old Roy, gay or not. Where did you even meet him?"

Marley answers how he and Jesse usually like to answer, the answer that's funny because it's almost true. "Church," he says.

"Nice," Greg says. "I've always wanted to write a story like that."

Chapter Four: Faith In Poison

The next day, The Homo Superiors are on the road again. They leave Darian's house with the van vacuumed out, fresh sheets on the mattress, and every item of clothing laundered and folded in piles behind the front seats. Miriam set them up with plenty of road snacks and canned goods for when they make late check-ins, plus she made sure they'd be okay in case the van craps out... which it does.

It happens about an hour into their journey, just south of Fort Myers: a sweet, hot smell fills the van, like oatmeal on an open stovetop. Then white smoke starts to curl out of the engine.

"What the hell is that?" Aaron asks, leaning close to the front windshield to get a good look at the smoke.

"Anti-freeze," Darian says, signaling to get off the highway. "It'll be interesting to see if we make our gig now."

Missy starts to rouse herself away from her music player. If they're going to be dealing with mechanics, Missy will want to brush her hair and put on a touch lip gloss or something. Funny thing she's noticed: she gets treated a lot better by men when she's a little dolled up. It's not an ideal circumstance, but it's not an ideal world, and Missy's not afraid to make sexism work in her favor whenever possible. She locates and assembles a bra, starts cracking jokes about parts and labor.

Darian laughs. Aaron starts to pout and says something about, "Grumble mumble charging for *your* parts." He gets moody whenever Missy tries to flirt up a discount.

They can't even find a chain auto shop when they get off the highway, that's what kind of swamp shanty town exists in this corner of Florida, or so Darian says.

"There's nothing interesting between here and Miami," he assures his band as they turn off of Corkscrew Road onto another that can't decide if it's Old U.S. 41 or South Tamiami Trail, since it has signs for both. "God it's so Florida-tucky out here."

They finally find a section of town with a couple of places that purport to fix cars. Darian passes up the first few in favor of a place called Kenny's Garage, maybe because it's not as slick as the others, or maybe because it looks a lot less busy, Missy doesn't care to ask.

"Okay," Darian says, cutting the engine as the sweet-smelling smoke starts to overwhelm the view through the windshield. "Let's try not to sneer at the locals, y'all."

Everybody piles out of the van. Missy thinks she can hear her sandals start to sizzle on the pavement as soon as she sets her foot down. Even the shade of the two story interior of the garage offers little relief from the heat. Three oscillating fans only serve to move around the trapped air, which feels heavier with greasy stink of road metal filling it up.

Missy can barely see after stepping in from the bright sunlight, and by the time she blinks the green out of her eyes and gets a good look at who Darian has started talking to, somewhere in her memory she's already recognized his voice. At first she thinks horribly that it's a visitation from the ghost of one-night-stands past, but then... no. No, it's older than all that.

"Oh my god," Missy murmurs as she recognizes the cold-sky eyes of Jesse James McGrath. Those eyes squint at her, can't quite place her, then move past her to where Aaron has followed her in. They were best friends once; Aaron he knows.

"Whoa," Jesse says. "It's you guys."

"Hey, man!" Aaron says, laughing, a sound Missy hasn't heard out of him in ages.

Missy holds up a hand between the two of them. "Is Marley here?"

"No," Jesse says, and Missy's heart falls, a wet beanbag at her feet, for the cruel second it takes Jesse to add, "He's at work right now."

"Ooooh!" She runs over to hug him. "I've never been so happy to see a fucking psycho in all my life!"

Jesse accepts her invasion of his space and shows his teeth in what he obviously thinks passes as a smile. "I guess it's nice to see you too," he says, but Missy's already let go and forgotten about him as he and Aaron fist-bump or however boys express ecstatic wonder.

Missy's about to see her best friend after two years of thinking they wouldn't meet again until heaven or hell; she's got to get ready.

Her tight stack of clothes is immediately demolished in the search for her best dress. Miriam commented that it was nice to see a girl these days who didn't live in pants, and Missy had to agree with her. While wearing mostly loose sundresses during the biggest months of a summer pregnancy, Missy was enlightened to the benefits of the dress. A dress and a pair of panties is an entire outfit—easy to get in and out of, easy to sleep in, easy to launder, easy to pick up cheap in thrift stores; just the thing for such an easy girl.

She spends a lot of time in Marley and Jesse's bathroom teetering on the edge of the tub, trying to see her torso in the portrait mirror above the sink. She's got to find the dress that best fits her body as it's shaped this very moment. Though Missy has stayed rather comfortably busty since growing that baby, her weight fluctuates in conjunction with the band's prosperity; feast or famine, up and down within about a twenty pound range. Missy is happy to carry the weight voluptuously, mostly in her hips, like Marilyn Monroe, but it still must be accomodated.

The tight dresses make her cleavage look way too aggressive, and most of the looser ones look frumpy without a belt, and Missy doesn't want to feel at all constrained tonight. She ends up in a dress she rarely ever puts on because it's so dark (Missy prefers bright colors—they pop better in the dark places the band plays), but the sooty black-and-gray poppy pattern makes her hair look amazing. The next problem is how to wear her hair: tied back and braided the way Marley would remember it, or spiraling down to show off its lustrous splendor?

Missy decides that on this night (as with most others) she doesn't want to be hampered by it, and puts it in its same old braid. She puts on her makeup—just a hint of eye liner, as-needed dabs of concealer, two swoops of lipstick. While putting on the lipstick she remembers her one and only previous sleepover with Marley, tears up, and has to reapply the eye makeup. That sort of behavior just won't do at all.

Marley would laugh to see her acting like such a hysteric. She never used to be like this! He'll remember that bit of flint she was during the most trying summer of her life. Now she's older, a little more jaded, softened by alcohol. A drink! How could she forget? A drink would take the keen edge off of this severe, painful happiness.

Careful to waddle around while her toe polish is drying, Missy gets into the back of the van with a tote bag to pull out all their liquor. It's going to be a party tonight, and Missy wants to get ahead of it.

"Wow," Jesse says as she starts setting up her chemistry set on the coffee table. "You know that me and Marley don't drink, right?"

"Unless you guys are in recovery, then you just don't drink yet, and I'm here to show you the wonders of potion-making."

Darian snorts and Aaron comes over with his worried house-mother expression and Jesse just blinks at her like a fucking dog. Missy clusters the glittering spires of bottle necks and admires them for a moment; they're the prettiest things in this shooting gallery Marley calls home. She shakes her head thinking, *Boys*. It just never ends with these boys.

Her disapproval amplifies when she goes to the kitchen to evaluate the mixer situation. No soda, no juice but a pitcher of home stirred Kool-Aid crap, not even ice cubes, Jesus. She'll have to send Aaron to the store for supplies. Missy takes the Kool-Aid as a chaser—a spoonful of this ought to help her medicine go down.

Missy trades off doing swigs of vodka and Kool-Aid to cut the intensity until a pleasant tingling nestles within her. Jesse and Aaron take Jesse's truck to the store, and Missy is left with Darian and a lightheaded, precipitous feeling. Darian stretches out on the ground across the coffee table from her and picks up one of the SoCo bottles to join in the fun.

"I've never seen you like this before."

"He's the one that got away, Darian," Missy tells him through the encroaching blear.

"Probably something to do with him being gay, don't you think?" he asks cheekily, wincing at the taste of his swig.

"What am I, a couple's counselor? It just didn't work out." She and

Darian snigger quietly as they work at the business of getting drunk. In the comfortable silence, a closing door echoes in the cavernous garage below them. At first Missy just assumes it's Jesse and Aaron, but... what if it isn't? It might be *him*.

Missy rushes to the door, turns off the room's one brilliantly white mood-killing light, and opens the door as quietly as possible. That *must* be him, those tiny shuffling steps. Missy tucks herself onto the other side of the door, standing at the top of the steps and counseling herself not to tumble down the things in the dark. She stood up awfully fast and is moving in drunken swaths. She takes a deep breath.

The tall air of the garage is full of his steps. The sound of her own, ringing as she descends, rise up to meet them.

Marley walks back from work holding *Wish I Were At Home* like a talisman. He started re-reading the book as soon as Greg asked him out, trying to see it with two minds, past and present.

The first time he read this thing he was a freshman in high school. Every memorable line comes with a snapshot of where he was when he first read it and stopped to meditate on its significance: hiding in the periodicals section of the library during lunch; sitting on the bus hoping the person on the aisle side of the seat had to get off before him so Marley wouldn't be forced to speak; hearing his father get home and quickly stuffing the book under his pillow, unconcerned with losing his page if the alternative was his dad reading the back and finding out the thing wasn't about cowboys as the cover might indicate, but *gay cowboys*. Marley was never able to read any of the sexy covers until he got his job at Purple Prose, and by then he'd been ruined by literary stuff and didn't like half of it anymore.

It's not just being older himself, but understanding that this book came from a real person, that makes Marley read it so differently now.

This story didn't come to life out in the rural towns it takes place in, but instead on a keyboard in South Florida. Marley doesn't know yet if he likes having so much insight on an author; the more he understands about where a story comes from, the less it seems like magic.

He's thinking about this when he walks into the garage, trying not to imagine that something's about to jump at him from the darkness between the machines, when for once in his life of anxiety and fret, something actually does.

"Tell me you love me," she says, "or lose me forever."

It hits him in fast pieces: that strawberry-gold hair, that big mouth full of a mischievous smile, those pale legs running towards him beneath the sway of a skirt... Marley throws his arms around her a second before he knows her name.

"Missy," he tells her. "You've come back to me!"

She only laughs in response and lifts him off his feet. God, she still smells the same; different shampoo, different detergent, different lotion and makeup and perfume, but it's still *her* underneath it all. It's been two years! Two whole long short mere vast years, and here she is! Like she's been long dead, like she never left. It's like, Bogie and Bacall eat your hearts out.

Jesse and Aaron manage to come home to them canoodling in the dark; someone Marley's never met stands watching from above, curious and amused. Wiping her eyes and taking Marley's hand to lead him upstairs, Missy takes over the night.

"No tap outs, no blackouts, gentlemen," she says as she empties the bottles of soda and juice from the grocery bags. "So." She gives Marley an extra special long look and asks, "What's your poison?"

"I've never tried any before," Marley says. "I'm not twenty-one yet."

Missy rolls her eyes and waves her hands dismissively. "Nobody's twenty-one." She orders Jesse to bring her some glasses and starts concocting drinks.

"Rum and coke for my sailor, Darian," she says, handing a dark drink to the new guy. "A weak gin and Sprite for my grandmother over here," Missy says, handing a clear drink to Aaron. He rolls his eyes and retreats to the kitchen table with his drink. "Jesse I'm thinking whiskey and Coke for you? We only keep bourbon, no scotch, I'm sure you won't mind."

"I'm sure I won't know the difference," Jesse says, taking his glass and sniffing it suspiciously.

"Marley, try my vodka cran, see if you like it. I can't peg you as easily."

Marley, still watching Missy with a dreamy wistfulness, takes a sip before he thinks.

It hits the back of his mouth like lighter fluid. He's never had a liquid dehydrate him—even as he splutters he feels like he's wheezing dry.

Missy laughs throatily at him and saves the drink out of his fluttering hands. "I guess that's not for you then."

Jesse pats Marley on the back as he sniffs alcohol back out of the unsuspecting membranes of his nose, and Darian gives him a round of applause. Marley can feel his face turn red even as he smiles and tries to be a good sport. He cannot yet tell if what he's feeling is alcohol or choking, but he's got all night yet to figure it out.

Next is a gin and Sprite, which Marley likes quite a bit better, since he can hardly tell where one taste ends and the other begins. Some of Jesse's whiskey is an absolute bust (it makes his lips go numb), and a taste of Darian's undiluted Southern Comfort reminds Marley too strongly of his bitchy grandmother's perfume. It's not until Missy lets him smell the top of a rum bottle and he's surprised into saying, "Oh! It smells like a cupcake," that they've found his date to the party; Marley will be dancing with the girl on the back of the Sailor Jerry label.

Marley feels himself start to detach from his body. He begins to notice its movements only after he's in the middle of them: When did I start laughing so hard? When did I start rocking back and forth? Likewise, facts about other people's movements come gradually through a brown liquid obscurity, like manatees rising to meet him out of briny depths: Jesse and Aaron refuse second and third drinks; Darian is suddenly playing a guitar; Missy gets up to start singing. She's singing to Marley, and by the time he takes in the meaning of the lyrics, he's laughing so hard he can't stay sitting up anymore and flops over on the ground.

"You know I wish that I had Jesse's girl!" Missy rocks, her braid swinging dangerously. "Where can I find a woman like that?"

After a while Darian stops playing, but Missy keeps singing as she tumbles down next to Marley, her hair falling across his neck like a rope.

"And she's watching him with those *eyes*, and she's lovin' him with that body, I *just* know it..."

"Are they going to bed?" Marley asks, surprising himself with the volume of his own voice. The other boys are cleaning up and making noises that sound like, *Well we could get a hotel, nah hey just crash here,* etc. The three of them look over at Marley when he speaks, and they all have the same sort of smiling tolerant look people get when they're stuck listening to someone either very old or very young, a look that usually drives Marley insane with irritation; the outrage of knowing that he's being humored! But right now he couldn't care less if he knuckled down and tried. It's way too blissful to just lie here peaceably.

"Come, my love," Missy says, rolling herself up off the floor. "We'll take this party down to the van." She yanks Marley up to stand beside her, but stumbles back with his momentum into the door. "We don't need to be around a bunch of sober people, all remembering shit tomorrow."

Marley giggles again as he follows Missy carefully out of the door; railings or no, he's never been so unsteady on his feet; it's amazing! He decides to sit his way down the steps, sort of sliding and inching, very safe, very slow. He's halfway down when it occurs to him to say goodnight to Jesse first.

All care for avoiding accident is abandoned on his way back up the stairs, where he nearly slams into Missy coming out to follow him. She's carrying a bottle in each hand and manages to swerve wide and clear of Marley, so that he lands on Jesse instead.

"Hi!" Marley tells him.

Jesse's smile seems more understanding than it did before, not a judgmental sneer like Marley assumed it was. Why does he constantly think people are against him? Especially Jesse, who always seems like he understands what Marley *means* to say, instead of what he inevitably fails to say well. Marley's books could only take him so far; his comprehension is enviable, but his communication is usually insufficient. He knows more than he can describe to anyone else, but talking to Jesse feels superfluous anyway. He just gives you that quiet, knowing smile, and you think, why ruin such perfect sympathy with a bunch of muddling words?

"Hi back," Jesse says as Marley, despite his best efforts to support himself, starts to lean on Jesse, and then slide down him. Jesse presses the both of them up against a wall, and once again Marley can tell he would normally feel self-conscious. This is an intimate display of affection in front of other people, one of whom is a perfect stranger, but right now he doesn't care. By embracing him, Jesse has made the room go away. It's like not being anywhere except in his arms.

"I feel like a ragdoll," Marley says, hearing his words come out thick, accented with alcohol.

"Yes, you do," Jesse tells him. He reaches up behind Marley's shoulder and turns off the bright fluorescents above them. Marley can still feel people moving around them, using the dim light from the kitchen to see about their own business. A clang behind him reminds Marley that Missy is still out on the stairs. The world is starting to come back into focus, but Marley finds that he can block it out if he wants to, and only be in the vacuum tube of Jesse's embrace.

Marley closes his eyes, and before the desire to kiss Jesse can even begin to translate to his mind, his body has moved him forward with instinctual precision.

Right away Marley notices a difference. Not that it's ever a chore to kiss Jesse or anything, but most of the time Marley's too aware of himself to *only* kiss Jesse. Like, along with the kissing there's always a voice in the back of his head sighing and reminding him to not make a scene about his affection.

But now it's like that voice has passed out, it finally isn't talking and analyzing and criticizing endlessly. Instead, Marley can listen to his body and the sweet silence of its self-expression.

Marley can concentrate the world to an even smaller area now, just the inside of his and Jesse's meeting mouths. Jesse tastes like whatever he was drinking (Marley has long forgotten such small details as that), and together they make this dark, syrupy flavor, slow like the mixing of honey and molasses.

"Hm, you're fun like this," Jesse murmurs when they pull apart.

"I'll keep that in mind," Marley thinks he says.

He runs his hands through Jesse's hair and starts to bite his neck like a teething baby when Missy shakes a bottle in his ear.

"Okay, you've had enough," Missy says to Jesse, her voice a little round on the edges, a little slurred. She tugs Marley away and Jesse waves goodbye as Missy shuts the door on him.

She brings Marley cautiously downstairs and installs both of them in the van. She slams the doors behind her and clicks a button somewhere, turning on white Christmas lights that are strung up on the interior of the van's roof, like ribs inside of a whale. He stares around at her child's fort of a home the same way he used to stare at the merry-go-round at the fair: amazed, and a little jealous that this is someone's real experience, since his dad never let them on the ride (once it was because his sisters were wearing skirts and he didn't want to temp any creeps, another time because it was apparently overrun with Mexicans).

"This is really awesome," Marley says, flopping back on the mattress.

"Yeah," Missy says, turning on a portable player and popping in a CD. "It sort of sucks that the rest of them punked out on us, but it's nice to have some time to ourselves too. And, well, good for them anyway, right? Sobriety is a virtue, isn't it? For other people."

Marley snorts and manages to dredge up a quote from some book he read: "Give me chastity and continence, but not yet."

Missy laughs as she lies down next to Marley and throws several of her limbs over him.

"I've missed you so much," she says, kissing the side of his face. Marley closes his eyes, and for once feels totally present in his own life. He hopes for nothing, regrets nothing, and is for a moment... happy.

He's listening to the hum of 'Jesse's Girl' in his ear as he fuzzes into black.

Jesse opens up the back of the van the next morning and tries to keep a straight face as he watches Marley and Missy extricate themselves from their rat's nest. He sees at least half a tit, he sees everyone's underwear, and he watches their unhappy faces as they blink at the light and start to comprehend where they are.

"You guys look like fuck pie," he tells them with a smirk. Missy flips him off and rolls over to avoid the light. Marley digs towards him and pulls himself out of the van by Jesse's shoulders.

"Still drunk, or hung over?" Jesse asks him softly. Marley smells like he slept inside of a wet gym sock. The scent of drunk sweat reminds Jesse of his father, of getting up early for school and having to peel the old man's face out of the puddle of drool that was gluing him to the couch, asking really loudly if he could have a ride.

"I don't know," Marley groans. The poor kid; he's a real amateur at this.

"Here, can you stand on your own?" Jesse slips out from under Marley's weight and watches him weave a bit before his knees give way. Jesse catches him before he falls. "You're still drunk."

"Sorry," Marley says, but nothing's his fault. Jesse doesn't want to blame him for bringing up memories of his father; Marley might not even remember that Jesse's father drank, it's not as if Jesse ever talks about his dad. Dan McGrath is pretty long gone from his son's life.

But the smell of whiskey brought him back to Jesse's mind in an instant. He didn't want to be gun shy about alcohol just because of Dan, so he accepted the drink Missy prepared for him. Everyone else tipped easily into their beverages, including Aaron, who made plenty of disapproving noises about the way Missy drinks even as he joined her. Jesse might have asked Aaron why he stuck around with her then, but he was too distracted by the sudden whiff of his past.

His father drank cheaper whiskey than what Missy gave him, but it wasn't that different. Jesse had never tasted it before, only remembered the sour way it leeched out of his father's skin, or the way it's caustic splash would make the kitchen sink smell like the inside of tumbler whenever his mother poured it out in a huff. Jesse never tried a drop of it until last night, and even then it didn't seem to have the same effect on him as it did on everyone else. He and Marley especially had a bit of a Freaky Friday moment, with Marley finally unwinding, and Jesse tightening up uncomfortably.

He gave it until the bottom of his glass, but Jesse has already decided he doesn't like the stuff. It leaves a bad taste in his mouth.

Marley sort of mumbles in Jesse's ear that he's something something, and then starts sleeping on his feet. Jesse nods goodbye at Aaron over Marley's shoulder, and Aaron jumps into the van to deal with Missy. Apparently she still doesn't give him the time of day any more than when they were kids. Jesse gathered that bit of information between listening to Aaron complain, and listening to Darian explain in small asides that this is what they're like all the time.

The three of them had a nice dudely bonding session last night; it wasn't the same love fest that Missy and Marley obviously had, but Aaron and Jesse have their history too. They talked about cars (Jesse is going to donate his labor to his friend's radiator, in his infinite kindness), they talked about music and money, they mostly avoided the topic of sex.

Escorting Marley upstairs, Jesse figures he'll have to play nurse all day, just like he used to do for his dad. He'll have to keep the lights off and the noise down, wet a few washcloths, find a puke bucket for the inevitable sickness... But once Jesse gets Marley alone, suddenly the boy isn't so lethargic. He wakes up, and his eyes are bright, and he doesn't look sick at all.

"Good morning," Marley says, stretching luxuriously and running his fingers through his hair. He's not wearing his overshirt and he's not even self-conscious that his arms are bare, exposing the self-inflicted scars from his little stress episodes. Marley strips off his T-shirt and smiles at Jesse before jumping onto their bed and winding himself up in the sheets. How inviting.

Jesse follows and tries not to snort when he finds that Marley has gotten tangled up for real. He kneels on the bed and starts to unwrap him. It reminds Jesse of a winter in Loweville when he and his father found a litter of abandoned puppies, wrapped up lovingly, but still dead from the cold. Dan had let his son take the dogs home as pets for the day until his mom found them and ordered Dan to bury them before he made their son weird.

At last, Jesse finds Marley's face again. "Hi, sweetheart," he says.

"Hi," Marley says before dissolving in laughter again. Jesse lowers himself to kiss that giggling mouth. "Wanna fool around?" it asks.

"Don't you have work later?"

"Bleh, yeah, I guess I do."

"Well, do yourself a favor and drink some water, sleep it off a little longer." Jesse starts making Marley comfortable, gathering the pillows up off the floor where he had leant them to Aaron and Darian.

"We should do this just you and me some time, don't you think?"

"What, get sloppy drunk?" Jesse asks on his way to the kitchen to get Marley a glass of water. He gets water from the faucet, which Marley would usually hate, but Jesse knows it won't matter to him now. He returns and hands the glass to Marley and tells him, "No thanks," as the boy drinks down more than half of it in several long gulps.

"Why not?" Marley asks breathlessly. He'll be lucky if he doesn't make himself sick doing something like that. Jesse watched his father retching up water the day after a bender more than he ever saw him puking up alcohol.

Jesse just shrugs, rather than answer. If Marley doesn't remember that his dad was a drunk, he doesn't want to bring it into the room with them.

"Seriously try to sleep some. If you listen to me, you won't be sorry."

"Fine you talked me into it," Marley mumbles, finally settling down into bed. "Who knew you could be so motherly?"

Jesse gets up to turn off the light for Marley thinking, *Probably only my father did.*

61

Chapter Five: Drunken Vigil

Tristan, in spite of his insistence that he doesn't care about what Marley does *or* who he does it with, keeps a very precise accounting of his comings and goings at the store during the first weeks of September.

He doesn't mean to care, but with him and Lindsay suddenly estranged, he has nothing better to distract himself. Rita keeps telling him over his increasingly neglected dinners that he should get over himself, he should just call her. "A simple *mea culpa* is all it would take. I'm sure she misses you just as much as you miss her, but you can't blame a girl for feeling hurt that you just dropped her like that."

Sure he stopped answering her phone calls, Tristan acknowledges that, but it's not like she came to his house to find him or anything. She obviously has someone else to talk to now, doesn't she? Tristan loves her, but he's not going to beg, and he's not going to be a burden. He's lost his family once before, he can do it again if he has to. And if it's so easy for her to forget about him, then Tristan will pretend it's easy for him too. But he's got to keep himself busy somehow so he doesn't eat his own heart out brooding about her.

So here he is, in the horrible silence of Not Talking To Lindsay, of neglecting to meet her at their usual spots in school, of spending his lunch time hiding in the secret smoking nooks around campus, of wasting his afternoons first in bed, and then in the back of the store to keep Rita from worrying about him. Tristan's heard her on the phone to friends both gay and straight, baffled about what she can do to help him. It's not any standard break up, is it? Tristan did once smile to hear her tell someone laughingly, "No, I don't regret adopting him, I like a hard case." She hasn't run out of patience for him yet.

So Tristan starts watching Marley. It keeps his eyes open, keeps him engaged, and it cuts down on Rita's worry.

At first he starts marking Marley's movements with scorn. Marley wanders in late one day, stinking of booze. Tristan's parents, though they both pretty much drank themselves to death, weren't much for hard liquor. His mother was only ever a wino, but she had inherited a genetically bad liver, and she couldn't help making it worse even when it started failing on her. His dad was healthy, but depressed, and didn't switch from beer to liquor until his endgame was clearly to die.

Marley wafts by Tristan completely ignorant of all the memories he's dragging up, but when the outrage of it all completely erases Tristan's sadness for a moment, he feels an odd, begrudging thanks. He latches onto it; any port in a storm.

"Don't tell me you actually had some fun last night?" Tristan asks once he gets his teeth unclenched.

"Oh, you have no idea," Marley replies, infuriatingly pleased with himself.

Kid's a fucking idiot, Tristan thinks. Marley may be older, but Tristan can't help but pity him. He doesn't know what he's getting into. There's no sipping sweet water out of a foul well.

But as one week and then another slowly pass, a dangerous sort of curiosity starts to grow in Tristan. Something about Marley's little hints that underneath his blackouts were brief flashes of "crazy" behavior, such as making out with his friend, a girl, "fooling around" and finding it all hilariously fun. Tristan waited for some tragedy to strike Marley down, a punishment for his hubris, like a dude in a Greek play. Anything from a nasty, retching hangover to a horrible fall, a crashed car, a ruined relationship with *somebody*; could Jesse really not care that his boyfriend has a girlfriend? Could *she* really not care that what drives Marley to mess around with her is a drug, a crutch? Could this really not bring him any consequence other than a few harmless gaps in memory?

If he can do it, well then... perhaps it would be possible for Tristan, knowing the extreme limits of alcohol, to very carefully make the substance his servant and not his master?

Two weeks away from Lindsay is all he can take before he's desperate enough to ask Marley for details. He finds a moment when Rita is in the back taking in a delivery, and he quizzes Marley about his drunken exploits.

"So you've been like, what, feeling her up? With breasts and all?"

"Well, she's got a couple of them, yeah."

Marley is idly twirling a magazine rack on the cash counter and Tristan firmly resists the urge to flip it into his face.

"So did it turn you on?"

"Kind of everything is a turn-on when you're drunk."

"Not necessarily," Tristan finally says acidly. "There's nothing very sexy about shaking and crying on a bathroom floor."

"How would you know?" Marley asks. "It's not like you've ever done it."

Tristan feels his lip twist in a sneer, almost a reflex independent of his will. He had a grandfather once with a phrase for people like Marley: an educated fool. Tristan's never met anyone so smart and stupid at the same time; Marley should get an award.

Tristan turns away, deciding to save himself a lot of trouble and never use Marley as an example to follow, but his path is blocked by Rita bringing a box up to the front, something she's always telling the boys not to do ("Use the cart, I don't want the store looking like a warehouse, okay?"). She's aimed at Marley with it. Tristan stops to see why.

"This is addressed to you," Rita tells him, "and there's a letter taped onto it. There's a bunch more boxes in the back, all from the same address."

Tristan stretches his neck to see the return address, written in black marker, says it's from St. Louis. Marley has to get a pair of scissors out to score along the tape that is laminating a letter onto the box.

Both Tristan and Rita stand and watch Marley unfold a few neat pages of cursive handwriting, and then they watch his face as it morphs dramatically from happiness, to horrified disbelief, to that little quivery pathetic face he makes when you ask him to answer a ringing phone.

"What's wrong?" Rita asks.

"Someone's dead," Marley says, looking suddenly, horribly sober (*I guess booze can't make everything rosy, can it?*). "This guy I knew, he was like a father to me."

Now Tristan grins a bit, because he's pretty sure he knows who the dead man is, Marley's first "boyfriend" or "man friend" or whatever you'd call a guy old enough for retirement who's messing around with someone in high school. Imagine thinking of him as a father! As if his faraway death is anything like losing a real parent! Well, fuck him!

As Marley starts to open the box on the counter, Rita shakes her head sadly and notices Tristan's inappropriate face. She reproaches him with her eyes, and in equal silence Tristan stands up for himself with a defiant shrug. It's so easy for everyone else to forget that he's the only orphan here. Why should he sympathize with Marley's sadness? Hasn't he had enough of his own? And who was there to share that with him, outside of Lindsay?

Suddenly Tristan no longer cares about what Marley's been sent or why. He's been enduring a long two weeks without his best friend, and though he's very careful never to be hyperbolic about any situation being the worst of his life (short of more bad luck, he's already had the worst days anyone can expect to have, one for the death of each of his parents), it's still made him pretty low. He's been thinking the whole time though, about how to possibly fix it.

It's a problem of sex versus love: Tristan wants to have sex with boys, but he doesn't love a single one of them; he loves Lindsay like a virus loves a host, but he doubts very much he can get it up for her. Because of that he thinks sex shouldn't matter very much. It's like, think of all the great things you could do with your life if you just forgot about getting laid and quit wasting all that energy and creativity and passion. But then he thinks that this must just be his damage talking. A normal life is a balancing act, isn't it? You love the one you're with, and you're healthy.

Tristan picks up his phone with the impulse to call Lindsay, to tell her that he knows things are weird, that he knows it's mostly his own fault, but... he can't yet. He needs to try something first. He needs some proof of what Marley says, a solution to his problem... a hair of the dog that bit his parents.

He needs a drink.

Mitch is highly uninterested in helping Greg with his birthday party, but they've always been the best man in each other's lives, and so calling people up to confirm their RSVPs falls to him. He calls everybody, including his ex, before he calls the kid Greg has invited for entertainment. Marley Kurtz.

There are two numbers for him written down in Greg's tiny handwriting, one for Marley's home and one for his work. Mitch decides pretty quickly to call the work number; with any luck he can leave a message with someone else, because for sure he doesn't want to get stuck talking to this kid's boyfriend.

"Yeah, Purple Prose," says an aggressive young voice.

Mitch asks for Marley, already sure that whoever has answered so flippantly isn't the kid he saw slouching in Greg's cell phone picture, or the kid Greg described submitting to his lascivious request for a kiss.

The phone is handed with no warning or ceremony to someone else, and on comes a soft little voice that fits more in line with Mitch's imaginings. He was not expecting the voice to be shaky, however, as if its owner is close to tears.

"Who is this?"

"Uh, hello, Marley? I'm a friend of Greg Haywood's, I'm planning his birthday party. I just wanted to find out if you're planning on coming."

"Oh, God, I don't know, I just..." the kid sighs heavily, and it sounds so close that Mitch expects to feel the exhale in his ear and moves the phone to the other shoulder. "I thought you were going to be someone else."

"Who were you expecting?" Mitch asks, his sympathy piqued. There's at least one kid in his classes like this every year, one who doesn't seem like he'll be alright with a pat on the head and a bit of good advice that'll be ignored. Those are the kids to whom Mitch always gives a copy of *The Giver*, as a teacher had done for him once; young Receivers, every one of them.

"I just... I don't know, it was stupid." There's a shuffling sound, the phone getting moved around, jumbled with other things. Mitch, sitting in his kitchen, watches Tasi jump up onto the counter and roll around on his mail. She likes a nice glossy magazine against her fur.

Marley comes back on the line with another sigh, his voice stronger. "I don't have a ride," he says.

Before he knows what he's doing, Mitch finds himself saying, "I could pick you up."

"Oh, well, I don't really know you."

Mitch smiles. It's okay for Greg to pick him up, but Mitch might be a creep?

"I'm Mitch," he repeats. "I'm Greg's best friend."

"Did he base any characters after you?"

"What?" Mitch laughs.

Marley gives up the ghost of a laugh too. "Sorry, that's weird. It's just if you were in one of the books somewhere, you wouldn't be a stranger, you know?"

"Okay. Yeah, he said I was the basis for the cousin in *Wish I Were At Home*. The one who went to Vietnam."

"Oh, that's pretty good, I liked him." Marley is quiet for a moment, and his next statement sounds as cheerful as Mitch has yet to hear, as if his curiosity has gotten the best of whatever is bothering him. "You weren't old enough for Vietnam, right?"

Mitch laughs again. Somewhere in the past two minutes this conversation became enjoyable, certainly the most entertaining one out of the batch.

"What year do you think this is?" he asks with a chuckle.

Marley makes an apologetic sound and says, "Well, if you're sure you want to give me a ride after that, then I accept."

"Alright," Mitch says. "I'll see you Saturday after next."

A beat and then, "Okay, bye."

The call dies in Mitch's ear. Looking at the phone, the timer flashes: *Call time 3:21.* Hell of a thing.

Mitch stacks all the party-related papers and weights them under the salt and pepper shakers so that Tasi won't bat them all over the room. He gets up from the table thinking that maybe he was too quick to judge Greg. Sure that was a short phone call, but the kid's personality came through like a beam: bright as light, solid as wood. It's not as if Greg is some sort of malevolent Pied Piper, but Mitch assumed that his pursuit of this kid meant a turn towards an unbecoming lasciviousness. Maybe he was being unfair; Mitch knows better than anyone that sometimes age is no indicator of maturity, going either way.

But even with that in his favor, Marley managed to remind Mitch of something else he doesn't like about Greg. The character in his book, Patrick, the cousin who went to Vietnam. Patrick is an amalgam of Mitch and stories about his actual cousin, Ricky, who died in Vietnam before Mitch was ten years old, and who used to play patty-cake with him at family barbeques. It's not as if Greg stole any of the information... he says everything he knows gets mixed and jumbled, and he reads new stories out of it all, like blocks shaken up in a Boggle box. It feels a little personal to Mitch though. He still reads every one of Greg's books first, and he still gets startled every time he recognizes bits of real life in them.

Mitch tries to sigh these thoughts away, deep breath in, deep breath out. Toxic feelings, toxic fumes, let them go.

Mitch texts Greg in a spirit of reconciliation: *The party is fully populated.*

Greg calls in the next moment.

"Oh, I'm so excited! You called everyone, they're all coming?"

"Yep."

"You called Shawn?" Greg asks in an arch voice. "How was that?"

"Fine. We're adults you know, we can be civil. We'll both be at your party next Saturday, and we won't be making any scenes, so don't expect a show with dinner."

"Party pooper."

"Your new friend will be there too. You know, the one who's *not* an adult."

"Eighteen is eighteen, Mitch. You'd probably like him if you could get over your ageism."

"I *do* like him, what I heard of him anyway. He seems smart."

"Doesn't he? It must be from reading all my books, because he didn't even finish high school. Ran away with that boyfriend of his, isn't that cute? You shoulda seen the boyfriend too, looks like the kind of guy that might fuck you or stab you or both. You know the type."

Mitch snorts along with Greg; there were more than enough of those guys in college, and remembering them only amplifies Mitch's curiosity about Marley. Greg can be very astute at times because of his writing. He sometimes finds the most unusually perfect word for something, a word that paints a picture, like the way he described Tasi's hen-like nestling on Mitch's stomach as "roosting". But that creativity has to be kept in mind when Greg is describing someone Mitch has never met; Greg can imagine a lot more than what is actually there, and sometimes it leaves Mitch attributing fictions to real people.

Mitch settles down on the couch where he sets his bag every evening. He gets out the papers he needs to grade before bed, and his day planner. Flipping to the weekend, he carrots in a reminder to pick up Marley, and draws an arrow down to the notes section.

"Tell me the kid's address," he says to Greg. "I'm picking him up on Saturday."

"He lives above Kenny's Garage, it's on Tamiami just past that enormous Walgreens. On the opposite side of the street, you can't miss it. But hands to yourself, okay? I saw him first."

"He lives above a garage?" Mitch has decided to just simply ignore Greg's flirty bullcrap. It keeps his blood pressure down.

"The boyfriend, he's a mechanic. He looked like he wanted to brain me with a wrench, I'm sure he'll like you too."

"If that kid murders you, I'm not gonna tell the news that you didn't deserve it."

Greg just laughs, a deep genuine one, not the polite little giggle he's learned to use when he's schmoozing.

"Hopefully I won't meet the boyfriend. I'm kind of interested in Marley now. He seems, I don't know, mature for his age?"

"No," Greg drawls. "Not mature. Weary for his age is more like it, sort of wary. And wayward. Hmm."

Mitch smiles to hear Greg clicking a pen. He'll write that down, he likes the sound of it. It's just a matter of time before Mitch sees some variation of that harmonious train of thought in a story somewhere.

"All right," Mitch says. "Leave me alone, you call here too much. Get a real job."

Greg laughs again. "See you at the party, Mitchell."

Rita insists that Marley leave when the store closes, and not stay later to straighten the stacks and close the register like usual. He doesn't particularly want to stay around Tristan any longer than he has to, since he's acting like this might be any other day, probably just to be hurtful. Marley doesn't want to leave Frank's books, but he doesn't want to call Jesse to come get them with the truck either. He'll do that tomorrow. He wants to walk home by himself today.

September is still warm and heavy. Marley leaves the air conditioned store and feels the artificial air come off him in a shallow slipstream. The afternoon, the evening, sleeps so peacefully. The sky looks like the sun's been melting hard candies together all day, and it's now cooling in a glassy sheet. Marley smiles sadly at the colorful ending of day. He feels so tired.

He blurted to Rita that Frank was like a father to him, and it's not untrue. That's sort of the easiest way to explain to a stranger what Frank meant to him. There isn't time to get into the Athenian way he was a both mentor and a lover. It's just like the opening notion in *Pet Sematary*: he met a man who should have been his father. And maybe it's weird that he had sex with someone like that, but hey, that's why he doesn't particularly feel like explaining.

Frank's letter was a little doomed, a little humorous, just like he was when Marley knew him. Marley thought it was just Frank's feelings towards him that were like that, because their relationship was so 'inappropriate' or whatever, but maybe that was just his personality. Or maybe he'd changed since meeting Marley, or since having to leave town because of Marley. Or maybe Marley is giving himself too much credit, but that *is* how the letter began:

I was never the same since meeting you.

To be fair, that makes two of them. Maybe Marley was too young to have really been somebody before meeting Frank, but at sixteen he definitely had enough personality to make Frank forget about how wrong everything supposedly was and let Marley experiment with him, to learn from him. Everyone who ever found out about them was especially scandalized that Frank should be a teacher. "A *professor*," Marley tried to stress. "A teacher, but not *my* teacher," he told everyone. But he had nevertheless been a teacher to him, and why quibble about it? It's not as if it could really matter now.

Nobody lives forever, and I've got a bit of a trick heart, as well you might remember. Frank had developed an irregular heartbeat at some point, a doctor told him about it; Marley used lay his head on Frank's chest and listen for it. *I just want to set my affairs in order while I can, and make sure my books will be well cared for and appreciated after I'm gone.*

No one but myself has ever loved these books as much as you. If my sister actually carries out my wishes (she has an idea of who you are to me and doesn't like it one bit), you'll get every book I've ever collected, after I die.

Marley spent half the letter unaware that he was reading the words of a dead man, and it was slow to filter into his mind. So wait, he's dead right now? Did he die last week? Last month? When did he write this letter? No date, no note of explanation from Frank's sister who, apparently, had honored her brother's final instructions.

Marley feels a little unsteady on his feet walking home, a little woolly-headed. He isn't jumping at every close-passing car though;

suddenly the volume on the world is turned way down. Coming home is surreal.

Aaron and Missy have been unofficially rooming with them for about two weeks. First they lived out of the van until Darian couldn't stand the incestuous in-joking with this Colorado crew and decided to go back to his mom's for a while. The closest Marley got to relating with Darian was a brief conversation about all the privileges and privations of growing up in Florida (fire ants, hurricane days, attending a swamp buggy race or two), but after a bit Darian decided he'd be more comfortable sleeping in his own room at home. Jesse patched up the radiator hose, said he'd replace it with the new one once the part came in, but that Darian would be good to go to Sarasota and back. They dragged the mattress out of the van and all the way upstairs for Aaron and Missy, and they moved Marley's bookshelves into the middle of the room to act as a divider, give the two couples some privacy.

It does a lot for the room; the space really is too big for a single room, and they're thinking about keeping the shelves there permanently even after Missy and Aaron take off again, use the created space as a nook for when Marley and Jesse need to get half an ounce of privacy away from each other. Maybe get a nice chair over there, create a sort of library by adding more shelves for Marley's growing collection. Coming home, Marley thinks it was a prophetic idea; Frank's books will need a lot of space once they're unpacked.

Marley manages to miss running into Kenny, though he heard him banging around somewhere in the garage. He's trying to compose the news in his head to tell everyone; he's always much more articulate in his head than outside of it, and he wants this to come out succinctly. When he walks in the door however, it's obvious that there's no need.

Jesse's standing, leaning by the phone like he just put it down. He looks like he does every time he's sort of pitying Marley for something. Aaron's got a look on his face like someone who's just watched you crash into a table corner. Missy's moving right towards him shaped like a hug.

"Rita called," Jesse says as Missy wraps her arms around Marley. Her body is warm but her exposed skin always feels a little cool, like her skin's too pale to hold a temperature. Marley hugs her back, looking at Jesse over her shoulder. "She said if you weren't home soon, we should go make sure you hadn't chucked yourself into traffic."

"Come on," Missy says to him quietly, stroking his hair. "Let's go drown your sorrows."

The suggestion of a new location draws Marley's focus away from thoughts of Frank. In the past two years, Marley has been in fewer than ten buildings in South Florida. The grocery store, his parents' house, Kenny's house, Rita's house, work, home... and he went to the hospital last year when he broke his arm. He's never been to a bar anywhere, but that is where Missy is demanding either Aaron or Jesse drive them to, because she plans to get them both profoundly wasted. Sounds like a good plan to Marley; alcohol has yet to do him wrong.

Missy finds the place, searching on the computer in Kenny's office since neither Marley nor Jesse owns one (Marley explores the internet tentatively while behind the counter at work, Jesse is completely uninterested in its existence).

"We want a place that's in between a club and a 'bar & grill' okay? Just a bar with a bar, nothing fancy, no sports on TV, no pick-up scene." She searches quickly, her eyes darting and narrowing as Marley sits on the desk watching her, wondering at her. There's somebody who's much better at growing up than Marley is, and she's always been younger than him. How to explain that?

"Oh, here we go," Missy says, a smile unrolling on her face like a welcoming rug. "Place is called Sunset Egret, it's in a shopping mall. God help us, it's perfect." She pulls a note pad over to her and snaps a pen out of the coffee mug on Kenny's desk. "Let's go."

Marley tries to ignore the drive—his time in Colorado, where he met every other person in this vehicle—was a strange divider in his life. For sixteen years his parents drove him up and down these streets, as far north as North Fort Myers, as far south as Naples. The road they're on now, for example, is the way Marley's parents used to take him to the pediatrician. He's trying to block out the quicksand suckage of the past and concentrate on where he is right now, the value of having these people here when it was so unlikely that they would all ever meet again.

"You'll be okay," Missy says. She and Marley are sitting crammed on the passenger side of Jesse's truck, sharing the same seatbelt.

"How do you figure?" Marley asks quietly.

"You've been through worse haven't you? And you've got me to take care of you." She squeezes his knee, and they ride the rest of the way in silence.

Sunset Egret really is in sort of a strip mall center, a squared-off horseshoe shape of rental spaces, the same kind that Purple Prose is in. The windows of the bar are blacked out with some kind of opaque film, little bubbles in it like it was put up by hands that only marginally knew what they were doing.

Marley keeps his eyes down when he walks in. It's still slightly twilit outside, but inside it's the middle of the night. Hooded orange lights pick out the bar on the right side of a long room. Aaron steers Marley discreetly over to a table and has him sit with his back to the bartender.

"You don't look at all like you're old enough to be in here, and neither of you guys have fake IDs, so we may not be staying long," he explains.

Missy goes up to the bar with her ID and money already in hand, and Marley scoots to the very back of his booth across from Jesse and Aaron. Jesse slides his foot over to Marley's side and nudges his sneakers sympathetically. It's the best he can do, and Marley nods at him for it. Missy does a lot more.

"Marley, meet a Long Island Iced Tea. I'd tell you to be careful and not drink it too fast, but we have been asked to leave in ten minutes or get thrown out. I've never had anyone pick and peel at that ID so hard."

"Fine by me," Marley says. "It smells like a wet dish rag in here."

"Does it?" Missy asks, taking a big pull at her Long Island through the straw and pushing the plain Cokes they requested over to Jesse and Aaron. "I love the way bars smell."

"It smells exactly like the gray ratty rag they used to wipe down cafeteria tables in high school."

"Hmm," Missy considers, sniffing the air. "I guess so."

The table gets quiet. Marley can feel everyone's attention creeping over to him and takes a sip of his drink. It doesn't taste like liquor, but it doesn't taste like iced tea either. He knows it's alcohol by the way it coats his stomach in a strange, emanating warmth.

Marley is suddenly thankful, ever so thankful, that alcohol exists, because he knows that in a few minutes it will cure what ails him. His painful self-consciousness gone, his sadness banished, and in their place is an optimistic feeling, like hearing the burbling sound of fresh water after being lost for days in a wilderness.

Or not water, Marley thinks with a smirk as he takes another, bigger sip of his drink, *but liquid all the same.*

Part Two: Remorse

Chapter Six: Unresting Death

Jesse expected Marley to self-destruct over the loss of the old guy. Not to be mean, but the boy just does not handle things well at all. Jesse's seen him take a few days to recover from the horror of an hour's change one way or the other in his work schedule; he would have guessed that something as serious as Marley's first death would demolish him.

But he's always been a funny kid. That's what Jesse continues to like most about Marley, the element of surprise. Jesse thought for sure that hell would come home with that dead man's books, but it hasn't, not really. Marley bought five more bookshelves, Jesse put them together as Marley sorted and alphabetized the books, and the boxes they came in went out to the trash, all very systematic. Jesse finds he likes the look of the 'library,' which now walls itself off into the nook behind the bathroom (which juts into the front left corner of their room in a six-by-six foot square). There are three shelves on the side wall, two at the back, and four doubled back-to-back to divide the room into two separate areas. Marley says he'll consider un-doubling those once Missy and Aaron and their mattress leave, and perhaps they'll open up the room again by pushing all the selves to the wall. Marley says he likes the idea of sleeping surrounded by bookshelves. He's very practical about it all.

"Hell," he says, "a few more shelves and we can make a maze. Frank used to tell me that you have to get older, but you don't have to grow up."

That's it, as far as Jesse knows. He simply hears about Frank more now, little stories, asides, anecdotes. Even Frank would have found Marley's system of organizing needlessly complex; Frank used to say you could judge a man by the state of his book covers; Frank liked to keep this and that author together on the shelf because they were friends in life. It's as if Marley feels like he can talk about his previous relationship to Jesse now that it's one hundred percent over, or maybe Marley's just been reminded of Frank because of all this, and eventually he won't talk about him so much anymore. It certainly doesn't bother Jesse to hear about the man, he's not what anyone would call a jealous type.

It seems healthy in a way. He's talking about it with everyone, and the books are up where they all can see, not hidden away. Jesse should but doesn't really understand the emotions Marley is going through. After all, his mother died when he was growing up, he knows a little something about death. He can relate to the circumstances Marley is in, but not the emotions. Never the emotions.

Understanding that they were built differently and trying to predict Marley's behavior objectively from what he's observed so far, Jesse has been waiting for the cutting to start up again. He knows Marley still does it sometimes, when he's inordinately stressed about whatever keeps him idly eating the skin off his own lips and fingertips, whatever makes him press his back into the corner of large rooms. But nope; for all the worrying Marley does about unlikely tragedy, when something traumatic finally happens it's like Marley's prepared for it. It's like when Jesse's father used to toothlessly threaten him with pre-spanking, in case Jesse did something naughty when he wasn't looking. Marley experiences all his stress, his mourning, and his worry every day, so when something horrible finally does happen, it doesn't knock him off keel. Jesse doesn't know it, but this is how Mithridates lived so long.

The books go up. Marley and Missy spend their evenings mixing new poisons in the kitchen. Marley and Jesse spend more nights than not trying to fuck quietly, not that it makes much difference. Missy is either passed out unconscious or giggling at their attempts to stay muted, and Aaron, as usual, is just shit out of luck.

Something's different in the way they do it now. Jesse had already started noticing hills and valleys in the frequency and intensity of sex over the two years he and Marley have been together, but this is something strange. In the past if Marley or Jesse's interest flagged, the other one just took up his own slack again. Masturbation's more instinctive than riding a bike must be, not that anyone ever taught Jesse how to ride one, but they say once you learn you never forget. Jesse has an impression that there's something very civilized and modern about the way they leave each other alone without complaint; something about hippies and feminists and some other stuff his father used to talk discordantly about, like he wasn't necessarily a fan, but he definitely thought Loweville was lesser for not having such people.

The way they're doing it now though...

Marley's become more aggressive. Not dominate (Jesse would like to see him try), but more assertive, pushing or pulling Jesse's shoulders in the dark when he used to tuck his arms under the pillow. He's started wrapping his legs around Jesse's waist and holding him in place, when he used to just get out of the way. Jesse's distant sometimes, but he isn't dense. He knows Marley's trying to tell him something.

It's something about the old man, and this author, Greg Haywood. It's something about Marley not getting what he thinks he wants, and Jesse feels mostly confident that Marley will get over it. Last year Marley tried to return to his father's house, and eventually he came back to Jesse, didn't he? And now he's looking for a father figure again, and what should Jesse assume? That he'll come back again, of course.

"I bet you could come to this party too," Marley says, putting his hair up, then down, then half up, then down, then in a ponytail like most days as he waits to be picked up for Haywood's birthday. "I mean, does anyone want to come with me?"

Missy, who has just woken up—that girl sleeps over 10 hours every day, Jesse can hardly believe it—shakes her head, but smiles at Marley.

"Have your own fun, Marley," she says. "Make me jealous."

Marley smiles, and Jesse sees him relax to one notch lower in his anxiety. She's done a lot of good to Marley by coming back into his life, though Jesse had at one time clean forgotten her name because it's not like Missy was ever *his* friend. She doesn't even like him much, still holds a grudge for the one time Jesse quit talking to Marley for barely two weeks, just because Marley spent a few days in the hospital during that time, and Jesse never broke his silence. Regardless of that though, Jesse's starting to really appreciate Missy's influence now. She makes his boyfriend, and thus his life, run smoother.

Marley turns to Jesse; does *Jesse* want to go to Greg Haywood's birthday party with him?

"I'll walk you out," Jesse says to Marley's plaintive face. Jesse doesn't want to go at all, and no amount of pouting will change that.

Marley goes back to the mirror, back to smoothing his perfectly smooth ponytail, with his bottom lip is in his mouth, getting chewed on. Jesse pats his shoulder and meets his gaze in the mirror. He'll be okay, even if he doesn't know it.

After approval from Missy on his outfit (which she didn't actually look up to see, and why bother, because they all look exactly the same), he and Jesse go downstairs to wait out front for his ride.

Jesse opens the garage door, thinking idly that there's a chance Marley has never touched the thing. If it isn't open, he uses the side door. It takes a bit of conviction to raise these wide, heavy doors, you can't just nudge them open like Marley usually goes in and out of places. He looks sort of rung out already, twisting the pointer finger of his left hand like it will unscrew from his palm eventually.

Jesse kind of wishes he carried a flask, so he could offer Marley a pull of courage. His father always carried one, and never got rid of it even when he quit drinking. He kept it empty for a while, and he took it with him when he left. Maybe he keeps it full now. He said it was a good way to make friends, offering people a drink. Not that Dan had many friends. But then, it's not as if Jesse does either.

Mitch pulls up right on time, and Jesse already likes him better than Greg because he has a regular car like someone who doesn't think too highly of himself. A silver Taurus, a bit of an old lady car, but he probably bought it used. He gets out and shakes hands with both Jesse and Marley, looking around at the dark garage and the empty parking lot like he can't quite believe this is a day in his life.

Me too, brother, Jesse thinks. It turns out that you can't really help who your friends are after a while. Mitch, who seems perfectly aware that he's too old to be 'hanging out' with teenagers, ended up best friends with Greg Haywood. Likewise Jesse, who's never once done anything he didn't want to do, is best friends with the saddest punk bitch he's ever even seen in real life.

Oh well; maybe whiskey makes you better friends, but Jesse will never find out for sure.

Marley enjoys sitting in the passenger seat of Mitch's cozy little car. It's low to the ground, has cloth seats where Jesse's truck has vinyl, it has an air freshener and even little decorations—a tassel on the rearview mirror, and a picture of a cat on the inside of the passenger sun shade, which Marley saw when he flipped it down hoping to find a mirror. It relaxes him to be in here, and it relaxes him that Mitch doesn't feel the need to make casual conversation, because it's never casual for Marley. Casual conversation is the most stressful part of his daily life working at Purple Prose. Some people must walk around talking about the heat to every bank teller and barista they come into contact with, and why? Why not just be quiet if there's nothing interesting to say?

Marley naturally worries that he doesn't have the first idea how to interact at a party. The last 'party' he was at was a sleepover when he was in middle school, and all the other kids tricked him into playing hide and seek so they could go play spin the bottle in another room. Marley, who had started reading in his hiding place, thought he had slipped *them* until he realized that they had engineered him away. He barely had his feelings hurt, actually. Those kids were dead boring, and at eleven they were all way too young to really care about making out with each other, if you asked Marley.

But after a couple minutes of being introduced around to people, and finding that it's impossible to sink completely into Greg's luxuriously thick couch, someone asks if he'd like a drink. Yes. Yes, he would.

"What'll it be?" asks a be-spectacled man whose name Marley cannot remember because it was in a line of four others. It's either Ted,

Shawn, or Keith. It doesn't matter.

"Well, I mean, a rum and coke is what makes me fun around my friends," he says, and the man smiles agreeably.

"That was my drink when I was in college," he says. "Good choice."

Marley feels bolstered, first by the praise (good choice, good job, good good!) and then by the sugary burn of his drink. This is Captain Morgan, Marley saw the bottle it was poured from—not like the slim bottles Marley was used to seeing Missy carry around by the neck, but a big ol' jug with a handle, the kind Marley can imagine people blowing hillbilly music into. It tastes fine to him, though he still prefers Sailor Jerry and can see it too in the cluster of the bar cart in the corner. He won't ask for it though. A Captain and Coke is just fine, really. Missy says you can get into trouble mixing brands, mixing liquors. "Dance with the one that brung you," she said to him with a throaty laugh one night, about five minutes before she decided she was too hot and took off her shirt. She's a real sport when she drinks, Missy, she's game for anything.

His drink cupped in both hands like a mug of hot cocoa, Marley makes himself a little hidey-hole in the corner of Greg's huge, plushy couch, and he doesn't emerge until he's about three drinks in. At first he's too distracted by the buzzing, static feeling in his face and fingers, that alchemical magic—it burns and spreads, a slow lava in his veins; it fills up the space around his brain and makes it float. But after a while Marley is happily surprised to find that he isn't where he left himself.

In a jump he's leaning out of the pocket he made for himself, talking to someone about books—beginning with Greg's books, which Marley's gushes about, and then about other books like them. There's a chunk of time where Marley wonders if he isn't talking too loud? These men all seem to be leaning away from him while he deluges about the lovely books he's read, all the connections he's seen between them. But they're all smiling at him, no matter how far away they are, so it must be okay.

After a while Marley becomes a puddle; he's a liquefied human boy, he's thickly melted flesh. He keeps talking, but no matter how loud he gets now, he can't hear himself at all. Except for Greg and Mitch, the whole room starts to seem like a parade of the same middle-aged guy. They're all wearing nice button-down shirts, or is that just the one sitting next to him, the one whose buttons Marley twiddles idly until he realizes that people are laughing at him. But it *is* funny, isn't it? And no one seems to hold it against him. In fact, they're all looking at him with the same smiling head-shake, fond and wistful, the way Frank used to look at him.

The clearest memory out of all this party blur is when Greg asks if Marley brought him a gift, and since he did not, Greg says, "How about a birthday kiss, then?"

Marley stands fluidly up out of the well in the couch—it suddenly seems a lot deeper, since reaching his own full height makes him a little dizzy. He probably wobbles all over the living room to get to Greg's seat, but to him it's a graceful weave, a snake through tall grass. What makes him doubt his own perception are the arms that reach out of the orange dimness of the room to support him, to tug him away from the coffee table because it's covered in spillable drinks and glass.

Greg is sitting regally, waiting for the only gift Marley could bring him. A kiss, an unsophisticated and damp little kiss. Marley knows he can do better—he's kissed Jesse a hell of a lot better than that in the past couple of years—but maybe it isn't okay to kiss other people that well? Eh, he'll worry about it tomorrow.

He must have done well enough however, because he can hear a discussion about the kiss sort of reverberate through the group. *Murmur murmur, something something, kiss me that way ha ha ha.* In the next moment Marley finds himself going in a circle, starting with the man who sat right next to him, Satiny Button-Down. Marley lands a kiss on the corner of his cheek, but it seems to satisfy him. Marley moves on.

Next is Sweater Vest, and Marley does a better job with him, at least getting him on the lips. After that is Faux Leather Jacket, and after that is a man standing at the counter with a wine glass, catch-and-release all around the room. These guys don't seem to be drinking anywhere near as hard as Marley, and though it's mystifying that they don't want to have as much fun as possible, Marley doesn't care too much. There are two more guys in the kitchen, and they seem to be happy with only cheek kisses. And at last there is Mitch, standing discontentedly by the stereo.

Marley tries to throw his arms around him because it's Mitch! Mitch from before! Mitch that he knows by name! But Mitch isn't having it. He catches Marley's wrists and smoothes down his shoulders like a bed sheet that's just fluttered down over a mattress. Smooth, smooth, tuck. It's such a finishing gesture. It injures Marley sharply, the idea that someone won't even let him kiss them, not even just on the cheek! Ouch.

Mitch is talking to Greg. "It's time for him to go home. He's not even old enough to drink, is he?"

Marley wants to protest—he's tired of being too young for everything! He's finally eighteen after a lifetime of being a child, and now people want to keep one more thing from him. Outrageous.

But before he can really form an argument (or even the coherent thought around his indignation), everyone is waving goodbye to him.

Mitch places a bottle of water in Marley's hands and stows him back into his car. Marley feels like he was just here, though it's a much deeper dark out than it was last time.

Time slows down during the drive home. Marley first is aware of the silence in the car, after the barrage of music and conversation of Greg's party. Next Marley takes a sip of his water and thinks about how much more delicious it is when he's drunk and dehydrated than it ever manages to be the rest of the time. Third, Marley notices that he's terribly hungry. He wishes he had some McDonald's like when he was a kid *right now*. It's an intense need, but he still can't bring himself to ask Mitch to go through a drive-through. Marley will probably never be *that* drunk.

But he can get pretty close:

"So," he says to Mitch. "You don't want to kiss me, then? Or was it just a bad time to ask?" Marley is equally confident that his words are coherent as he is suspicious that he just can't hear the slur.

Mitch doesn't answer, but instead lifts the lid on the center console and pulls out another bottle of water. He hands it to Marley and says, "Drink this or you'll have a terrible morning." Marley hadn't realized he'd finished the first one and dropped it on the floor.

Marley rolls his eyes (he thinks) but opens up the bottle after fumbling the cap a few times. He feels sort of compelled to keep drinking *something*.

"There's a couple more bottles in here, help yourself," Mitch says. "You ought to pace yourself, you know. Have some water in between every drink, that way you don't lose control."

"But that's the point," Marley says, shaking his head slowly to feel his brain swim around. "Why not just drink soda if you don't want to lose control?"

"You're still such a kid," Mitch sighs. "It's not right for grown men to... take advantage of you like that."

"I'm not a kid," Marley says petulantly, and he supposes that's as far as his treatise on ageism is going to get tonight, at least out loud. He's heard this sort of speech before, people telling him he lacks the ability to make his own choices because they want to make all the decisions for him, and fuck that! "I was just having fun and I don't feel like being judged, okay? In fact why are you even taking me home? I wanted to stay."

"I doubt you'll feel that way tomorrow. Besides, we're almost there."

Marley looks out the window, but everything's moving too fast for him to nail down any identifying landmarks. In fact, at some point he blinks for so long that he doesn't realize he's back at the garage again until Mitch turns off the engine. Though he thought he was energized enough to go back to the party, now the prospect of rousing himself enough to even get upstairs seems impossibly exhausting.

Mitch nudges his shoulder gently. "Are you okay from here or should I walk you in?"

"It's upstairs," Marley sighs heavily.

Mitch gets out of the driver's side and comes around to help Marley out. "There's no way you'd make it up a flight of stairs. What the hell is wrong with Greg?" he murmurs.

"What's wrong with you?" Marley counters as he slumps out of his seat after the door is tugged out from under him. Mitch catches him, and Marley's arms wrap around Mitch's neck in complete contradiction to how he's thinking right now. He's annoyed, but his body is friendly. It's the strangest feeling, but Marley goes with it. The sensation of Mitch's strong shoulders sliding beneath his arms, the rush of being dipped and twirled *a la* a ballroom dance as Mitch moves to keep Marley upright. It makes him like Mitch all over again. "What kind of person doesn't want a free kiss?" Marley asks.

Marley goes for Mitch's lips and lands on his beard. The combination of thinking 'oh I've missed' with 'oh he's rejecting me' strikes a blow of pain even deeper than before, when there was so much else going on. God, it's like the time in high school when someone pretended to pick him first for a kickball team (not that he knew how to play really, or even thought he would be chosen ahead of the kid who had his knee in a brace). It's like the time his little sisters started playing a game he invented and then told him he couldn't play with them anymore, and he can't even remember the game now, but the feeling of being excluded is starkly present. This happens *all the time*. Marley's whole life is people snubbing him like he's nothing.

A sob escapes Marley's throat and mouth, but he isn't crying, because a second later he's moving towards the building with purpose. He meets Jesse in the light of garage, a bunch of blah blah happens between him and Mitch that Marley stomps right past. Missy is by the stairs, with a lot of blah blah and gestures upstairs. Aaron is at the door to their loft with some blah blah don't fall down or something.

Marley yanks off his clothes.

Marley trips trying to take off his shoes.

Marley falls onto the bed thinking he could use some more water.

Marley doesn't remember anything else.

Missy is charged with babysitting Marley the next day, nursing his egregious hangover, and counseling him with some sage alcoholic advice.

Missy's experience helps in almost every aspect of Marley's day. He thinks he wants to eat two bowls of canned ravioli? "Kiddo, you have never thrown up canned ravioli, and trust me you don't want to," Missy tells him. She brings him slices of white bread, she brings him a Gatorade and gallons of water, she brings him half a pack of crackers. Even this very careful diet makes him feel sort of sick, however. Once he feels overwhelmingly uncomfortable, Missy runs him a bath.

"So, how much of last night do you remember?" Missy asks him as she eases him out of his clothes and modestly turns away to put some bubbles in the tub when he drops his underwear. The boy is half sober now, no telling how he feels about being naked anymore. Missy enjoys her own nudity, but not everyone respects that.

She would have thought that Marley, as shy as he is, would be really uptight about his exposed body, but either Missy is an exception for him or the kid is still inebriated. He flumps into the tub, spilling a little bit of water over the edge that Missy wraps up with a towel. He puts his hand over his eyes like he thinks he can contain the shame that way (no way) and answers:

"I think I made out with the whole room. I can't even remember their names."

Missy snorts, and then apologizes for being so loud when she sees Marley flinch. "Sounds like you're a bit of a good time girl when you drink. Don't worry about any of that. Most likely everyone appreciated the tongue-time, and if they haven't done the same thing when they were young, then they haven't lived as much as you."

Marley smiles at her, even peeks out from under his hand, though the light still hurts him and he's squinting. Missy turns off the bulb so that the room is filled with only the filtered light coming through the rippled glass of the tiny bathroom window. Her eyes adjust slowly, though she can hear Marley moving around tentatively in the water. It's like she's found a mer-boy and brought him back to keep; this world is strange to him, but Missy is here to help him learn.

"Besides," Missy rejoins as she kneels next to the tub. "Mitch wouldn't have let you do anything too crazy. We met him, he's a nice guy."

"You met Mitch? Really? He's like the only person I can even remember from last night. When did you meet him?"

"Marley, he's the one who brought you home, remember? He told me everything you'd had or might have had to drink, and he stayed talking with Jesse for a while too, first about cars, and then about you."

Marley covers his face again, and Missy dips her fingers into the lukewarm bathwater to stir up some more bubbles. She painted her nails the night before as she watched Marley sleep it off, thinking fondly of the time she painted his fingernails once, when they were kids, or at least younger than they are right now. She never stopped missing him, and it's been a strange thing, because Missy has had friends before, but never like this. She loves him. He's her best friend, for life. She trails her fingertips though his bathwater and knows that she'd do a lot for him. Not anything; Missy doesn't write any emotional blank checks. But she'd do the most for Marley, she knows that for sure.

A knock vibrates into the door, way too loud for this drunk, marinating boy in front of her. Missy stands up and slides the door open maybe an inch, just enough to hiss, "What!"

"Are you guys okay? You've been in there a while," Aaron says on the other side.

"We're fine," Missy says. "How much are you going to bother us?"

Aaron's mouth lemons up and he murmurs that he was just checking, that she didn't have to be mean. Missy shuts the door on him. He may or may not have caught her rolling her eyes. She doesn't care.

"That wasn't very nice," Marley says quietly.

"Well, I'm not very nice then," Missy says. "And you should talk; how much does Jesse appreciate you kissing other guys?"

"He'll live," Marley mumbles. "He doesn't have my problems."

Missy hikes up her dress and sticks one leg in Marley's bath, sitting down on the tub's edge. He starts trailing his fingers up and down her shin. As her eyes adjust more and more to the light, Missy watches Marley's face. His expression gels back and forth between a fuzzy fondness and a wincing embarrassment. Missy knows what he's going through.

The bottle is a steep learning curve for some people. She never would have guessed she had any natural talent for drinking, since her mother never had more than a glass of wine on Christmas, but it was absolutely intuitive. None of this nonsense about moderation for Missy, no reasonable limits, and no big problems yet. Missy was able to hit the ground running. Poor Marley looks like he hit the ground with his face.

It's time to get him out of the tub when the water gets cooler than tepid, but Marley somehow manages to start sweating. She definitely gets to look at his junk this time because he's too dizzy to be demur; he has to hold on to the wall while Missy gently dries his hair. It's going to be a long day for him.

Aaron and Jesse keep well away once they're out of the bathroom, fleeing downstairs so they won't be conscripted into being hangover nannies. But once Marley feels better they go downstairs to hang out in the relatively mild weather. The cold snap that had come through in the second week of September cleared out in a hurry, but the summer is still falling away, and Missy sits up on a tool bench out back to watch Jesse try and teach Aaron how to change the oil in a van much like Darian's, check the tire pressure, maintain the battery. Missy brings Marley up onto the bench with her, and he lays his head down in her lap. Jumping up on the bench made it throb again, so she's rubbing his pulsing temples.

Missy has a moment... just one of those snapshot moments where her toes are waving in the breeze, and there are fluffy clouds all over the sky, and she's reunited with her boys all together again, and everything's perfect. She had a couple of dreams like this after they first left Colorado, when she was plagued by self-doubt and sleeping badly. Missy wondered how much of this she had given up by leaving—hanging out after school with Marley, sneaking booze and cigarettes under the bleachers or whatever, giggling in church. And it might have been like that if they hadn't all been under the intense scrutiny of the adults in Loweville, or if Missy hadn't been burdened with a child. But here she has everything she was afraid she'd left behind forever. She can now easily say she regrets nothing, and the feeling is a relief.

Missy starts twirling a piece of Marley's hair as Jesse and Aaron go back and forth pointing at engine parts, saying their names so that Aaron will learn. Missy smiles and leans down to whisper at Marley, "They sound like Adam and Eve, naming the animals."

Marley laughs, but then immediately cradles his head in pain. As wrecked as he got, he doesn't look that worn out—same boyish cheeks, same girlish eyelashes batting at her over eyes that are only a touch bloodshot. He'll turn out all right, just like she did. Missy's sure of it.

Missy and Marley start inventing their own names for car parts (*wang, bent wang, accordion thing, tube, other tube*) and getting Aaron and Jesse to roll their eyes at how stupid they're being, when Jesse's boss comes out carrying a phone. They'd heard it ring, but with Kenny in his office, no one took any notice of it. Kenny is looking at the phone like it just changed colors on him. How does that guy run his own business? He looks like he's the owner's half-wit son to Missy.

"It's somebody named Miriam."

Aaron wipes his hands (delusionally, because he never really touched anything on the van) and takes the phone from Kenny, who looks even more confused now that his hand is empty.

"Yeah, hi, Miriam," Aaron says, and then, "Oh." He turns to Missy with the same look on his face that he wears when he has to tell Missy and Darian that there is no money left for booze, they need it all for gas to the next gig. It's his Bad News face.

"What is it?" she asks Aaron.

"She says it's serious," Aaron tells her, handing her the phone. "An emergency."

A cold crash of dread shakes through Missy as she takes the phone. Darian's mom isn't calling so they can have more girl talk, so what does that leave? Missy and Darian always worry, with all the sex they have, what they would do if they ever caught something. Even being careful has its limits statistically, and they both have contingency plans. Darian says he would quit the road and stay home with his mother, supporting her and wallowing in abstinence. Missy would kill herself if she got something incurable, no question.

"Is it Darian?" she asks right away, as Aaron backs off and Marley sits up because she was jostling him in her reach.

"Ohhh," Miriam says, drawing it out sentimentally. "No, sweetheart, he's just fine, but I do have some bad news. Are you okay to hear it?"

Missy looks around. Everyone, including Kenny, is hanging around pretending not to listen. But she's sitting down, so Missy thinks she must be ready.

"Go ahead," she tells Miriam.

Miriam takes in a large gulp of air.

"I got a call from some people in Colorado, they called about a little girl, your little girl. Natalie? Darling, she died. She had leukemia and she died a few weeks ago. I'm so very sorry."

"Huh," Missy says.

"I guess they were trying to reach you to see if you were a match to donate marrow, but they didn't track you down until you guys stopped here for a while." Miriam is quiet for a beat and then asks, "Do you need me to let you go?"

"Yes," Missy says, and she hangs up the phone. She can't look at anyone, but she can feel all of them looking at her. She vaguely wonders why until Aaron asks her, "Is Darian all right?"

Missy opens her mouth, but... no. Just no. She shakes her head yes so that no one thinks Darian is dead, but when they ask her what *is* wrong then, she still can't say.

She can't seem to catch her breath.

Chapter Seven: A Standing Chill

Lindsay can hardly tolerate a month of mingling with the normal kids.

Jordan and his friends welcome her into their lunch table circle, but Lindsay has a difficult time taking them seriously. They're nice enough; the girls especially make an effort to be friendly towards Lindsay, but it's because they assume she's dating Jordan, and thus no competition in their games. They are malignant bitches towards everyone else, and the boys don't turn out to be much better. It's like they can't even communicate except through fart jokes and dangerous pranks (blasting someone who has asthma in the face with body spray, for example). She can't enjoy anything in their company. Just listening to them talk about the way the cafeteria pizza is shaped ("Pizza's supposed to be a triangle, man! What's this square shit?") is more disheartening than the actual congealed mess of overcooked cheese.

"I can't take this shit anymore." Lindsay slides her tray away and stands, even though the lunch bell is nearly ten minutes away, and they're supposed to stay in the cafeteria for the duration. Jordan tries to get up with her, but Lindsay rebuffs him with the tray, nearly jamming it into his neck as she picks it up to keep him in his seat. She looks around and finds that one of the exit doors is being guarded by a female teacher: bingo.

"I have my period," she tells the woman, throwing away her uneaten food with a snap and slamming her tray down in the caddy. "I need the bathroom."

"Name?" the woman asks, already opening the door to let her out. Her face is full of weary understanding.

"Lindsay Kurtz."

"Okay, Lindsay Kurtz; I better not find out you were doing anything else."

Lindsay nods. Tristan hasn't been at lunch in weeks; if he can get past the teachers in the hallways, then so can Lindsay.

She walks out of the lunchroom purposefully, keeping her eyes lowered, but glancing everywhere as she goes. If Tristan's not at lunch, he's got to be hiding somewhere. She doesn't worry about him being in a classroom, he doesn't like any of the teachers. He might have snuck into the library somehow, but Lindsay will only end her search there if she can't find him anywhere else. Marley used to barricade himself in the library here, and Lindsay feels somehow that Tristan will not want to follow in his footsteps.

East Arrow High School does its name justice by looking a bit like a compass rose from the sky—two floors surrounding the courtyard, and hallways shooting off three of the four corners, so that in making her way through the open-air halls, Lindsay winds in and out the courtyard, trying her best to skirt around in the shade. First she walks past the clock tower and turns down the hall with the butterfly garden and the fitness utility rooms, where even the scent of hot Florida flowers can't overpower the smell of sweaty mats. Tristan wouldn't like it out here, but regardless, Lindsay's eyes rove for him.

Next she goes by the athletic fields, looking out past the junior parking lot, towards the football bleachers and basketball courts, but Lindsay doesn't waste her precious few minutes going out there to look, knowing Tristan's distaste for sports. She reenters the courtyard, passes quickly in front of the cafeteria windows, shielding her face with her hair. She came out through a side door and knows there's nothing back behind it—unless Tristan is socked away in the handicap elevator. She hurries down the next hallway towards the senior parking lot, noticing much prettier flowers out this way, maybe because seniors are optimistic enough that they don't feel the need to stomp every plant that's set down to beautify the school.

She doesn't see him out here anywhere either though, and there's only the front of the school after this, a dangerous place to loiter unless you have big brass balls, because administrators never stopped coming and going. She's thinking of turning back to the nearest staircase and searching the upstairs before parking herself in front of the library in case he emerges at the sound of the bell, but in her hesitation, she spots something: a tiny little four-tree orchard right in front of what must be the cluster of counselors' offices. She sees a fence... might there not also be a gate?

Lindsay keeps moving, a little slower this time, feeling exposed because on her left stretches the senior parking lot, and on the right is an expanse of grass all the way to the iron fence enclosing this little alcove. There's no sidewalk leading over there, Lindsay would have to cross grass to go examine it, and though she could get to the gate door—yes a door, and yes open—with her back to a windowless wall, anyone could still spot her from the sidewalk, and as soon as she poked her head in to look around at the dark corners behind the trees, anyone daydreaming out of their office window might see her too.

She checks her watch, sees she has no more time to look anywhere else, and figures: fuck it. She'd at least be able to cross this place off her list for when she breaks out tomorrow.

Lindsay creeps along the wall towards the gate, hearing the Pink Panther theme music in her head as she sneaks, and smiling sourly at the thought that if she was in fact pink, she might blend in better with the side of the stucco building, which is painted a stomach bile, terracotta pink.

Lindsay can see half of the enclosure from the corner entrance, half of a diagonally cut sandwich. Tristan isn't over there, although she does see an empty bird's nest in one of the tiny trees. The trees must not get much sun over here, since most of the daylight is stopped by three surrounding concrete walls. Tristan might be in the darkest of the corners, and Lindsay pokes her head in to see.

It's all green for a moment after staring at the heinously bright daylight, but in a moment her eyes adjust and there's Tristan, sitting with a textbook over his knees. He's looking up at her like he's been watching her whole approach. He looks like he can't help but be amused.

"Get in here quick before someone sees you. I like this spot, I don't want to be chased out."

Lindsay darts around the side of the building and throws herself into Tristan's corner, sliding uncomfortably down the textured wall so that she can't be seen through the windows at her back. Tristan tightens himself into the corner, and Lindsay tucks in closer to him. He's lucky; it's too close a fit for her to punch him in the face.

"Where's Jordan?" is the first thing he says to her.

"Fuck you, really? I come all the way out here just looking for you, and this is how you treat me?"

Tristan shrugs. He tips his chin up in defiance, away from her. He looks like an angry little kid.

"It's like you can't see yourself! You can't see what a brat you're being to me. I haven't done anything wrong, and Jordan is boring as hell, and you should have been there to find that out with me!"

His haughty face breaks into a one-sided sneer-smile, what Tristan himself sometimes calls a stroke smile. It looks like he isn't speaking to her, so Lindsay stops speaking to him right back.

Tristan's got his hands crossed and dangling over his knees. Lindsay reaches for the left one, the one on her side, and she holds it. Fingers laced firmly in his like a comb in tangled hair. She confronts him with full eye contact. That brings him out.

He cuffs the side of the wall he's leaning against with his sneaker, pissed off in some injured way. He'll explain it any minute now, and Lindsay sits patiently in the dirt, uncaring of ants or sandspurs, waiting for him to find the words.

"I love you," he says, as if it's news to either of them.

"You don't know how to show it very well," Lindsay tells him.

He slants his eyes at her in a way that says, *Don't interrupt me.* He's staring out at the gleaming windshields in the senior parking lot, the school road beyond, the still-empty apartment complex that their history teacher says used to be all trees, and in which he might be forced to live next year, since apparently the teachers don't make very much money. Problems of money are starting to trickle down to Lindsay, young as she is. Even Rita is starting to partner with local colleges to sell textbooks, and she's started getting in a lot more books on spirituality and alternative medicine, for the local housewives. Selling books on gender and sexuality is unsustainable, she says, especially in this town. Rita says she doesn't care if the store has to change; the bookstore led her to adopting Tristan, and whatever else happens, it will always have been worth it. Lindsay loves him that much too, she knows exactly what Rita means. The question is, what is Tristan still so insecure about?

"I'm sorry," he says starkly, finally. "I want to see you this weekend, but not before then, okay?" He takes his hand away from her and slithers roughly up the wall. "Come to my house on Saturday while Rita's at work. I'll try to be... better by then."

"Fine," Lindsay says. "Saturday. I'll be early."

"I'll be waiting for you, trust me."

And Lindsay does. Like, heaven help her, but even as he walks away in a storm cloud of his own making, Lindsay knows she'll go wherever he asks her to be.

Tristan skips school for the rest of the week. Rita won't like it when she finds out, but it's really for his own good, Tristan knows. He has some very serious business to attend to.

Tristan is grimly satisfied when Lindsay finally comes to seek him out; it's what he meant to achieve in abandoning her. How could he make demands on her without knowing that she demanded him just as aggressively? He needed to make sure he wasn't burdening her, and now he knows for sure: they burden each other. Good thing too, because this situation is going to be heavy.

Tristan spends his unauthorized week off looking up some of his old associates from the boys' home. There's a guy Tristan knows, his older brother aged out of the foster system and makes money now selling bathtub shine to kids through a network of foster connections.

Tristan has to talk to three people he despises just to get in touch with this guy, and then there's a two day relay to get the goods to Tristan. He has to sit in the park across from the middle school, a place that has bad memories for him, and wait for some peon to deliver a Mason jar of hooch.

Tristan feels utterly disgusted by the whole exchange (plus it cost him forty dollars of his allowance) but it's all for Lindsay, and Tristan sticks it out until he has what he wants—a jam jar full of clear, toxic-smelling bisexuality.

The plan doesn't go so well after that.

Tristan gets his jar on Friday morning, and since he knows Rita will be home later that night, he writes her a note saying he doesn't feel well and to let him sleep when she gets home, knowing that what he has now is a dangerous compound, unpredictable and volatile. He needs to know he has some time and space to experiment with it. Rita will be at work for a while at least. He utilizes the kitchen while he can.

He pours equal amounts into three tall glasses and recaps the jar, setting it aside. In one glass he mixes in Coke, in one Sprite, in the third, fresh squeezed Florida orange juice. Tristan watched his father go about the business of getting drunk, methodically, with purpose. Tristan is very acutely aware of his parents' flesh surrounding his core self. Sure he's being adopted by someone else now, but he'll always be their son.

He starts sipping. The liquid in each glass is as vile as gasoline, but the Coke and gasoline is the least painful. He starts there, and as the alcohol dulls his ability to taste, he moves on to the others.

Tristan starts to feel sick right away. First it's the foul taste, but then the sickness goes deeper. No matter what the ratio between booze and mixer, Tristan can feel it burn him all the way down. A dull fire highlights the tube of his esophagus, allows him to feel its diameter. It hits his stomach and goes down around the inside of that sack like the drizzle over a cake. He feels like it's killing him already. He never should have let a drop pass his lips, not him, not with his family's history. The stuff is too loaded for him; a loaded drunk, a loaded gun, cocked and ready. He never even has a chance to enjoy it.

Far from being pleasurable, the effect of alcohol only serves to enhance his pain. It must be different for everyone, because Tristan knows his mother drank to feel good, and that his father drank to forget. It isn't working like that for Tristan. He's obviously inherited some terrible hybrid gene from the two of them; he feels awful, and it's making him remember everything.

Tristan hasn't cried about anything in over a year, not since he and Lindsay started school together last year. But suddenly he's thinking of some of the worst days of his life with horrible clarity. Not being able to wake anyone up to take him to school no matter how much he shook them, a congealed layer of vomit on the kitchen floor that no one had sobered up enough to clean and which Tristan refused to touch no matter how much it disgusted him to smell it, going hungry the rest of that night no matter how much his stomach ached because there was no way to step around it. His stomach hurts now, almost like it's remembering too, but then he realizes that his stomach is empty except for this drink he's nearly done with.

With tears on his face, and a babyish keening coming out of his own throat, Tristan is still paranoid enough to clean up. He rinses out the three glasses he's used, smelling them furiously to find out if Rita will know what's been in them, and hides them in the back of the dishwasher. He takes the two-liter of Coke and his Mason jar of cold fire back into his room with him and continues drinking. His father was right, he really can't taste it anymore. Mostly he tastes the jellied salt flavor of sobbing. That too takes his memories back pretty far. Only little kids cry like this.

Tristan passes out about a third of the way through his jar, with snail trails of dried tears on his cheeks. Daylight leaves and Rita comes home some time while he is unconscious, but she doesn't check on him.

He comes to a few hours later in the deep dark before dawn. He hasn't dreamed, and he hasn't gained any rest, but he's wide awake again. His insides feel like they're fermenting. His brain is a dry, crispy, degraded sponge. His mouth is gluey cotton. Tristan goes to the kitchen and tries to quiet the scald of his stomach by eating buttered bread and drinking milk. It feels right going down, but he quickly overloads his stomach and has to run to the bathroom to throw up, another bodily discharge he hasn't experienced in a while. He gets to the bathroom in time to splatter the inside of the toilet in undigested lumps of bread. He spends the whole next day in bed, only getting up to use the bathroom. He pours out the rest of the jar as soon as he can stand straight without becoming dangerously dizzy. That's that plan aborted.

In a way, Tristan is glad for the experience. It isn't pleasant to spend two days feeling tender and beaten on the inside, but now that it's done it's almost as if this was something Tristan needed to do, a purge of some putridity he had been holding in way too long. He shed some tears, evacuated some bile, and he's absolutely sure now that alcohol holds no appeal for him, thank God. He doesn't want to say he'll never try the stuff again (he's heard "I'm quitting" too many times from the same people to believe that), but at least it holds a lot less mystery for him now. He's found more magic in getting the fucking flu than in that jar.

There's still the problem of what to do about Lindsay, what he's capable of doing for her. He can't have her meeting him like this, sick and sweating and miserable. He texts her to say, *Don't come over this weekend, see you on Monday, promise.* He's pretty sure he's lying to her again, and that he'll have to find a new place to hide on campus come Monday, but he just isn't ready for her yet. They're closer to where they need to be, what with Jordan deemed unfit and both Tristan and Lindsay so desperate to knit themselves back together.

He just needs a little more time.

The end of September brings a welcome bit of cool weather, what Floridians call a 'cold snap' though Jesse would disagree with both cold and snap as descriptive words for this temperate chill. If it were really cold, then it would really snap, like the crack of an icy whip. Colorado had cold snaps, they'd blow down off of the Rockies some years and mess up every wife's garden in town. Florida knows no cold snap.

But the sort of collective delusion everyone falls into—wearing sweaters and scarves and allowing their teeth to chatter in 65 degrees—is only a primer for what Jesse is made to experience at home.

Jesse vaguely remembers that Missy was pregnant when he first knew her. He doesn't think he ever knew it was a baby girl. But after she got that phone call and poured herself a stiff drink, she faced the whole lot of them and said, "My daughter's dead." At some point it had stopped being a baby and turned into a daughter.

All eyes were on Missy, and after a time, on Marley, since it's clearly him that she meant to receive comfort from. Surprisingly, Marley seems to think he is perfectly capable for this job. Jesse's seen him hide from a ringing telephone, but he steps right up to deal with this mess. How can this stress him out less than a telemarketer or a wrong number?

Marley and Missy partition themselves off from Jesse and Aaron, make an exclusive club for the recently bereaved, start sleeping on the other side of the book cases and whispering to each other every night after lights out. Aaron can barely stand being boxed out even further from Missy's attentions, but Jesse is very glad to see Marley take his grief out on someone else, someone who can reciprocate with him.

Marley and Jesse's relationship scales back a bit, but it doesn't concern him the way it does Aaron. Maybe they don't fuck for a couple of weeks, maybe they go days without talking or even making eye contact as they pass each other going to and from work. He doesn't worry, because whenever Jesse seeks out his hand to squeeze, Marley squeezes back, and whenever Jesse pats his shoulder to find a kiss, he gets one. Perfunctory for now, sure, but that can't last forever.

Missy doesn't take to grief as well as Marley does, and that's not saying anything against her either. It really shouldn't come so easy to anyone, but it's hitting Missy especially hard.

"I juss, like," she says on more than one occasion, her voice rarely crisp anymore, more often softened with drink. "I juss keep thinking that if those fuckers would've let me abort her when I wanted to! This could have sucked a lot less. I mean, it looks like she was meant to die anyway, right? But at least it still gets to be all my fault, that's what matters most."

Marley gives her this new wise, sad smile he's acquired, and he agrees with her. "Bet you never stop feeling like shit about it either, even though you wanted to avoid this whole thing."

"Egg-zactly," she snorts humorlessly, and over-splashes her next pour. That's how they spend their evenings.

But even so, it's all manageable until Darian comes back to collect the rest of his band. Jesse knew their friends weren't going to stick around forever, but it comes as a shock to Marley, as do so many obvious things.

They rustle Missy out of her nest, disturbing Marley in the process, and Darian says, "Hey, we got a gig in Alabama, time to move."

Missy gets up automatically, rote in her ability to rouse herself from a hangover and get back on the road again. Marley is much slower to wake up and to realize: his friend is leaving. She's leaving *today*.

"You're going?" Marley asks her, but his answer comes from Darian.

"We've got a gig in Alabama," he repeats.

Missy is pulling clothes out of the bed by the legs and sleeves, like scarves out of a magician's mouth. She looks pretty single-minded in the search for clothes and keys and wallet. If Aaron's to be believed (and as far as Jesse knows he's never lied to anyone, probably can't figure out how), Missy spends a lot of time scraping her clothes up off the floor of strange places. Jesse can't bring himself to be surprised or judgmental; he learned his father's practical brand of misogyny years ago, and was told that slutty girls should never be shamed, that unlike most other women, they're a friend to all.

Aaron and Darian are mostly packed and in order, and they're waiting for Marley to get off their mattress so they can take it back down to the van, but they're not going to say anything to him. Since Marley and Missy got their bad news, both have been more than a little off-limits. Like a shook-up soda bottle, or a still mug of water that you know is boiling hot, and the second you break the surface tension, it'll burst scalding water all over you.

Not that Marley would be *that* volatile. He's unstable, but not unpredictable, and he slides off the mattress when he feels the body language of those who are waiting around for him. He sits with his back pressed hard against the edges of his book shelves. He watches the boys in the band strip the sheets and fold up the mattress. They head for the door, leaving the room looking much more bare than it did before. Marley is like a pet in the corner, just realizing that his owners are moving.

"When will you be back?" he asks in a small voice after Darian and Aaron have gone downstairs. Jesse, who up to now has been leaning against the center shelves and looking in on the show, decides to melt back into the 'bedroom' such as it is separate from the library nook.

"Oh, who knows," Missy says, and Jesse can hear her flump down onto the floor, probably continuing her sort from the space left by the mattress. "Darian usually lines up a bunch of shows in different towns so we can do little looping tours. We always end up in some town I've never even heard of, but he's got at least one friend who loves him enough to put up all three of us. I don't know how he gets away with so many people liking him. When I leave a town, I always feel like I'm sneaking away, never to return."

Jesse smiles. What would it have taken for him and Missy to like each other? Somehow hearing her voice detached from the person he's grown to tolerate makes her seem almost appealing. Probably the only thing missing is what Marley says he loves about her: that she likes him best of everyone in the world. Missy is a sun; if she pulls you in, it's a warm revolution, and if she lets you go, it's more time in the cold black void of space.

"So you're leaving me?" Marley asks.

Jesse can hear Missy's movements slow and stop. An uncomfortable stillness seeps from where they are into Jesse's area. He's reclined back on the pillows with his hands behind his head, but once the room goes all stiff and weird from Marley's side of it, Jesse brings his arms down and crosses them over his chest.

Missy's voice lowers, but Jesse can still hear every word when she says, "Hon, you have to work. And I have to work. And I work on the road. We'll come back, don't worry. Darian lives just two hours north of here, I'll always come see you when we're nearby."

Marley's only response is a snotty sniffle. He has never been able to cry with dignity. Jesse's father cried a couple of times while Jesse knew him, but the tears just leaked down the side of his face like they were boiling over. Jesse himself hasn't cried since his own early childhood, but Marley? Marley can still cry like a baby.

He hears Missy moving to hug him, and Jesse sighs silently, knowing that once she leaves, that sniveling collapse of boy in there will be his to deal with. They'll be alone together again, finally, but Jesse won't have Marley to himself for a while yet.

Marley and Missy stop slobbering on each other when Darian and Aaron return. Missy starts flinging clothes out of the nook at them, and whenever anyone gets a handful they leave to secure it in the van. When at last there's nothing left of Missy's in the apartment, the boys go off whistlin' Dixie because they don't want to watch Marley and Missy say goodbye. Jesse does though. He hides himself in the kitchen for this show.

They pull each other into a tight hug. Missy's breasts squish against Marley and bulge out from between them like wet mortar between two bricks.

"I'll send you a cell phone on my account so we can talk all the time, okay?" Missy says in the muffle of Marley's slept-on hair.

"Yeah," Marley mewls back at her. They pet and whisper for another half a minute or so, too softly for Jesse to hear, and then Missy (of course) disengages first.

She holds Marley back by his shoulder, keeping him at arm's length as she reaches for the door knob, as if he might glom onto her again and insist on being taken to Alabama too.

Jesse goes over to the sink and starts flipping dishes around, making noise until she's gone, hoping that she didn't spot him at his study. Marley is used to it, but Missy might hate him forever if she sees her doing something she thought was unobserved. Some people get aggressively private, and Jesse's never been able to predict who or when. He hides to save himself the guess work.

With the sound of the door shutting behind him, Jesse stops with the dishes. He turns the water on and off, rinsing his hands. He dries them on a square of old t-shirt they use as a dishrag before turning around and holding his arms out towards Marley. The kid looks abysmal, eyes bright with the sting of salt, face flushed and damp. He looks even sadder now with the distance of his friend than he was at the death of his old guy.

He comes to Jesse's embrace for comfort, and Jesse kisses his forehead and thinks something he hasn't thought in a long time, something his mother used to say: *Well bless your heart and best of luck with all that.*

Chapter Eight: The Anesthetic

A sad song about summer comes on through her earbuds as Missy rides away from Florida, and from Marley, and it ought to, because this song has always reminded her of him and their first ill-fated summer together. It almost doesn't apply anymore, because they've met each other again, but still it resonates. A song that owns you once will own you forever, and never mind that it isn't summer anymore.

As the song waltzes along, Missy smiles grimly and turns the player off. Enough of that for a while; she doesn't want to cry, and certainly not about Marley, who isn't even dead. She still hasn't shed a tear for her daughter, and she knows it's coming, but now is not the time.

Missy spends the drive through Florida to Alabama in a numb state.

It's over half a day's drive to get to the Alabama gig, and Missy is buzzed the whole time. Never fully hydrated, though she makes an effort every few hours to suckle at her water bottle like it's some life-giving teat, and maybe nibble at a bit of food, before resuming her doses of alcohol. It's just like when she was in the hospital, really: keep up the medication to keep the edge off the pain. Too much too fast and you're wrecked, too little too late and you're in agony. Missy finds the balance right away; she's been drinking for a while now, she's good at it. She knows how to ride the edge between sick and sober.

Novocain for the brain, the sweat of grain which numbs our pain, Missy writes in one of the lyrics notebooks they keep for stray ideas. She may want to write about what's happening to her sometime, but right now she's too close to the situation (and too far in the bottle) to really produce anything coherent.

But it is like medication, Missy muses on their long drive, in much the same way that it's like being ill. She feels sort of clear and waterlogged at the same time, the way a fever will cause you to feel clear-headed, but will absolutely prevent you from focusing. It's all an idle speculation for Missy, something to keep her mind out of the well of her body, out of the depths where it feels like her heart has sunk. She would tell anyone that she doesn't feel guilty, that she knows she shouldn't, and so she does not.

But knowing and feeling are two different things, that's what Marley tells her when she talks to him about the baby, or child, as she would have been by the time she died—like a whole nearly two-year-old old child with little shoes and a mop of hair and likes and dislikes. Marley says that's just the way it is with his little going-outside problem: he can *know* it's useless to be so fearful, but a lot of good that does to how he *feels*. They've got more in common than ever now, even though they're parted once again. Marley was upset at the idea of her going, and Missy might have been too, before they became aggrieved together. It's so easy when she's on the road for Missy to forget that she was ever anyone's daughter or mother or friend, but that won't happen now. Sort of a consolation prize, considering what it's cost.

The gig in Alabama is in some nowhere town in an even more nowhere bar that Darian found by accident during his travels before they became a band, and where he had curried enough favor to be invited back and paid. They like to get cute on the road, so in Alabama, they sing "Alabama Song" by The Doors. Missy gets through it wryly (and would be doing it rye-ly if whiskey weren't disgusting as hell to her). She's lost her dear young daughter and must have vodka, oh, you know why.

The next gig is in Louisiana, and in Louisiana it's fun to sing "Moon Over Bourbon Street" (even though they're in an obnoxiously hip venue in Baton Rouge where songs about New Orleans are met with worldly eye rolls) with Aaron whistling in place of the horn. This song really is all about murdering a young girl, and that doesn't help Missy either.

It gets especially bad when they hit a gig on the edge of Austin. Missy tells Darian she wants to sing "The Bluest Eyes In Texas" and he and Aaron look at each other like, *Oh man, this is a bad idea*. Her hands shake when she tries to grip anything, because she asked for this favor before taking the first day's drink. She's in that pre-hysterical state that tends to get her what she wants, within reason. One too-sad song is all she asks, and if she's denied that, she might have a total meltdown, so Darian nods yes, and Aaron winces but says nothing.

That's why it's in Texas that a few tears leak out while she's on stage, as Missy is just *laying* into the most painful parts of the song because she starts to wonder: *What color were my daughter's eyes?* But fuck trying to remember now! She hands one of the bartenders a twenty when she's coming back from the bathroom and asks for a bottle of vodka in that price range.

The girl takes a hard look at Missy, either looking for signs of age or signs of sincere need, and whatever she needs she finds.

Missy gets another bottle of forgetfulness.

By the time they reach the Oklahoma panhandle, Missy is calling the entire set list. Darian might have protested if this were a real gig for the Homo Superiors, but they aren't officially booked in Oklahoma, they're just stopped there, and sometimes they like to use unsuspecting open mic crowds as guinea pigs anyway, so Darian indulges her. So it's Oklahoma, and it's some shitty place where the stage lights are only old supermarket Christmas lights taped along the stubby stage, and it's there Missy sings to a small group of pudgy folk her slightly slurred bunch of songs (*lips feeling thick*, Missy writes in her notebook later that night, *like lips that have been bitten or kissed*). The last song of the night is "The Freshman" by The Verve. There's an abortion and a suicide in that one.

Missy gets off stage feeling like the audience watched her murder someone (instead of just the tunes), full of an overwhelming shame—at her bad performance, her sloven drunkenness, her absolute failure as a mother.

Next stop: Colorado.

"There's a gig in Denver, but I don't know if she's up for it," Darian tells Aaron quietly at the front of the van.

"Our old town is just north of there," Aaron says, even more quietly.

Missy is in the back, trying to hold her head still with her hands while the van moves around her. They must think she's asleep, though she's really just buried under the blanket to save herself from the light. She can't breathe so great in with all this trapped air, but she can hear just fine. She thinks it's funny that Aaron thinks of Loweville as his 'old town' even though he's from Michigan. But he's perfectly right: that really is where they originate from, now.

"You know I can hear you assholes, right?" Missy croaks. She burrows in the direction of their voices, trying not to lean an elbow on her own hair as she searches for air and light, but not too much of either. She peeks out at them through squinted eyes.

Aaron looks ashamed of himself as he says, "We'll be passing right through Loweville soon if you wanna, you know..."

"No," Missy cuts him off. "We won't be passing right through Loweville, we'll be stopping there." She can't not go back.

The road into Colorado is horribly familiar. Not that she ever came or went from Loweville by the south highway—Missy was flown to Cheyenne from her distant home in Vermont, and she and Aaron left by the west-bound highway when they skipped for California—but she remembers this place all too well.

Fuck you, mountains, Missy thinks in greeting as they approach the town. *Fuck you, welcoming sign, General Grocery, First Baptist Church, you wretched cunt: howdy and fuck you all.*

Missy has a straw in a cup full of vodka, trying to drink it onto the back of her tongue so she can't taste it as much, trying not to throw it right back up again. She imagines she can feel the outline of her stomach, burning with alcohol and acid, no food for hours, no water at all. She doesn't care how sick she gets, she's fueling up for something. In fact, it's time to let her ride in on her plans.

"Drop me off at the graveyard," she tells Aaron. "Go and do wha'ever you want, I don' care. I'll come back to wherever you lef' me at dark."

"Missy it's cold out, and you don't even know where she's—"

"Shuh," Missy says, cutting him off with the beginning of 'shut up' and not bothering to finish because he's already quiet, and she'd never get out the sound of the T with how inebriated she is anyway.

Aaron slows his speed on the slope of the hill after First Baptist. The cemetery falls gently down the hill away from the church and the rec. center where Missy and Marley and Aaron and Jesse all first met each other. He drives the winding road through the cemetery for a while and stops roughly in the middle of the bury patch.

He opens his mouth to say more but, "Nah in-a-rested," is Missy's final word on the subject. Darian lays his warmest jacket, his leather jacket, over Missy's shoulders without a sound. She takes it and gets out of the van, happy right away to have it. Her bare legs are freezing in the afternoon breeze, and she knows her canvas shoes won't save her toes from becoming tiny ice cubes in a matter of minutes, but the jacket will help keep her warm in her thin gauzy dress. All of Missy's clothes are dresses, and they double conveniently as night gowns, but they are every one of them inappropriate for cold weather.

Missy doesn't wait for the van to leave before she totters off the road and onto the grass. Let them sit there until she gets back if they're so worried, it doesn't bother her. She finished her cup in one burning slurp as she got out, and now she has a long-necked bottle tucked close to her body under the jacket. She vaguely understands that, with the help of vodka, she can finish something here.

In fact, the bottle's cool surface is right next to the scar from her appendectomy. She thinks it's too bad she doesn't have a cesarean scar to go with it, only the faded mottle of stretch marks, which might be from any kind of bodily growth, contrary to what one moron she fucked around with thought. He was convinced girls *only* got stretch marks from being pregnant. Missy might have told him he was an idiot, if it weren't for the way he revealed his ignorance. He asked her out of nowhere, "So what's your kid's name?" So suddenly, so sure that he knew she was keeping something from him, with that little sneer in his voice that everyone gets when they're judging you for being a slut. He might as well have slapped her for all that Missy knew what to say to *that*. She certainly slapped him and told him to get the hell out of her van.

No scar for the baby, though. Too bad. Maybe she could create one in honor of the painful occasion. Isn't that what Marley does? His arm looks just like a tally of every horrible moment he's ever had to get through, and damned if Missy doesn't now understand why someone might do that. Just like giving yourself a memorial tattoo.

Memorials. Missy is lurching past quite a few of them. She's headed for the recent graves, easily spotted because there are soldiers from whatever war the country's in these days planted there, and their graves are covered in flowers and flags and scraggly deflated balloons. The sky is getting a dark cast as Missy steps off the path and onto the grass at a bit of an upward hike. She'll be around here somewhere, surely.

Missy gets the bottle out now, not giving a shit who sees her or what municipal laws there might be about drunken carousing in the cemetery. She has to stop and lean against the higher markers for every swig so she doesn't overbalance and go rolling down the hill, but she is making an effort to walk along the backs of the graves so that she isn't walking over the coffins. A sign of respect, the best she can do.

She's looking for a name, checking every engraving, but looking at the dates too, and only finding adults. People who died this year, born in the 1930s, the 40s, the 50s, the 60s even, and surely their families would say they died horribly young. Not as young as the girl Missy is looking for though. Not even close.

But there is no one under eighteen out here, and as Missy winds higher and higher on the hillside, she starts to look around from her better vantage point. She sees something. She sits down on one of the flatter tombstones to settle her vision and concentrate. It's a little grove across the street, nestled in among other graves. There is a gap among the gold and brown and dull-leafed trees, like a natural courtyard. There's a banner or something across the entrance, and Missy has to go closer to know for sure, but she suspects she knows what that is. When she gets close enough to read, she laughs joylessly and thinks: kindergarten. Her daughter managed to make it to kindergarten after all.

The banner says: The Children's Garden.

Missy steps inside. The wind is gone in here, though a still chill remains. There is a pebbled path sectioning The Children's Garden into quadrants. Missy crunches along slowly, reading every name this time, knowing that the dates will all be short in here, and that paying attention to all these little pops of time will only make her start crying, and she just can't yet. She'll never have enough time to weep over other people's dead children.

She tries to ignore them, but still she sees: a baby that died the day it was born, siblings who must have gone in an accident since they died the same day. She ignores the numbers harder, even trying to physically block them by holding the bottle out in front of her eyes, but fuck knows she can't hold it steady. But that trouble is moot when she finds what she's looking for. Dates with significance to her, and a name she hasn't annunciated even in thought since the last time she was in Loweville.

Natalie Naomi Baker. Missy's daughter.

She got one name from each of her parents: Missy, and her host parents in Loweville, Ellen and Rob. Missy's forgotten the name of the biological father (she thinks it started with a 'T' maybe?), but he was never really all that significant, and he certainly doesn't matter now. Missy picked her first name out of a song, which seems fitting considering what she ditched motherhood to do. Ellen, Missy's housemother while she was entombed in Loweville, chose the middle name from the Bible. Rob provided his family name. They were going to adopt Missy eventually (they thought), and so the family name went right on the birth certificate. It made it so much easier for Missy to leave the baby with them, and disappear as if she'd never been there at all.

But she left her DNA. There's a 50/50 chance that it was the male contribution which made the baby sick, but Missy will never believe it wasn't her. Her bad blood, her bad luck. If Natalie had grown up she might have gotten pregnant by accident too, just like her mother, and her mother's mother before her. Looking at the grave, Missy can't bring herself to think she's better off dying young, but she still thinks the abortion could have saved a handful of people a heaping lot of pain.

Missy kneels at the grave, partly out of a sense of tradition and partly because she's having a hard time standing independently and there's nothing to lean on. A moment later she's on all fours, her thumb over the mouth of her bottle to keep the liquor from escaping. She rests her forehead against the polished stone. She maneuvers the bottle to her mouth, takes one more swig, and it doesn't get halfway across her tongue before she throws up a horrible burning bile on her daughter's grave.

Missy knows the tears will come soon, from the burn of the booze and from the unmentionable misery she feels. It seems she can't have one without the other! Sickness and sadness, the two things she never wants but must crawl through to be rid of.

Missy sits back, away from the spatter of vomit, wondering how different it looks from the baby spit-up she never wiped from her shoulder, wondering what those bilious flakes are in the otherwise thin, watery upheave she's produced. Looking at it, Missy longs for a hose that would make it run into the grass, go away. She'll never, *ever* tell anyone about this. Not Marley, not a priest, not a single other living soul in the world. She even takes another swig from her bottle, careful to put it down easy, hoping for a complete blackout of this moment.

It only makes her puke more, although this time she heaves it over the back the tombstone. It burns coming up, and it isn't over quickly. She's finally crossed the line and poisoned herself, something she hasn't done in over a year, not since she first started drinking and was still getting her sea legs. It takes her so aggressively by the throat that true weeping begins: a leaky sting in the seams of her eyes that becomes a deluge.

Her water is breaking.

Sobs wrack out of her. Her gingery hair is braided back and trapped by the jacket, which is all that saves it from getting covered in bitter gobs of slobber. The tears are all that come out of her smoothly, streaming down her face in regular gushes with every blink, the way blood beats out of a wound.

Missy keeps pushing out tears, even though she's already dangerously dehydrated and her head throbs hard whenever she comes up from sobbing to breathe. It's just that whenever she starts to sniffle up and regain herself (which is when she starts to feel like a dried-out, salty, water-starved, landed sea creature), her mind forces up another tragic thought the way her body keeps forcing up bile. This *needs* to come out of her. It's toxic and it must be expelled, and it's now or never; Missy knows she'll never be this vulnerable again.

Missy flops over on her side (she's too dizzy with her head in the air) and gets a faceful of crispy, dying grass. She thinks of what being dead is: never experiencing the excited charge of crunching leaves again, the sort of sound you can feel, like the snapping of static energy. She thinks of never smelling the honk of summer grass, never kissing the waxy petal of a tulip, never getting rained on and showing up to work or school with wet hair and that feeling of triumph. Missy wonders how many of those moments any person might potentially get in a lifetime, and she wonders how often people get horribly short-changed.

Then Missy's thoughts get more specific. Her crying becomes breathy and almost ladylike as she imagines a crib, used and rumpled by a squirming little life, but now and forever empty. And then not a crib, but a bassinet, the one that was in Missy's own room for less than a week, and the little pink girl who might have grown up to look just like her mother.

And the images blur together; Natalie never made it to kindergarten, of course not, it's been barely two years since Missy left. It's *felt* like such a long time though, and Missy can imagine Natalie wearing the same goofy dress she herself wore on the first day of school—the sleeves, skirt, and body all different bold primary colors, and covered in white polka dots, neckerchief attached.

Missy sees that girl and knows she would've looked around the classroom and realized her parents were not like everyone else's. Missy had only one sour mother, whereas so many other kids had mommies *and* daddies, and that the daddies were getting especially soft-eyed if they were there with a daughter. What would Natalie have noticed?

That the blonde kids had blonde parents? Would there even be another redhead in the whole room, and would she start to get an inkling if she were the only one? Or would the Bakers have told her she was adopted, that her birth mommy was around somewhere, they just didn't know where?

With a stab of childish pain that makes Missy flinch and curl up tighter, she remembers that her father never promised to show up and it was her own dumb hope that had hurt her. And Natalie, who never got old enough to say the word adoption let alone understand it... would she have felt the same way? It didn't happen, but if it had? Missy is almost grateful that the abortion she originally wanted finally went through. Feeling abandoned isn't something she'd wish on her own daughter, but being the one to run away? That shit runs in the family.

Missy feels herself start to sober up, and she doesn't fight it anymore. She hasn't cried like this since she was a little kid, not even when her appendix burst and she was in massive amounts of physical pain. She feels a little like she did right after giving birth, a little woozy and exhausted, but better. Something has been forced out that was getting too big to keep inside anymore. The worst of it is over.

Missy scrunches closer to the headstone and sets her forehead against its smooth face again. The coolness of the stone calms her throbbing head, and her tears dry into a light crust that Missy rubs off once she sits up. She'll want to find her way back to the van before it's full dark so she doesn't get lost. Missy picks herself up very carefully and turns to say goodbye.

The grave is as impassive as she found it, seemingly unimpressed by her living tantrum. Missy pats the top of the headstone lightly and opens her mouth to leave it with some parting words, but none are there to come out. Instead she closes her mouth and starts humming, just to mark the occasion with some sound, and swoons away from the grave. She stops under the sign for The Children's Garden and physically resists the urge to look back. She realizes she's humming "Believe Me Natalie" and clips it off with a gasp. The gasp starts her hiccupping. She shoves off in a hurry.

Missy weaves her way back as she came, feeling like a cartoon drunk and expecting bubbles to float up from her mouth with every little spasmed yelp.

The van never moved, it's right where she left it. Missy opens the back door, climbs in to find Aaron and Darian trying to look casual like they wouldn't have seen her lurching towards them from a mile away.

"I'm gonna sleep this off," Missy tells them as best she can. "If you want to help, find me water, park the van somewhere dark, and leave me alone tomorrow." She picks the bottle out of her jacket, warm at last with the heat of her body, and holds it against her frozen cheeks. She slops down on the mattress and adds, before letting the sweet dumbness of passing out overtake her, "Don't leave town."

When Missy resurfaces, she stays bobbing on a sea of precarious sickness. She wants to eat, but she knows better than to try and keep down anything but water, of which there is an abundance, along with a container to puke in and a wet rag that she applies over her eyes. It blocks out the orange haze of the daylight that is seeping through the window like blood in her ocean.

She rolls over slowly, time to stop treading water and just float. She's too warm, but she nudges the blanket down slowly with the tips of her fingers rather than just kick it off. No sudden movements, and she might suddenly turn cold if someone opens the door, and that's a chance because she can feel no one in the van with her. She dips into blank sleep again.

When she returns, her stomach feels calmed but her head is dizzier than ever. Even just laying her head to the side to let the rag fall off her face is disorienting (warmed by her skin, it has started to smell like mildew). She blindly feels for a water bottle and starts sucking it through the side of her mouth. It makes her think of a baby with a bottle of formula, and she doesn't like that imagery at all. She studies the squiggles that move across the inside of her eyelids and remembers how she once tried to draw them as a child, hoping to ask everyone else if they saw them like that too. She somehow never got around to that.

Missy flickers in and out for another bit of time. Her eyelids shutterspeed open a bit when the boys come back, and again when they start the van and drive it somewhere else, but once Missy realizes that driving over the hills isn't making her hate all the world and life itself, she starts to come back. She tunes into Aaron and Darian's muted conversation in the front seat.

"I know people in Cheyenne," Darian says. "Or, you know, I know this one guy and his people. So whenever we're done here that's the next stop."

"I've certainly had enough of being back here," Aaron tells him. "I don't know what she wants to stick around for. In fact, if we're here too much longer I could probably still get arrested for stealing all that money from Deputy White."

"You robbed a cop?"

"More or less, it's sort of a long... Missy?"

Missy groans in salutation. She rolls over holding her breath, just to keep the nausea at bay, and gets her knees under her before lifting her head.

"Where are we?" she asks, her voice croaking out over the matted carpet inside her mouth.

"Hiding in the grocery parking lot," Darian says. "We picked you up some recovery food." Darian points at the grocery bag with corn chips and plain bread and vitamin water sticking out of it. Missy grabs for the supplies and is already trying to lick a mushy bit of bread off the roof of her mouth when she looks out the window at the King Soopers center. She almost feels like spitting her food right back out. She had really hoped to never come back here again.

"I have to go back to the Baker's place first," Missy says, mostly to herself and partly to Aaron, since he knows who she's talking about. "Then we can fuck off out of here."

"You want to go now? We still have daylight left, or else tomorrow, but it'll be Monday and they'll be at work..."

"Now, then; I won't be able to stand waiting."

Darian stays quiet, just gets out and switches seats with Aaron. He's probably had as much information as Aaron could feed him all day, wherever they went. Missy wasn't planning on asking them about it, but Aaron volunteers the info as he drives.

"We parked at the lake for a while. No one was out there, the water's too cold. Then we sat around at the Dairy Queen before coming here. You'll never believe, but we saw Billy. Remember Billy? Jesse's cousin? I barely recognized him since he thinks he's gay now and he died his hair purple and had on some, like, cut-off belly shirt under his jacket. Darian says he seems legit, but I don't know. I mean, it's not like he was gay before, right? When we were around? And what are the chances that he and Jesse are both gay? He's probably just trying to piss off his mother, which that really, really would. She'd probably rather he got someone pregnant."

Aaron falls quiet after that, maybe startled that he managed to say the one thing they have all Not Been Talking About for... ever. Since he and Missy first met, even. She was fully pregnant back then, but they never really talked about it.

The Baker's house hasn't changed much. Same American flag flying beside the garage, same unimpressive flower bed. They've lost the juniper tree in the front yard, which they were always worrying over. They needed a kid in the worst way; they could never be busy enough without one. A birdbath now stands where the tree used to be. It's dry as a sun-bleached bone in the desert.

Aaron pulls the van in behind the Baker's car, the same one they had when Missy was here, the one they'd bought a car seat for. It isn't in the back when Missy looks in through the glass, and it isn't in their open garage as far as she can see. They must be moving on after Natalie's death. Good for them?

Missy takes the lead walking up towards the front door, with Aaron trailing tentatively behind her, and Darian keeping the engine running just in case this becomes a peeled-rubber situation. Aaron's half hiding behind some ashy, puckered cactus that Missy doesn't remember. She rings the doorbell and remembers that she used to have a key, but doesn't remember what she did with it. Probably they changed the locks anyway.

There's a commotion behind the peephole. Missy closes her eyes, bracing herself, reminding herself of what she must look like right now: she's got a hangover that is almost as tactile as a cloak; it crimps her clothes, it red-rims her eyes, it stinks in a cloud around her. Her hair is a detonated area, her usually pristine braid is one long dreadlock after days without maintenance. Her skirt definitely has puke stains on it. But hey, whatever. Fuck these people anyway. She was only fifteen when she lit out of here; it can't all be her own fault, no matter how the pain in her gut tells her otherwise.

It's Rob who opens the door. Ellen is there too, her hair cut shorter, her dated bangs finally gone, hiding behind the door and hissing at Rob, nudging him, hurting him by the wince of his face every time she jabs him. She's definitely angry, but Rob seems sadly pleased to find her back. He speaks first.

"Hello, Missy. We haven't seen you in a while."

"Tell her what happened, tell her! See if she even cares!" Ellen strangles out of herself from behind the door.

"I think she knows, hon."

"I guess it shows?" Missy croaks out.

Rob smiles painfully and shakes off his wife so he can step outside to meet Missy. He closes the door behind him, and he and Missy both jump as Ellen slams against it, probably imbedding the peephole in her face like a monocle.

"I guess you heard about Natalie, huh?" Rob says to her.

Missy nods (kind of feels her body start to follow her head too much as she does it, has to touch the house to stay on her feet).

Rob looks like he got a lot older than two years should have aged him. He looks tired, gray in his temples, defeated where he used to be annoyingly optimistic. Missy feels herself relating to him much more than she ever did while living here. What was that program thinking, putting jacked up kids with normal people? How were Rob and Ellen ever supposed to understand Missy when they had experienced nothing but a bland sort of happiness their whole stupid lives? *Now* they're really her family, ironically. Missy wants to raise a toast and welcome them to the club.

"You know, she was our daughter for two years, and so were you for that one summer. That's more than God has ever seen fit to give us naturally, and for that I'm thankful to you."

"What about Ellen?" Missy asks.

"She..." Rob starts. "She wants to think you could have saved her. We hadn't been looking for you for hardly a month before the leukemia took her, and the doctors told us there's just no hope for a case that aggressive. They say nothing could have saved her, not even you donating marrow, if you'd even been a match, which we don't know at all."

I know. Missy thinks. *I think I know that.*

"Look, she doesn't really want you here, but wait just a second." For the first time Rob looks over at Aaron and nods at him like he expects him to watch out for Missy while he's gone. It feels a little like being given away at a wedding, but it's an impression that leaves Missy's thoughts pretty quickly as another flare of sickness and heat hits her insides.

But it's not the booze this time.

"Oh, I'm getting my period," Missy murmurs. "Fantastic."

Aaron goes straight to the van to get her some Advil, but it's already too late. She hadn't noticed the signs of cramping because she was too egregiously hung over, and now she knows she'll be in pain for at least another day. She feels like it's this place that's done it, all of it; this shitty town that yanks out the absolute worst in her.

Rob comes back outside with something in his hand.

"Ellen actually started making this for you, thinking you'd come back someday and want to see all you had missed. I finished it up after Natalie passed away from us."

He hands her a photo album, small and pink and thick.

Hell, that's just how her daughter had been, once.

She nods at Rob, then starts backing away as the door handle rattles, and he waves goodbye without another word.

Missy climbs into the passenger seat of the van now, too revolted by her behavior to want to return to the back.

"I want to go..." Missy begins, but stops when realizes she was going to say 'home.' She has known no such place. "I want to get away from here," she says to Darian, and he nods, already driving them down the road.

Chapter Nine: People or Drink

Mitch is getting absolutely sick of finding Marley over at Greg's, hearing the kid's voice over the phone, finding his hair ties in Greg's key dish. He stopped bringing it up pretty quickly, because Greg loves to do what other people disapprove of, it makes him feel cool and rebellious, which he'll never truly be again. He's more childish than Marley with the way he lies to himself; at least Marley is still young enough to not know better.

Mitch goes over to Greg's one evening to pick up his latest manuscript—Mitch still reads them all first, a sort of frontline editor even before his agent sees it, and sometimes before Greg himself has read over the raw material. It's really more of a habit at this point, one neither man can break without hurting the other one's feelings. Mitch is irritated but unsurprised to see Marley and Greg sitting together under the overhang of Greg's front door in a couple of iron chairs. Mitch has already refused to read a short story 'inspired' by Marley that started out like this. Mitch is rolling his eyes whenever his back is turned as he gets out of his car; got to get that out of his system before he faces them both.

He is sorely tempted to do it again anyway when he sees the drinks on the table. Greg is probably still on his first, while Marley's eyes are filmed over with inebriation.

"Oh Mitchell, I forgot you were coming over," Greg lies. "I promised you my new book, I have to go print it." He gets up and smirks at Mitch as he leaves him alone with Marley. The boy seems to be pretty far from the world at the moment. It's like being left alone with an aquarium holding one very odd fish.

Mitch sits down and pushes Greg's drink away from himself. Marley, who is just polishing off whatever's in his glass, seems to take the gesture as an offer and picks the fuller glass up the way a ski lift picks up a car full of people, with a jolt and a wobble.

"Marley?" Mitch says, deciding to ask something he's wanted to know for a while. He figures he'll get the most honest answer now.

Marley finally looks him in the eye at the sound of his name. "Why don't you have any friends your own age?"

"I do, I've got, like, one." He smiles horizontally, no upward bend at all. "I'm juss really mature for my age."

"Okay, right now? You're not being mature for any age. It's the middle of the week and the middle of the evening. This is not how adults drink."

Marley shrugs in a jerking motion, his glass sloshing just the merest drip over the side and onto his hand. Marley licks the liquid off the side of his finger, as if he wouldn't want to waste a single drop. It makes Mitch look away with a grimace. It's one thing to see kids drinking in big, happy gaggles, but quite another to watch someone so young be so solitary about it. Only winos who sleep on bus benches should pull a move like that.

"You should really drink less, you know. It can cause a lot of health problems, especially if you're starting so young."

"I don't feel like I'll live very long anyway," Marley says baldly.

"Why do you say that?" Mitch asks after a shocked pause. If Marley were one of his students, he'd already be sitting in a counselor's office.

"I don't know, I just get the feeling like I'm not gonna to make it. Don't you ever feel like that?"

"No," Mitch says with surety.

"Hmm," Marley muses slowly. "I used to think everyone did sometimes."

"But not anymore?"

Marley shakes his head, and the motion is almost too much for his neck to contain. If he wasn't sitting down already, he definitely would have fallen over.

"I think I might be different from other people. Like, not the way I used to try to be different, but more like there's something wrong with me. I'm sad all the time." He looks at Mitch like someone on a small, pitching rowboat watches someone on the shore. "I think my grandfather was an alcoholic."

Mitch is stunned by the non sequitur for a moment, but wants to keep Marley talking. He starts twisting a bit of his beard, what he thinks of as an active listening move. He was never trained as a therapist, but you spend enough time around kids in the throes of hormones, you learn a few things about calming and counseling.

"What makes you say that?" he asks judiciously.

"Well, my dad and my aunt both seem pretty traumatized by something. No one ever talks about him, but they do, you know? They say something about how their father used to do this or say that or how he was so much harder on them than they were on me, but they won't talk about him normal. I'm not even sure of the guy's first name."

"Why are you thinking he was an alcoholic though?" Mitch asks. Marley puts away the last of Greg's drink before he answers. That's an answer in itself.

"It's a family thing, isn't it? Genetic or nature-nurture or whatever. I'm just suspicious." He mangles that word almost beyond recognition. "They talk about him like he's Voldemort or something, I never noticed it before, but now it's so, like... of course."

Marley picks up one of the empty glasses about three times before he realizes that they are both indeed empty. He looks around at his chair like he wants to but also doesn't want to get up for more. It's so uncomfortable to watch him *think* about getting up that Mitch is almost willing to offer to refill the drink himself. However, he's saved from this uncomfortable dilemma by Greg's return with a fat stack of warm pages.

"Here it is. Marley's going to read it for me too, aren't you?"

Marley says something with an agreeable intonation that sounds like, "Whibble d'heur." Mitch sucks on his tongue to keep it still as he takes the pages carefully—they're not bound and might flump all over the place if he lets them go.

Mitch is reluctant to stand and leave, but he can't think fast enough for an excuse to stay as he slowly pushes back his chair. It's an agony of suspended, unending time where Mitch is waiting for his Child In Crisis training to kick in, but this isn't a classroom, and Marley technically isn't a child, and there's just no protocol on something like this.

Mitch finally gets to his feet and opens his mouth hoping something deliberate and authoritative will come like it always seems to do when he's got to control a room full of human monkeys, but he is quite sure he would have been left hanging dumb if Marley's cell phone hadn't gone off at just that very moment.

Marley answers it like Mitch and Greg aren't even there, and starts to crawl up out of his seat, telling the person on the other end that he's going inside for some privacy.

He gets to his feet okay, but when it comes time to straighten up he almost plants his face in the ground.

"Watch it, don't fall over," Greg says, while Mitch actually reaches to help, hoisting Marley by the elbow and steadying him.

That's right, Mitch remembers, scolding himself for lolling around thinking of something to say. *Talking isn't helping, and helping means doing something.*

By the time Marley makes his way inside, Mitch knows what to do.

"If I find him over here drunk on your liquor again, I'm reporting you to the cops."

"What?" Greg asks, his face scandalized.

"You're actually not allowed to get people under twenty-one drunk, Greg. It'd be one thing if you let him cadge a beer or two, but that kid's so blasted he can hardly stand. Why do you think that's okay?"

"He's old enough to vote and join the army and screw just about whomever he likes, why can't he decide how much he wants to drink?" All fine points, and Greg is just as quick with his words and arguments as he might be sober; it takes a fearful amount of alcohol before Greg isn't good at talking.

But this isn't a debate, and Mitch won't be swayed by impersonal logic. "How about because he clearly has no clue what his limits are?"

"Um, hello? How do you think anyone learns their limits, Mitchell? How did you and I learn them? That boy never finished high school, he's not going to college, so where is he going to find a few years to figure out how to drink?"

"Don't pretend you're doing him a favor," Mitch says, an uncustomary sneer marring his face. "You just like his attention."

"And he just likes mine!" Greg says brightly, smartly snapping up the glasses on the table and heading towards his front door. "All the booze in the world won't keep young men entertained by me if they don't want to be."

The front door slams and the bolt is thrown before Mitch gets all the way through Greg's quick speech. God, how he remembers hating him at times in college, hating how easy it was for Greg to be clever; he read fast, thought fast, typed his papers with satisfaction and ease, even when he was tired or hung over or (as he seems to be right now) actively buzzed. Alcohol only ever made Mitch feel fuzzy, even duller than he usually felt around Greg. One mercy would have been if a few shots dampened Greg down to the level of everyone else, but no: some people got all the luck. What rusted Mitch's engine lubricated Greg's. What drowns others, buoys him.

Mitch goes back to his car and only notices Greg's manuscript is still in his hands when he goes to open the door. He sets the pages on the floor behind the passenger seat and knows he's going to 'forget' to bring it inside when he gets home.

Missy excuses herself away from the boys for some peace and solitude up on the roof of Jim or Tim or Tom or whoever's apartment building. It's not cold out in California like it was up in the Colorado elevation, and Missy is happy to be back in a place that feels more like home than not. The smog and balm of west coast air gives her a hug as soon as she steps out into the late afternoon light. She was happy here when she first escaped Colorado, and she was happy in Florida, when she found Marley. Maybe the coast brings her good luck.

She decides to call Marley, unite her worlds. She extracts her cell phone carefully from her bra, and squints one eye to make sure she's not drunk-dialing anyone but her best friend.

"Hi," Marley answers after a couple of rings, a short word that somehow manages to sound long. Missy assumes it's because she's half-crocked; time tends to warp a little when she's been drinking.

"What's goin' on?"

"Nothing, I'm just over at Greg's house. Here, hold on a second, I want to go inside."

Missy listens to scraping and rustling and hears someone who she imagines can only be Greg say, "Watch it, don't fall over." A couple of doors open and close and then the sound coming through the phone sounds closer, more intimate, like he might have tucked himself in a closet. Didn't he used to do that? He maybe once told her that he used to do that.

"Marley, are you drunk?" she says with a grin slowly seeping from the cracks of her teeth.

"Yes," he says with humble victory.

"Oh, hon, I love you so much, that makes two of us. What time is it on your coast?"

"Six or seven, I don't know. It's evening. Of course I started drinking a few hours ago, but, whatever."

"It's a few hours ago here, and I'm drinking, so don't feel bad. We're in the same boat."

"Hmm," Marley laughs minutely. He sighs a long one, and the line goes comfortably silent between them.

Missy settles back against the cold concrete of the roof housing. She fights the chill emanating through her back by concentrating on the sunlight that's buttering her face and body. She starts to hum "Here Comes The Sun" in between tiny little sips of her martini, sips as small as the amount of saliva you might pick up from a kiss. She's not sure how much she likes her vodka salty (the drink sort of tastes like the inside of her mouth during a good cry), but she was willing to try something new if their host was offering.

Banks, that's his name, Tim Banks. Missy remembers because she thought it was funny to be named Banks and then study economics. He looks exactly like she might have predicted; awkwardly tall, glasses thick enough to fry ants with, his collar stiffer than his personality. He's still a graduate student, he's not all the way gone into full professional adulthood, but he's not hanging on very tight. It's still mystifying to think that this guy was Darian's first love, and that Mr. Nebbish had ever even seen a guitar up close, let alone been the one who taught Darian how to play.

But that's people for you; everyone has a past.

Missy starts making clucking noises when she realizes she's still on the phone, just to fill the space. This is the great thing about Marley; all that shit that just passed through her mind? She feels like she shared it with him anyway. He finally wakes up on his end, too.

"I have no idea how long I've been in this bathroom," he tells her.

Missy squints at her phone again. "We've only been talking for three minutes."

"Really? Jesus. Missy, just look at what you've done to me."

"You're welcome," Missy says to him, closing her eyes so that she can feel close to him. Space, like time, bends a little more freely in her perception when she's halfway down a bottle.

"I think Greg just came in," Marley says. "I should try to find my way out of here."

"Try the door, lover," Missy says, and is flushed with happiness when she hears Marley giggling.

"Okay, I'm going. Bye, dude."

"Yeah, goodbye." Missy doesn't bother to hang up the phone, she lets Marley deal with that, thinking what she always does when she finishes talking to him lately: *That kid is not going to make it.* But in a very literal sense, no one is going to make it, so... cheers!

Missy goes back to concentrating on her drink, tries to pour it down her throat like an easy waterfall, but it's too strong for that. She balls her left hand into a fist, trying to fight her gag reflex, and just manages to hold it down. She'll need to do a few shots of water if she doesn't want be sick.

Missy breathes deeply, closes her eyes and focuses on the feeling of osmosis, of the molecules of alcohol trading places with her blood. With the applied meditation that any heavy drinker will teach herself after a while, Missy ignores the way her stomach lining burns, and the salted slug feeling in her frontal lobe, and the god awful gluey fur feeling on her tongue. Instead she lives in the dizzy swirl behind her eyes and the way her bones feel suspended in the jelly of her flesh.

It's all pleasant in its own way until she sits there long enough for the sun to shift an octave lower. That's when she becomes aware that her buzz is starting to ebb, and her higher mind is starting to stir, and the most atrocious feeling of emptiness and horror starts to rise in her chest, obscuring even the discomfort of her poisonous habit. Once she realizes what's happening—that a fearful eruption of guilt is trying to find its way to the surface—Missy gets up immediately.

Marley makes it out of the bathroom. It really wasn't that complicated, as soon as he got his hand on the doorknob, it just *looked* a bit like a funhouse hallway from his seat on the toilet.

When Marley reemerges from the hallway, he gathers that Mitch is gone and the party has moved inside, with Greg rinsing glasses from the sink to the drying rack. The sun has gone away, and the living room is lit by lamps, and Marley can see himself reflected in the sliding glass door that leads out to the back patio. *Oh, no you don't*, Marley thinks towards the reflective surface before turning his face away. *Not interested in looking at that at all.*

Marley sits down on the couch, then lies down on it (and he's pretty sure he made that decision himself, that it wasn't made for him by tipsy momentum). He lands on one of the plush pillows and realizes his hair is down because it sprays out comfortably around his face, like a bed of laurels. He worms and snuggles down into the nest comfortably.

"Hey, if you want another drink," Greg says from the kitchen, "I can make you one with a dash of cherry liqueur and a couple of maraschinos. I've got a few in a jar left over from my party and I don't like them."

"Sure," Marley says. Greg would have made a great politics or PR guy, he's got a real deft touch with every word he says. He's never once blurted, or misspoke, or blathered off into silence. He pretends to be shy or at a loss for words, but it's all too smooth and charming. Marley knows people who are really awkward. There are a lot more crashing, horrified silences and what-the-fuck-did-that-means when you aren't engineering every social situation to go off without a hitch.

Marley might not have been surprised to find that his favorite writer couldn't talk for shit. Sometimes actors are like that; brilliant on the screen, painful in an interview, like they're uncomfortable being themselves. Oscar Wilde said as much, that a man is least himself when he talks in his own person. Speaking for themselves, people are hampered by the thought of consequences for their actions, but as soon as it's established that you're playing a part, you can act naturally without repercussion. Even Marley does it, on a smaller scale. He's already caught himself saying, "Sorry about that, it was just the booze talking."

Greg comes over with the cherry drink. It's got a little red coffee straw with three cherries impaled on it so Marley can drink it without sitting up. It tastes like it's right out of a soda shop, no sting of liquor until it burns the back of Marley's throat where, against his more sensitive membranes, it can't hide anymore. Marley realizes halfway through eating the cherries off the straw that there's no way to do it without it seeming sexy. See, that only goes to confirm what he already suspects about Greg: none of this is an accident.

"Nice that it's finally getting chilly," Greg says. His body movements are like origami, the way he folds one leg over the other, pops one arm into his lap and the other over the back of the couch, hand twisting back around like a swan's head so that he can lightly rest his cheek there.

"I've started my Halloween reading list," Marley says slowly (getting his tongue to cooperate for the word 'Halloween' takes a second). It doesn't seem like a non-sequitur to him. Cool air means the cool air holidays to Marley—any temperature below 75 degrees makes him feel like Christmas is approaching. "*Frankenstein, Jekyll and Hyde, The Picture of Dorian Gray.* I never read *Dracula* anymore, I don't like it. Probably I've been spoiled with all the other vampire books I read in high school." He found it a little dry actually, even compared to other books from the same time period. He found it a little... bloodless.

Every other time Marley has told people about his themed reading lists they've felt duty-bound to inform him of his strangeness (and some breaking news that is not), but Greg simply says, "Hmm." Probably he's not listening, or perhaps Marley didn't manage to form proper words at all. Greg goes on as if Marley hasn't made a single sound.

"Now you won't look so conspicuous wearing these shirts." He flips the tail end of Marley's overshirt off his body, opening up his torso area. Marley keeps sucking his drink through its tiny straw until he's slurping nothing but melted ice. He reaches towards the coffee table to set the drink down, and Greg chases after him so he doesn't accidentally drop it onto the carpet (a real possibility).

The glass makes it safely to the table. By the time they make it back to the couch however, Greg's hand has found its way to Marley's crotch. Maybe an accident, maybe he thinks it's resting on Marley's thigh, but who really believes that? Marley starts to laugh without smiling.

"What's funny?" Greg asks.

"I was thinking of what Jesse would say in this situation."

"What situation is that?"

Greg's hand squeezes a bit, and Marley gets hard in response, not that it's any big compliment; he was getting a little turned on by the feel of his hair down around his face too.

"Jesse would probably be like, 'Get off my jock,' and his face would be all serious." Marley laughs again, picturing it in his head. That stern face that Jesse has, the one he obviously learned from his father. Now that Jesse's got long hair, he mentions once a week that he looks just like his dad. That man's probably pretty good-looking, wherever he is.

"So that's what Jesse would say; what do you say?"

Marley sighs and reaches for Greg's hand, wanting to just set it down somewhere else, but ending up with their fingers laced together. That's maybe not the right impression to create, but then again...

Greg comes over him in a heartbeat. His lips cover Marley's mouth so fast he gets confused about trying to breathe through his nose, but Greg moves on quickly enough after that. He kisses Marley's cheek, then neck, then settles his weight down over Marley like a smothering blanket.

So long as every last item of his clothing stays right where he put it, Marley is fine with this. In fact, it's almost kind of funny, like, it's such a teenaged thing to do, necking and grinding on a couch, and Marley's not even the one doing it! He starts to giggle.

Greg pulls back, leaving only enough space between their faces for a whisper.

"Do you mind?" Greg asks him.

"Apparently not." Marley attempts to sit up (yes, he forgets for a moment that he can't very well sit up with Greg lying on top of him), and it sends a thick, painful pulse of blood into his head. That's officially a headache. Missy says he has to butch these out because Tylenol will shred his liver. Marley still hasn't learned how to walk the line.

"You want another drink?" Greg asks him, taking Marley's struggling as a hint to back off.

"Can I get it to go?"

The answer is happily yes, for by the time Marley is delivered back home to the garage, the fast swigging of his to-go drink has obliterated his headache (or more likely eclipsed it; no one feels a paper cut when his leg is broken).

Marley gets out of Greg's car without saying goodbye (he's already concentrating on getting up the stairs). Greg departs with a wave and an amused chuckle as Marley lurches off around the corner of the building towards the office door.

This is one more great thing about alcohol; usually this alley makes Marley feel like he's about to be ambushed, but now it's just his good friend the side alley. He's lived above the garage for two years and nothing more terrible than a sour whiff from the trash cans has ever happened to him here. He can think about that one of two ways: either something awful becomes more inevitable the longer he tempts fate by being here, or it's just a safe place. Alcohol is an optimist.

Marley is lucky to feel safe at the moment, because it takes an overabundance of time to unlock the door, step his body around to the other side of it, and make triple sure he relocks it. Getting upstairs, while hard to do in the dark, is somehow a little easier with his eyes fully shut. He feels his way carefully when totally blind, and doesn't try to rely on all the lying, swirling shadows.

He doesn't bother trying to keep count of the stairs, just feels ahead on the railing to know where it bends into the platform. He gets to the loft door and is relieved to find it unlocked. He probably already made enough noise on the stairs to wake Jesse out of his coma-like sleep, but he's happy not to be flopping against the door and grinding the key in and out of the lock. Not that Marley really has any idea of how loud he's being. He has to assume very. Missy says you're always a hundred times louder than you think.

Marley lets this door hang open. He hits the bed by sliding down the wall so that he doesn't accidentally land on Jesse. It's a successful strategy, because Jesse doesn't move an inch even after Marley is horizontal. And Marley? He's out with one shoe on and one just barely hanging off his toes, an unevenness that would have driven him half to madness in a sober state. Now though he's so thoroughly turned off to the world that he has no conscious knowledge of Jesse getting up from bed less than a minute later, walking out and slamming the door loud enough to startle a rat in the trash cans outside.

Chapter Ten: Courage

Jesse doesn't sleep the rest of the night. He spends the time before dawn dismantling car parts and putting them back together again, like cleaning gun after gun.

He's turning his thoughts in and out of place too, going over each one independently from the interlocking, revolving whole.

Jesse's officially tired of watching Marley skirt around cheating on him. Surely he's been as understanding as anyone could hope to be. He realized when this began that Marley was just dazzled by meeting a minor celebrity, and he realized (once he heard Missy explaining it to Aaron) that it got a little deeper once the old guy died. Marley has been projecting, he's been using Greg as a surrogate for all his unresolved crap. It's all fine by Jesse to a point, but how many nights is he supposed to go to bed alone while Marley gets sloshed with another guy? And how long before getting sloshed with that guy turns into sloppily making out with that guy, if it hasn't already? How far is it going to go before it becomes a serious betrayal? Sex? Honesty? Probably Jesse could forgive a handjob before he'd be okay with Greg seeing Marley's scars. If Marley could share that with Greg, he wouldn't need Jesse anymore. There'd be nothing special about being with Jesse that he couldn't get just as good somewhere else.

Marley's skin is starting to smell like the sour mix Jesse's father used to put into his first drink of the day, the one he had to sneak past his pukes from the night before. Sometimes it wouldn't work and he'd hurl it right back up into the kitchen sink, and for the rest of the day Jesse would smell it: getting a drink of water, rinsing his plates after meals, making his dad more ice cubes... the ghost of it haunted.

When Marley spends all day in the bathroom, Jesse remembers

having to take his childhood leaks in the weed-choked flowerbed out front of their crunchy little house. When Marley hits pockets of ravishing hunger, Jesse remembers Dan talking about that craving. He told Jesse once, said, "Even though it feels like you're burning a hole through your guts, eating will only put you down, and you have to resist that, because you've got a lot more drinking to do."

In the early morning Jesse takes an unhappy nap on the couch in Kenny's office. He's dissatisfied, but he's pinpointed why now, and he's formulated a plan for going forward. He's going to take this situation to Rita. He doesn't know her that well, but she's one of the few older folks in their life who keeps a level head when some bullshit's going down. It's probably because of the whole foster situation. She can understand that drinking too much doesn't mean you're an immediate alcoholic. Sure, that's how you get there, but someone like Kenny's wife would be calling rehabs right away, all dramatic and having kittens. Jesse wants to talk to someone a little more calm and battle-weary.

The book store opens at nine. At eight thirty Jesse takes a head-clearing walk down the street to mention some of this to Rita. This is the road Marley walks every morning, the road he hates. He says he can't stand the barreling trucks, says he feels like he's about to be sucked into the road like an inflated grocery bag on the wind and flattened beneath the tires. Jesse likes it though. The rush from the passing semis brings a much appreciated breeze, but he's always liked big trucks, probably the same way some people like big dogs.

The doors aren't open when Jesse shows up, but the lights are on, so Jesse knocks and loiters until he's noticed. He's expecting Rita to be the one here, but it's Tristan, her foster kid.

Jesse and Tristan only know each other by sight, but it's enough for Tristan to come unlock the door and let Jesse in when he knocks. The unwelcoming look on his face might be the early hour, or general teenage moodiness, or intense personal dislike, Jesse can't tell. Tristan locks the door behind him.

"Marley's not here, even though he's supposed to be," Tristan says. "He's late a lot these days."

"I know, he's still sleeping it off. That's why I'm here, to talk to Rita about... all that with Marley."

"Hmm," Tristan says, hopping up onto the counter and eyeballing Jesse, adding him up like a series of short numbers. He's got his mouth puckered around something he's clearly weighing whether or not to say. Jesse waits to be decided upon.

"Your boyfriend's starting to develop a nasty habit," Tristan says. He makes a spade's-a-spade face and starts tapping a pen on his knee.

"I know that, but he doesn't."

"You don't know crap, nobody around here does, it's starting to really piss me off."

There it is. People always bristle up at him eventually. Even Marley is starting to get that same affronted attitude, but Jesse's almost certain that's about something else. Marley liked him well enough before he met Greg, and before he started imbibing alcohol. Jesse's not the one who's changed, he's sure of that. He's the same as he's ever been.

"My dad drank a lot," Jesse says with an odd note of... almost pride? He feels a sense of achievement in having made it through his upbringing, like surviving a tour of duty.

"Too many beers in front the game?" Tristan sneers.

"He shot my mother." He did that particular deed while stone sober, but that detail won't wipe the derision off Tristan's face.

"Nice," Tristan concedes. "My parents only used booze to kill themselves." He sets down his pen and squares himself, squeezing his knees through his tattered jeans and giving Jesse a small measure of respect. "So you're not okay with the way Marley's drinking?"

"Not particularly."

"Do you drink?"

"I don't think so." Jesse runs his fingers over his head, gets them snagged lightly on his curls. He's still not used to them. He grew all this hair just for Marley; what would Marley do for him? He could always ask him to stop drinking, or to stop seeing Greg, which would amount to the same thing. He's just disinclined to turn into his mother, especially knowing that all her nagging did precisely nothing to influence his father's decisions.

"What does that mean?" Tristan asks him. "Either you drink or you don't."

"I tried it, when our old friends were in town. I think it would take a lot of practice to learn to like it, and why bother? Shit's poison."

Tristan nods an Amen. "I tried it too, on Marley's advice. He said it makes you more sexually loose, all it did was make me sick." Tristan gives Jesse another appraising squint. "What bothers you more, the booze or the fact that he uses it to screw around on you?"

Jesse smirks at the impertinent question. Tristan reminds him of himself at that age, the smart way he used to talk to people when he was still trapped in the rote and ropes of high school. He hasn't heard that fresh little tone since it stopped coming out of his own mouth.

"What were you trying to use it for? Trying to get sexually loose yourself?"

"That's none of your business," Tristan says, quicker to anger than Jesse has ever been, hopping down from the counter to erect a more hostile stance. "Rita's not here yet, okay? And she'll be a while in coming, so don't feel, like, obligated to wait around."

"Hey," Jesse says, opening up his body by resting his arm on a shelf, gesturing open-handed with other, like how he was taught to approach a wild animal. He feels like he was halfway to making a friend just now, or at least a friendly acquaintance. He wants to keep that going by letting out a piece of truth, a show of good faith. "Marley's not messing around on me, not yet. It's not exactly charming me that he's thinking about it, but it's not a deal breaker yet."

"He said he got really close with that girlfriend of his, like making out and shit."

Jesse lets out a chuff. "I'm not worried about what he does with girls."

"Don't be so binary," Tristan says. "Not everyone's sexuality is exclusive, right? He probably won't leave you for just any girl, but for the right girl, don't be so sure."

Jesse grins. "You're speaking from experience?"

Tristan's face tightens right back up, and his fists ball up, and Jesse drops his grin in defeat. That's a situation good and botched right there.

"Guess I'll take off then," he tells Tristan. No one's ever hit him in the face yet, and Jesse wants to keep that record going. "Tell Rita I stopped by," Jesse says, knowing full well that she'll never hear a word of it.

Jesse is once again (as ever) on his own.

Tristan is indeed unamused by Jesse's questions. Jesse might know what it's like to be born out of alcoholism, but he doesn't know anything about Tristan's real problems. He doesn't know anything about the subtlety of girls, or about the gray area between a guy's label, and his imagined self, and his true heart. Jesse is simple. He doesn't even read, Marley's said so. He doesn't question himself, or dig through his own motives. He doesn't delve because he isn't deep. He's got as much depth as a mirror.

He might be Tristan's brother in an alcoholistic upbringing, but so were a lot of the assholes at the group home, so what? Jesse can just fuck right off if he thinks he knows anything about Lindsay, about the way Tristan feels for her, about the constant learning it takes to really love someone you've never wanted to have sex with.

He and Lindsay have been talking again. Shallowly, and only face-to-face at school, because somehow it's easier to bullshit her when she can look right at him. It's so easy to text her the truth, knowing he won't have to deal with her real-time reaction to his opinions, and so even though they eat lunch together again, and even though they spend private time together, times *perfect* for truth, Tristan just never gets around to telling her. He doesn't ever want to spoil his own moments with her.

Rita is going to have a party here at the store for Halloween. Tristan's been helping without complaint, putting up decorations and cleaning the store, clipping coupons for Halloween candy. Rita knows what he's up to; he's told her already that he and Lindsay are going to spend Halloween together, not tick-or-treating (they went last year and both agreed that they were at last too old to be dressing up and going door-to-door), but hanging out at one house or the other. They haven't decided which yet, maybe they'll just... float.

Tristan feels like he's been floating for months now, and he drifts through the early part of the day until Marley finally oozes in, well after their first few customers. College kids hang around in the chairs up front now, mostly drinking from the two pots of coffee Rita keeps going behind the counter. It's basic cheap diner shit, nothing but kitchen brewing pots and packets of sweetener from the grocery store, but each mug is only a dollar. Students like to kick off their shoes and study and sometimes even cruise Tristan if they think he's older.

Marley is matted down from sleep, but he still looks utterly exhausted. After the night and day Tristan spent with his Mason jar, it just makes no sense to watch Marley come in the mornings after his own benders. How much fun can he have the night before that this crap is worth it? What is he made of that's so different from Tristan, who's supposed to be the predisposed one due to nature or nurture or neurosis or whatever?

He and Marley stand behind the counter like two strangers in a bathroom. Tristan rolls a question around in his mouth for a while before he finally turns to Marley and discreetly lets it out.

"Why do you keep doing this to yourself?" It's probably the first authentic question he's asked Marley since meeting Lindsay, since switching every last bit of his loyalty to her.

Marley sighs, and appears to take the question to heart. When Tristan speaks to him flippantly, Marley usually responds in kind, but Tristan has softened this one for him. Out of the goodness of his heart, of course.

Marley's hands come up; he uses them to talk a lot more now that he drinks, like it's loosened him up just the way he says it does. He spreads them out the way church people do when they talk about the light of God which shines down everywhere, except Marley isn't full of peace and love.

He says slowly, as if picking out just the right words, "I'm just... really tired of being... so entrenched here."

"What? Here on earth?" Marley shrugs and his hands fall away immediately, closing him down. "You know what that sounds like, don't you?"

"The world's a prison," Marley says dismissively, "with many confines, wards, and dungeons."

"What's that from?"

"Hamlet."

"Oh. I think we're supposed to read that senior year."

"Read it before then if you want to like it," Marley says. "I always hate a book that I'm *supposed* to read." He walks off, and Tristan thinks that's the end of their interaction until Marley comes back with an annotated copy of Hamlet from the new textbook section and sets it down in front of Tristan, tapping it twice with a bitten down fingernail before getting someone a refill.

Tristan decides to give it a shot. He wasn't going to do anything but stand around today anyway.

It's kind of slow going at first. It's harder than reading a book because he has to stop and try to picture the stage directions. He has a hard time keeping minor characters in order, and he keeps forgetting to look at who is speaking when the dialogue gets short. But the footnotes help him to decipher all the old words, and there are summaries at the end of each Act in case he does miss something. By the time he's halfway through the play, he's pleased to find that he isn't lost. Rita always tells him he's smart, in spite of the way bouncing through the foster system has trashed his grades. He smiles to think that maybe she's right.

It makes him want to text Lindsay with a quote or something, but he hesitates before he does, and a moment later wonders if Marley isn't still sharp despite the dulling effects of a hangover. He would be one of these college kids by now if he weren't so weird. Jesse's boss or somebody made him get his GED, and he reads way more than even the students in here, who spend half the time on their laptops just dipshitting around.

The summary *just said* that Hamlet's all about indecision, and Tristan knows for a fact that he's been pulling his phone out to contact Lindsay like this for over a month and then putting it away again unused. Is this meant to be some kind of a lesson from Marley? What happened to him hating a book he's *supposed* to read?

Tristan can feel himself being condescended to and doesn't particularly like it, but he won't quit reading now. Rita looks so pleased when she sees what he's reading, and besides… Hamlet's avoiding his more-or-less girlfriend too. Maybe they do have a few things in common.

"I can't even *believe* how hot it is out here," Lindsay says, lifting the hair off the back of her neck as she and Tristan walk down the middle of the street, past little clusters of costumed kids. Most of them are experiencing extreme emotional upheaval: kids screaming to go home, kids screaming to keep going, kids screaming wordlessly, jacked up on sugar.

"Yeah, remember it was almost cold last month?" Tristan asks.

"But never on Halloween."

"I know, never."

She and Tristan have just left Lindsay's house after her mom and little sister returned to man the fort. At only eleven, Rebecca already thinks she's too old to trick-or-treat, at least while being accompanied by their mom. Lindsay's pretty sure she wasn't such an uppity little turd when she was that age, just three years ago. These younger kids are so anxious to be older; they can't seem to enjoy where they are in life.

It's a scenic night for a stroll. Lindsay is happy to see a set of boy-girl twins dressed as a prince and princess, and a little nauseated to see a pair of preteens got up as a football player and a cheerleader. Lindsay is in high school now, she knows actual kids who have chosen that for their identities, and they're mostly real cunts about it. The only ones worse are the ROTC kids. It's what happens when people put on a uniform; it's just their costume for everyday life.

Lindsay is musing on this when Tristan links arms with her, something he hasn't done since he got weird at the beginning of school. It comes back so naturally that it doesn't interrupt her thoughts, but after they turn off of busy North Cypress (and into the shabbier neighborhood where Tristan lives), something new happens.

Tristan's hand slides into her palm.

I mean... okay? Lindsay thinks. They haven't held hands since they were pretending to be a couple, but since people assumed that about them anyway no matter what they did, they quit play-acting a long time ago.

Oh well. He probably saw some guy giving her a lascivious look or something and just wants to scare him away. It's a night for frights, after all.

They get to Tristan's house, and it feels like coming home so much more than stepping into her own house does. It's mustier, the carpet's nearly worn through in high-traffic areas, and there are rust stains under every faucet, but Lindsay prefers this place over her mom's clean and uptight environment. Nobody hassles you here. It's okay to set your bag down where you please, it's not an act of war if you forget to take off your shoes, and you can put your feet up on anything your legs can comfortably reach.

"Wanna watch monster movies?" Lindsay asks, flumping down on the couch and grabbing the remote and a handful of M&Ms from a bowl on the coffee table.

"Um... no," Tristan says, touching his face a bunch as he sits down and turns to her. "I want to talk to you about something."

"Let me guess, you're coming out as straight, right?"

Tristan tries to laugh at what was obviously meant as a joke, but he only manages to cough out a puff of air. His already dark irises have gotten suddenly stormier, and his lips twitch in an apologetic wince when he looks at her.

"Just hear me out, okay?"

Lindsay feels her eyes grow large as Tristan picks up her hands and starts talking a whole flood of nonsense.

"Look, it's like, sex just isn't the most important thing in life, you know? It's probably the least important thing when it comes to being in love with someone. I don't want something as inconsequential as me being gay to be the thing that pushes us apart."

Tristan keeps talking in circles. Lindsay stops listening to every bend and dive in his argument in favor of looking at their hands, at the way Tristan keeps stroking his fingers through hers.

"Blah blah soulmates, mumble fumble transcend our bodies, something nothing always," she hears Tristan say, and right there she stops him.

"What are you asking me?"

"I... okay I thought I just explained it, but I was wondering if since we love each other, shouldn't we try to maybe make out or something? Because love is the hard part, and sex is easy, and so it's perfect."

Lindsay frowns, her mind at once stalled with shock and racing with picture-images: her concept images of 'making out' as she's seen it done on TV, or imagined it would be when she suddenly became older and cool, all colliding with her real-life memories of touching Tristan. It's not that they haven't been close; they've slept together in the chaste sense, they've hugged and snuggled and kissed each other, but it's been regular! It's been a part of Lindsay's same old uneventful life. She's skittish about meshing those two things together, afraid of life becoming too real, because it might be disastrous, or worse, disappointing.

"Is this what you were worried about the whole time with Jordan? Because I wasn't ever planning to get with him like that, I was just letting stuff play out."

Tristan cocks his head wisely at her. "That's exactly how it would have played out," he tells her. "But if you had chosen Jordan and wanted him over me, you would have realized that while I wasn't talking to you, and now it's plain that we both feel the same way about each other, right?"

"I can't exactly say I've ever wanted to make out with you though,"

Lindsay says. Her tone is apologetic, but Tristan doesn't need it.

"Of course not. We've always been so past all that nonsense, but Rita says that sex and figuring all that stuff out is an important part of developing, and she's right. I mean, I've already done it, but it's something you'll want to experience eventually, and why do it with some random jerk you meet in math class? Why don't we, like, shape our own destinies? Letting things play out is so passive; we should engineer our shit, don't you think?"

Lindsay wants to pull her hands back, but she doesn't want to injure Tristan. This is definitely hard to deal with while he's staring clear into her bones the whole time. She demurs for long enough that he continues the conversation without her.

"I knew it would awkward, right? So I went and got a jar of booze. It was your brother who actually gave me the idea, since he drinks now."

"Whoa, really?" Lindsay interrupts.

"Oh yeah, like a fish, he comes to work still half-soused all the time."

"That's... interesting. I figured he wouldn't want to drink because of our dad's dad being such a raging drunk."

"Was he? Marley keeps wondering about that, but you know for sure?"

"He doesn't *know?* How could he not, I feel like dad talks about it all the time."

"Well, you've met your brother, he's a little dense."

"Oh, for sure." Lindsay drums her fingers on the back of Tristan's hand. "So you got some booze to sort of grease the wheels? That sounds like a good place to start, I guess. We could try that."

Tristan's optimistic expression implodes. "I poured it out already. I tried it last month and it was awful, really," he urges. "Like not just awful for me, which it was, but gross and maybe even dangerous. Some redneck probably stirred it out of gasoline or something, but I have a much better idea if you want to try it."

Tristan leaves the couch, goes to the hallway to get a step ladder out of the pantry, and takes it into the kitchen. Lindsay follows to watch him. Tristan climbs to reach the cabinet above the stove, reaches back underneath the wiring for the stove vent, behind some dusty cornucopia-looking centerpiece, and extracts a bottle of red wine.

"Rita will just have to punish me if she finds out, but there's a real chance she's completely forgotten this is back here," Tristan says. "It's so weird. My parents never bought alcohol to tuck it away like this. It's just up here like a fire extinguisher."

"Cool," Lindsay says. She opens the cabinets looking for wine glasses while Tristan pans through the junk drawer to find a corkscrew. They return to the living room, leaving the kitchen light on for the ambiance of linoleum-reflected light, and Tristan eyes the two glasses she sets down warily.

"Okay, we can do this. It's not hard stuff, it's just wine." He pours an equal two inches into each glass and hands her one.

Lindsay smells the wine first, and then wonders why she did that, because it's got a sour honk that makes her reluctant to taste it. But Tristan throws it back with a tough pucker, and so Lindsay does it too.

It tastes a lot like grape juice and stomach bile. Lindsay sticks her tongue out trying to air out the taste and Tristan laughs at her, bumping her shoulder chummily as he slides down to sit with his legs stretched out beneath the coffee table.

Lindsay joins him as he tops off their glasses. Just that small movement has triggered a heady pump of alcohol-infused blood to her head. Lindsay tosses back another gulp of wine and endures the shivering disgust of its taste, but by the time it goes all the way down, she's giggling. Giggling and leaning against Tristan and thinking: *Human contact, so wild! Why shouldn't we make out?* He just smiles knowingly at her and kisses the end of her nose. Lindsay's giggles redouble.

The ceiling gets far away, and Lindsay stares up at it with her head resting on Tristan's shoulder. Her face and toes tingle as she realizes: *Hey! This is being tipsy!* Real life is happening to her right now. This is something she'll remember someday when she's old and think that she was once so young.

"I think maybe we can," Lindsay tells him. Her head is on Tristan's shoulder, and his cheek is against her hair, and he's breathing like he's smelling her hair. "I've got to lose my virginity at some point, right? And I do already love you. We should do it for Christmas, maybe. Over the break when the weather's nice."

"Don't say yes just because of this stuff," Tristan says, tapping the glass bottle with a muted ring.

"Why not?"

"It's not really you. Your brother says it's Dutch courage, 'cause I guess people didn't used to like the Dutch. Fake courage, just like a Dutch treat isn't a treat at all."

"My dad says nobody ever does anything drunk that they didn't at least think about doing sober."

Tristan's head shakes gently against hers, back and forth. "I don't know why either one of us is listening to your family anyway."

"I know," Lindsay says, picking her glass back up and thinking (though definitely *not* saying out loud), *I'd rather listen to yours.*

Part Three: Return

Chapter Eleven: Fellows Whom It Hurts To Think

Mitch is preparing for his after school tutee when the door to his classroom opens. He's surprised that Landon would be so early—Mitch is always having to call the front office to have the kid paged over the intercom—but it turns out not to be him. Marley's boyfriend is sidling into the room, his eyes roving everywhere as he goes, like any one of the historical figures on the walls might leap out at him and beat him to death with a scroll.

He starts in with a modest, "Hello, I don't know if you remember me," but Mitch cuts him off by grabbing his right hand in a shake.

"How are you, Jesse? How's Marley?"

Jesse smiles by showing a lot of his gleaming teeth. Those angelic ringlets in his hair make him look a lot sweeter than he would without them.

"I've been better," he says. "And Marley's who I'd like to talk to you about."

Mitch retakes his seat behind his desk as Jesse touches one of the student desks, thinks better of slipping into that right-oriented prison, and sits on the desk's surface instead.

"You're worried about him?" Mitch guesses.

"I think so. I can't tell if what he's doing is wrong or not. My father drank a lot and my mother never did, so I don't know what's normal."

"Marley's behavior shouldn't be considered normal by anyone," Mitch says, touching his newly bare face compulsively—he shaved his old beard right after getting Greg's latest manuscript. Everyone says it makes him look younger.

Jesse nods thoughtfully and says, "This morning I woke up and he was sleeping on the floor next to the bed. Just kind of rolled over and didn't come back up. And sure, the mattress is only a foot or so off the ground, but still."

Mitch sighs. He can just imagine little Marley passed out like a dropped doll. "Look, I told Greg that I'd get him in trouble if he kept giving him liquor."

"That's a nice try, but his friend sent him a fake ID last week. The liquor store told him to pound sand, but he lucks out at the grocery store more times than not. I mean, sometimes it's good to see him out of the house under his own steam, but he just comes right back and drinks until his vision's so trashed he can't read anymore."

Mitch tries not to laugh. "He gets drunk and reads?"

"And takes notes he can't decipher the next morning, yeah." Jesse shrugs. "He corrects his slurs too. It was cute the first few times, but he's been doing this crap for weeks, and some people never stop. He just took to it so fast, like a duck to water."

Mitch nods, realizes he hasn't stopped touching his face, and disciplines his hand away by grabbing a stress ball shaped like a red apple, a present for teacher.

"So you came looking for me... why? I've got some pamphlets on teen drinking you can give to him to throw away if you want."

"He likes you," Jesse says. "And I don't know you well enough to dislike you, and he might listen to you if you talked to him. I don't want an intervention to break out or anything, but I think he could stand to scale it back. Maybe some ground rules from someone who knows better than us."

"You think I know better?"

"Well you're old... older than us, I mean. And you're not an alcoholic, so you must know how you're doing that."

Mitch nods appreciatively. That's fine logic, although Jesse did just end Mitch's streak of being called young-looking. It had to end sometime—the kids always think he's forty.

"Here, why don't I write down my number, I'm usually free after school. Let me know when he's sober enough for me to swing by and lecture him."

"It might be a while," Jesse warns. "He usually starts as soon as he's off work."

Handing over the sticky note (shaped like a tiny open book), Mitch feels that he's doing Jesse enough of a favor to ask him a personal question.

"What do you like best about Marley?"

Jesse doesn't seem to take offense. He puts his hands on the back of his head and butterflies his arms as he considers an answer. The movement wafts air over Mitch's desk—chilly air over the top of Jesse's boyish stench like icing on a cake.

"He was the first really interesting person I ever met. Like, the people in my hometown are so simple, they might as well be a herd of cows, and then Marley showed up and was so smart, and so, I don't know, like deep and complicated. I guess this is all a part of that. I never totally understand him, but I think he wants someone who can."

"You mean Greg? Why he's so drawn to him?"

"Yes."

"That's nothing against you, Greg's very charming when he wants to be, it's why I still associate with him. Besides, if Marley didn't want to be with you he'd leave, right?"

"I doubt it," Jesse says. "This might be his way of trying, just act so bad that I break up with him, save him the trouble."

Mitch sighs. Why was it that he thought he wanted to be in a relationship again? It seems like every one has been just like this: unsure the whole time about your motivations, about his, wondering if you couldn't do better, mortified by the idea that he might be thinking the same thing, and what has it gotten Mitch? Does he have a relationship like a weathered rock, nearly infinite in its capacity to withstand erosion? No, it's gotten him to precisely where these teenagers are today—no wiser, no happier, and still wrapped up in the same old drama.

Landon finally arrives for his tutoring session, kicking the press bar on his way in and huffily dragging a desk closer to Mitch's. He doesn't acknowledge Jesse (who folds out of the way as if he doesn't like kids) and says, "Why are girls so crazy, god!"

Jesse snorts and tells Mitch, "I'll call."

Mitch waves him out of the room, and switches his attention to Landon.

"Why do you think girls are crazy?"

"Uh, because they are? They don't even know what they want."

Mitch smiles as Landon tosses his homework instructions across the desk. As if anyone ever knows what they want!

Coming home, Jesse doesn't know whether he wants to find Marley asleep or awake. His manic drunkenness can get annoying, and Jesse often avoids him after the second helping of whatever corrosive he's got stashed above the fridge. But there's something equally disturbing about finding him passed out and lifeless, something that's a lot more appealing in a way, something that fascinates Jesse.

He walks into the loft to find Marley flung out on the bed, sleeping with his mouth open, which he never did sober. Jesse tosses his keys onto the table, sure the noise won't wake Marley. He kicks his shoes into the wall and strips off his old jean jacket, letting the buttons clack loudly against the floor. Marley doesn't stir. His empty glass lies on its side next to his dangling hand, a little sticky spot underneath it, where the dregs of his drink slid out.

Jesse sits down on the edge of the mattress and rights the glass onto the table. He runs his fingers over his head, a nervous habit he's become more and more aware of ever since Marley asked him to grow out his hair. Every time it impedes his movement he thinks, *Oh, I must not know what else to do with my hands.* Doing it now, he doesn't think of the fact that he grew it out just to please Marley, and he doesn't resent the favor in the face of all that Marley is putting him through now. He understands that neither one of them goes too far out of the way for the other, and he *appreciates* that, it's what he's always liked best about their dynamic.

Jesse combs Marley's hair out over the pillow in a halo. He doesn't close his mouth for fear the boy might not be able to breathe, but he does get Marley out of his socks and pants, lolls him up out of his shirt and sets him gently back down. Once he's got Marley down to his underwear, Jesse tugs those off too, and then just looks at him. Hands still and steepled under his chin, taking it all in.

Marley's stopped cutting himself now that he drinks. The scars on his left arm are white and nearly undetectable now. The ones on his leg from their drive down from Colorado are brown and old. Jesse touches them, feels them under his fingertips like Braille. He walks his fingers over both of Marley's arms like they're ladder rungs, encircling the skinny limbs easily with his father's big hands.

It occurs to Jesse that he could do whatever he wanted to with Marley right now. This kid who doesn't trust anybody, who won't sit with his back to a room, has gotten so insensibly wasted that Jesse would be free to use and abuse his body without consent. Jesse would have warned him against this; so many people he's met before wouldn't trust Jesse to water their plants, let alone have access to their bodies.

But here he has all the access he could want, and none of the permission, and it makes Jesse realize again how much he doesn't care about bodies. The first time he discovered this, he was with his mother's vacant corpse. He looked at her just as intently on the afternoon of her death, he felt her cheek with the back of his hand occasionally, like his kindergarten teacher did to take temperatures, to feel her body heat leech away into the air. After that initial curiosity however, he covered her up and filed his mother into the dead folder along with the Founding Fathers and Jesus of Nazareth.

Jesse covers Marley with their comforter, a Christmas gift from Kenny and his wife, and decides to sleep downstairs again. There's no reason to touch Marley if he isn't there to participate, to react. Jesse might as well touch himself for all the thrill he'd get out of an empty shell.

Marley wakes up with no knowledge of how he got naked, or when, or why. He's not concerned about it, it's already happened a few times. He wakes up in pajamas he doesn't remember assembling, he wakes up fully dressed on the floor, he wakes up starkers and freezing on Jesse's side of the bed.

Marley massages the congealed drool off of his cheek, he steps in the tacky remnants of his spilled drink and thinks, *I better clean that up before Jesse sees it.* He doesn't want Jesse to get a bad opinion of him just because he's going through a rather messy transformation.

Marley woozes into the shower, starts laughing halfway through shampooing his hair, and that is how he realizes he's still drunk. Great! That's way better than a hangover.

When he gets out of the shower and the clock tells him he's right on time for work, it's another victory. He must really be getting the hang of this whole alcohol thing. He's finally an adult! He drinks just like the people in his books do! He can wooze himself all the way into work without a single goddamn worry or care! He's finally found the one-way ticket to feeling just like everyone else does, to going about his life as if it's his pure and given right. Frank would be proud of him.

Marley's work shift is beautifully swift—he's tapping a mechanical pencil along to the music Rita's started playing from some newly screwed-in speakers, he's laughing along with a customer who tells Marley he looks as fucked up as she feels and gives him the sunglasses off her face for his apparently blood-shot eyes. It goes gently, but snappily: a table cloth whipped out from under a full dinner setting without so much as making the wine glasses hum.

It's only on the way home that Marley feels himself start to dull and drag. It's all still very pleasant, but he's pulling his feet through cotton and cobwebs, and he's ready to crash when he walks into the garage.

Jesse pops up from the engine of a sedan.

"Hey, stick around down here for a sec, would you?"

"Ugh, why?" Marley asks. "I'm wiped out."

"I can see that," Jesse says, even though Marley is wearing that one girl's sunglasses, and he shouldn't be able to see shit. "Just do me a favor."

"Fine," Marley says, walking over and draping his arms around Jesse, assuming that Jesse just wants his company. This is when Marley realizes he is in short sleeves, and has been in them all day. Dear God! What is in alcohol that could make him forget about his scars? How terrifyingly wonderful!

Jesse dodges away from Marley however, and ducks into Kenny's office with one finger held up, requesting just another minute of Marley's time. Marley wants to crawl into this popped engine and pass out, but he stays on his feet through sheer force of will until Jesse comes back and helps to hold him up.

Marley lays his head on Jesse's shoulder, and being shorter than him, just rests his face against Jesse's flat pectoral. He's sleeping on his feet by the time another car pulls into the garage. Jesse pats him awake and turns him around to face Mitch.

"Hi, Marley," Mitch says, reaching to shake his hand like they've never met at all.

"Hey," Marley says, sacrificing one hand to civility and pushing up his new sunglasses with the other; they're great to hide behind, might become a new staple of his wardrobe. "Hope nothing's wrong with your car."

"Oh, no." This is when Mitch catches sight of his scars, and Marley watches his head bob over to Jesse, and sees Jesse's head nod back, and Marley realizes that this is some kind of low-rent intervention about all his problems, which only makes Marley start to giggle again.

"This is as close to sober as he'll get," Jesse says. "You guys can just go upstairs, he's on his last leg anyway."

Marley scoffs affectionately towards Jesse and then breezes past him. Let Mitch come if he's coming, Marley's done.

"Jesse asked me to talk to you," Mitch begins when they get into the room. Marley tumbles into bed and pats a patch of space next to him.

Mitch, after a moment's hesitation, sits.

"I want you to have your fun," Mitch says. "I've had mine, and Greg's had his, and everyone should be able to wreck themselves for a while, it's the American way. I just wish you wouldn't do it quite so young. The drinking age is a ridiculous demand, but the way you're... what are you doing?"

Marley has managed to hush Mitch's speech by taking up his hand and stroking his palm with newly grown fingernails. Ever since Marley started drinking, he has stopped gnawing his nails to the bed.

"I guess you still don't want to kiss me?" Marley murmurs, his eyes closed and his brain halfway to sleep and completely uninterested in propriety. His hand keeps moving in Mitch's hand though, fluid, a ribbon, with a life of its own.

"I feel like you aren't hearing a word I'm saying," Mitch says.

Marley doesn't hear him.

Chapter Twelve: Moping, Melancholy, Mad

Tristan gets downright scientific as November progresses, taking note of every gross couple on campus that he used to gag at, studying their techniques.

The tongue-tanglers are the easiest to find and catalogue. Everybody's so eager to prove how grown-up and sexy they can be that they're licking each other as soon as classes let out. Some couples overbalance, with one person aggressively choking the other, revealing the purple, veiny underside of their tongue as the struggle ensues. Some clearly aren't enjoying the experience of French kissing, and only stick the tips in and out like licking a new and unpleasant flavor of ice cream cone. The Christian kids don't use their tongues at all, and the kids who are good at making out keep their secrets lip-locked; their mouths move fluidly, suctioning back and forth, and their tongues must be doing something beautifully collaborative that Tristan can only guess at.

Then there are the couples who hide in all the out-of-the-way places Tristan found when he was avoiding Lindsay, who are going a lot further. Tristan once got shooed out of a nice hiding spot because too many kids are caught smoking and grinding back behind the auditorium's palmettos. Back there, kids are really up against it, hands in each other's pants, fingering and squeezing, probably more than a few blowjobs too. Tristan wishes he could get closer without them seeing—he's missing all the crucial details when he has to spy through the fronds.

Because sure he's had sex before, but it was just the once, and sure he's made out once or twice, but it was with people he wanted to take from, not give to. He wasn't worried about pleasuring Michael when they made out those couple of times; Tristan was finding himself, or he was forgetting himself, but it had very little to do with Michael. And Zeus? They fucked, okay, but that didn't teach Tristan hardly anything that he'll need to know to be with Lindsay. Maybe he'll be more sympathetic to how she'll be feeling, getting fucked being one of those sensations that you just can't truly know until you experience it, but still. Tristan won't know anything about being on top, won't know anything about pelvic rhythm, about the angle of her whole situation (and studying the textbook in health class does *not* help like it should). Tristan gets to be a double virgin. Lucky him.

It's okay though. The Christmas deadline, far from worrying him, has brought a sense of peace to his life, a window of methodical planning. It isn't even Thanksgiving yet, which means Christmas is many centuries away and isn't about to jump out at him. In fact, Tristan has almost the whole Thanksgiving weekend to himself, to run different plays in his head, because Lindsay will be going to the panhandle with her mother and sister.

"My mom's dating this new guy, and we're going to have Thanksgiving with his mom and stepfather, which is just great, it's like a big broken home tradition," Lindsay explains to him as they walk home from his shift at Purple Prose. They hold hands now very naturally. They must look so normal to everyone else.

"Rita always asks me if I want to go visit her family for the holidays, but... no. I don't even want to start dealing with that."

"Yeah," Lindsay says. "I can see why you wouldn't."

He kisses her hand goodbye as they separate towards their respective houses. Thinking about having sex with her has already caused him to notice more about her, things he never saw before, never pondered. It's strange, because while he surely knows her better than anyone else on the planet, there's an unending supply of information that comes out of her and probably everybody, not that Tristan would spare a second to think of any of them. Most people never even know themselves all the way through, let alone someone else, but maybe that's the reason why there are so many couples trying so hard: what one person doesn't know about himself, the other might notice and keep as her own secret, and vice versa, until everything about the both of them is known by either one or the other.

As much as Tristan can know Lindsay's opinions, and her contradictions, and her mannerisms, as much as he can predict which movies she'll like or tell her, "You'll hate this song," and be right, he's never really considered her body. Outside of the fact that she has to tend to it differently than he deals with his own (she has bras and tampons and a technique for shaving around her anklebone), he's thought of their bodies as unimportant. Like, why not transcend the things and meet on a higher plane? Why not leave behind all the thoughtless monkey-rutting that everyone else is doing and be superior together?

But now it has come to Tristan's attention that ignoring sex for his whole life is probably going to be impossible, and why shouldn't Lindsay have everything she desires, including sex? He'd never ask her to give up anything for him, but it *burns* Tristan to think of another guy knowing something he doesn't know about Lindsay. To think that there's a part of herself that can't be shared with Tristan, but could possibly be given to any other guy in the whole world. It's unbearable. Being gay is no obstacle at all compared to that agony.

So Tristan has started thinking of her body. Stuff like: she'll have pubic hair probably, so it's important to know that going in. Maybe one of her breasts is bigger than the other one, Tristan read that's just how most breasts are, though sometimes the difference is too small to notice. She might have stretch marks from developing. She'll probably smell vastly different from any boy Tristan's ever been close to. He's been studying her clothes, trying to imagine the landscape underneath, and imagining wild scenarios so that no matter what happens he won't balk, and won't freak out, and won't make her feel unattractive just because this doesn't come naturally to him.

When Tristan gets home, Rita is waiting for him. He thought for sure he would get here first, he usually does, even though he walks and she drives home. It's just she usually stays late doing extra work or has errands to run, but when she looks up from some bills she has spread out, Tristan knows she came home right away to wait for him. Maybe she found out about the wine he and Lindsay drank. Tristan sits down on the other side of the coffee table and lets his backpack straps fall from his shoulders so it can squat behind him and not pull him back. He's ready for punishment if that's what's coming, but probably he's only going to get a talk.

Rita smiles at him (definitely no punishment), and takes off her glasses. Some of the hair around her face is going gray, and it gets stuck in the hinge of her glasses all the time, and she just yanks it out. It's giving her this weird little halo of short hairs. She keeps saying as soon as she turns fifty and is 'legit old' she's going to lose the ponytail and cut it all short.

"I checked my internet history the other day, trying to remember some indie website that wants to sell through the store?" she says like a question, though it's not. "Have you been looking at porn? *Straight* porn? I thought it might be Lindsay, and I don't know how comfortable I am with her seeing that stuff at our house. Her mother might not like it and she could make trouble for me, for us."

Tristan doesn't say anything, only looks at her, willing her to read it in his eyes. He's not ashamed necessarily, but he doesn't want to go into detail.

"So whether it was you or Lindsay or you both were giggling over it together, just please make sure I'm not contributing to the delinquency of someone else's minor, okay?"

Tristan nods. "Okay."

"Thank you very much!" Rita says, basically dismissing him if he wants to leave. Tristan stays where he is though, and watches her shuffle bills and thinks, *Yeah, that looks awful.* At the boys' home he thought if life ever got too tough or he couldn't handle bills, he would just kill himself like his parents basically did. But now he knows he would never choose to die before Lindsay, which means eventually he'll have to focus some effort on all the petty crap that plagues a grown-up's life.

But not today! Tristan goes to his room, makes a note on his bedside post-its to learn how to wipe a computer's browser history. It was definitely him alone looking at all that straight porn. He hasn't even tried to masturbate to it, he just watches to see if he can turn himself on with the images. He looks for younger girls, with regular chests, and the hair color they were born with, and no manicures. Girls closer to Lindsay than the chicks who look like a series of bubbles: big blonde bubble hair, candy pink bubble lips, and tits like flotation devices.

On second thought, Tristan crosses out his note. Maybe he should stop over-thinking, just get drunk like Lindsay wants to, and figure it all out the old fashioned way. For the first time in years he almost wishes he had a father around, someone he could go to and ask about how to get with girls, how'd you and mom fall in love, do you have any tricks or moves to pass on?

That impulse fades quickly however. Tristan's parents aren't ideal models for how he wants his relationship with Lindsay to go, so once again he's left on his own to improvise.

Tristan feels like the only person who's had to deal with this very specific situation in all of human history, and in a way that's a comfort; it's not as anyone else knows better.

Marley goes home at his sister's request. She says the house is empty, that she needs to talk to him. Marley for the first time ever enjoys a walk outside because he's mixed rum into a bottle of soda and so can drink it as he goes, without attracting attention. He's already better at not falling down. He already doesn't feel numb in his fingers and face. He's already started correcting his slurs like the nerd he is.

Missy has congratulated him on maturing so quickly. It took her a lot longer to learn how to handle her liquor, she says, "But I started younger than you, so some consideration for that if you please."

He's thinking of her as he walks home, sipping occasionally, finally feeling like he owns these streets, like he belongs here. Is this what everyone else in high school had? It's supposed to be a kid thing, thinking you're invincible all the time, but maybe all those kids were on drugs and alcohol too? Either way, it's good to feel normal for a moment.

Marley opens the door presumptuously, doesn't even think that it might be locked, that he might have to knock. It's open for him, and in his current state, he thinks, *Of course!* Of course it is.

Lindsay is at the kitchen counter doing math homework. She smells the booze on him right away when he comes to stand next to her, but she fights to keep a disgusted look off her face. He's halfway to taking another swig from his soda bottle when she puts her hand over his.

"Let me have some?" Lindsay says.

Marley shrugs and relinquishes the bottle. He's got more at home, and how much would his parents hate this? So much. Which is awesome.

When Lindsay takes a sip, the look of disgust finally pushes to the front of her face.

"Ew! How strong is this?"

"Pretty strong, I'm getting good at it."

"I guess," she hands the mix back to Marley and they both move to sit on the couch. It's a wrap-around, and Lindsay sits on the short part of the L while Marley collapses on the long part, a discarded doll. "Who's that girl you're friends with, the one from Colorado?"

"Missy. It's weird that you guys have never met."

"Tristan says you've made out with her a couple of times. Why?"

Marley relaxes back in his father's old seat, amazed that this is a moment in his life: he's buzzed where he used to be a child! In fact he's so amazed at the situation that he doesn't spare any thought to why Lindsay's asking him all these questions, he just answers them honestly.

"Alcohol is why, it makes you very permissive." Marley tries to keep a smirk off his face when he quotes to Lindsay, "Did you know that alcohol, taken in sufficient quantities, produces all the effects of drunkenness?"

"Would you be serious please? I'm still mad at you for being such a jerk to me when I moved out, okay? I just want a little advice."

"Don't take advice from someone you don't want to be like," Marley says sagely, and gets up to explore his childhood home through the miracle sheen of drunkenness.

There are magnets from his youthful visits to the dentist on the fridge. He has definitely not been to a dentist in at least five years, he just can't see the point. There are his measurements on the height chart, and his school picture still on the mantle. He tips the picture face-down because everyone in this house can blow him.

He's about to go into his old room when he passes by the bathroom and realizes he's needed to pee pretty badly for a long while.

He sits down to go because, let's be real, there's no way he'll be able to stand and aim at the same time. It's gonna be a long pee, so Marley leans onto the wall to rest his eyes, and is jarred awake when the door next to his face rattles violently.

"Marley, are you okay in there? Mom is coming home soon, what kind of dump are you taking?"

"Mind your own business, Lindsay," he says, pulling up out of his slump and realizing that during his micro-nap he gently dropped his bottle on the floor; it slipped out of his hand so unobtrusively that there's only the merest puddle of rum and coke on the floor. He swipes it up with some toilet paper and flushes the whole mess away. Guess it's time to take off!

"Thanks for all your help," Lindsay says sarcastically as he heads past her for the front door.

"Yeah, well," Marley says in place of goodbye. Who promised her any help? What right does she have to expect it? None, and she'll do better to learn that now.

Marley runs out of fuel halfway home and chucks his plastic bottle into a ditch with about a dozen others. Fuck it! He's free to do as he likes.

There's a liquid pink sunset in the sky, like a watermelon Jolly Rancher in his mouth. The space between throwing his bottle into the ditch and arriving home to fight with the lock is lost to him.

It takes a long bit of struggling to get his key the right way in. Jesse's inside, but he doesn't get up to help. Marley lurches his way into the room, manages to get the door shut, and figures that's good enough. He slides down the wall next to the door and allows the room to soak into his consciousness at its own pace.

Jesse's taken the hooded light from Kenny's desk and put it on the bedside crate. He's got his pocketknife out, and is using the tip to carve something in the palm of his hand. Whittling and carving, it's probably something his father used to do. Jesse's taken it up since they've been living together, getting more intricate all the time, and Marley keeps forgetting to ask him why.

After a while of both boys being silent, Jesse scoots out of bed and pads over to Marley in his winter sleep attire: socks and boxers and white t-shirt, all of it smelling like laundry straight from the dryer, clean but hot against his skin when he squats down close to Marley.

Jesse turns the pocketknife handle-side out.

"Need this?" he asks.

"You don't have to be an asshole," Marley says, definitely hearing the word *ash-hole* in his slur.

Jesse taps the handle on Marley's knee, like a reflex test. The only action it produces is to get Marley to crawl away towards the bathroom.

"You're hurting yourself more with booze, if you're trying to replace cutting or something. Like, this isn't an improvement, it's the same, it's... you know, it's like a thing that's on the same level."

"Lateral," Marley says. He crawls into the bathroom and inches the door shut behind him. He must look like a pathetic fool the whole time, but he just can't stand the feel of Jesse looking at him.

He's sitting on the bathroom floor in the dark, and realizes that he spends a lot of time having this moment.

Jesse crouches down close on the other side of the door. Marley can hear him come to the ground, and feel him there, just outside.

"I hope you aren't like this forever," Jesse says. "I miss having you around, you know? You're just so gone."

Marley turns to touch the door, to lean against it. He's careful not to say anything. He's already learned that he's much more forgiving, and much more regular-giving, and much more generous with his affections when drunk than would ever wish to be sober. So Marley stays quiet, even though he wants to nudge the door back open with the toe of his shoe, and pull Jesse to his body, and make love with him on their mildew-y pink bath mat that Kenny's wife gave them after re-doing her daughters' bathroom, so the boys wouldn't rot the grout in the loft by stepping wet from the shower straight onto the tile and never wiping it up.

"Are you even awake in there?" Jesse asks after an unknown amount of time.

"I'm sorry," Marley murmurs, his lips on the fake wood grain of their bathroom door. "I just need more time, I need so much more time." His words are weak, vague. He's falling asleep again, and he wants to go to his bed, but he knows he won't go out there while Jesse is awake and wanting something from him.

That would be impossible.

Aaron puts some change in the jukebox, selects "Slide" by the Goo Goo Dolls, and looks over at Missy significantly, with every single one of his feelings on his big dumb face. The one day she decides to detox for a while and he's going to be like this about it. Soft and sentimental when all Missy wants to do after her little breakdown is to harden back up again.

Missy is sitting at a bar chugging water, and she's pretty unhappy about it. But she hasn't been completely sober for nearly a month, and after a while she noticed that the back of her skull stayed hot and prickly at all times, like her brain was on fire, and eventually even Darian (who isn't one to nanny a bitch) asked her what her endgame was, or if she just planned to drink herself to death.

Well, no, that's not the *official* plan. She's decided to sober up for Thanksgiving weekend at least, since Darian's mother is treating them to a feast with her credit card. Missy can replace drunkenness with gluttony for a while. It's the American way.

Aaron comes over and thankfully doesn't mention his song choice. Now that she and Darian have co-penned a few songs, Missy finds herself contemptuous of people who hear a song and blurt stupidly, "Wow, this song is so *me*." *Wrong, idiot*, Missy thinks towards Aaron. If your life was a song you'd write one, your life is a pity.

"Taking it easy, huh?" Aaron asks, sitting down across from her in the booth. "How's your water?"

"Shitty. Bars don't care about good water." Missy's drinking from a bottle, but it's definitely filled with tap water from the bathroom; the cap didn't crack and it tastes like the inside of a faucet, but at least it was free. This bar happens to be in a bowling alley, so it's the wrong place to be pushing a hangover.

Missy wishes they could have stayed on the coast, next to the sea. Now in Nevada, Missy can feel the desert stretching out around her on all sides, no freedom, just miles of rocks and bones. You dip back into the middle of the country, and suddenly places like this exist: a bowling alley with booze and shoes behind the same counter. Revolting.

"Oh," Aaron says, his face fallen. Guess he thought sobriety would make her more pleasant. What he doesn't know about booze could fill several handles. "Well, it may not taste very good, but it's a lot better for you than, like, an IV drip of liquor."

"Says you," Missy contradicts him, hoping to annoy him as much as he annoys her. "My grandmother took her coffee Irish every single morning I knew her, and she lived clear into her sixties."

"Missy, sixty isn't old. She probably should have lived clear into her nineties, but then didn't because she drank too much."

Missy doubles down. "When Nana was taking it easy, she switched from whiskey in her coffee to sherry in her tea."

"That's not funny." Aaron drops eye contact with her and starts looking around at all the orange and dingy that surrounds them. Every time someone's strike clatters throughout the building, it's like the sound of Aaron's shattering hopes. He should really know better by now than to set them up so nicely. Nothing ever goes up that isn't meant to come down.

"My mother never drank," Missy goes on, watching Aaron over her sink water. "Not even champagne on New Year's, not even wine on her birthday. She'll probably live forever, but she won't be happier about it than Nana."

"I mean, you'll use any excuse to keep doing whatever you want."

"I have been sober for about seven hours and you are seriously going to drive me right back to drink."

"Nobody else is responsible for your drinking, not me and not your family, and that includes Natalie."

He knows he's said the wrong thing as soon as it slips out of his mouth. Missy hasn't spoken the baby's name aloud since she left her in a basinet two years ago. Darian might not even *know* her name, that's how verboten it's been. Aaron would have been in trouble just saying it off-handedly, but to use it to try and call Missy out for her drinking? Like that even matters? Like this is supposed to be some come-to-Jesus moment where she breaks down and asks for help? Mistake.

Missy doesn't make a scene, she's never made a scene while sober (drunk, she can't always remember enough to say one way or the other). She calmly knocks the bottle of water over, letting that gross water spill across the table and into Aaron's lap. He has the nerve to look hurt by this. He's never really been hurt by anything, is why.

But... if he wants to stick around, Missy can fix that for him.

Missy gets up and goes straight to the bar. The man behind it looks like a bowling ball himself, his eyes and mouth like the finger holes, and filled with about as much personality.

"Double vodka on the rocks," Missy says, and he pours it just like any simple machine, and asks, "Sure you don't want a splash of anything else in it?"

"Positive," Missy says, staring right into his shallow little eyes.

She gets her drink and shakes it at Aaron over the expanse of cracked vinyl seating like, *Hey, cheers! Thanks for this!* Let him deal with that. Feel guilty, everyone should feel as guilty as she does.

"You shouldn't wreck yourself just out of spite," says Darian's voice over her shoulder. Missy tosses down a sip of her drink before turning to him, and clucks her tongue against the kick of it, which sends a puff of fumes into Darian's face. He winces at it, but keeps smiling at her. He understands this more than Missy would have imagined. She wants to know why.

Missy throws back the rest of her first drink and requests another with a few drops of cranberry juice this time, just to put it down easier.

"Darian," she says, already holding onto the bar as her dubious old friend burns down her neck and puts her insides right for the time being. "Did your mother drink while you were growing up?"

He leans into sitting on one of the barstools that Missy had to hop to get up on. He puts one of his long arms on the bar and the other across Missy's shoulders. He takes the first sip of her drink before handing it over.

"Yes, she did, but not so much that I noticed, not when I was little at least."

"Do you think she's an alcoholic?"

He smiles, and his teeth gleam white in the darkness, like his mouth is stuffed with his mother's pearls.

"I wouldn't say that," he tells her.

"I bet Aaron would." Darian nods and orders a beer. He's such a good friend, Darian. He's such a *sport*.

"Aaron means well, you know he does. He may not speak with any authority on the subject, but he's not just trying to piss you off."

"I know that, but I do not care." Missy throws the rest of her drink into her mouth and finds herself feeling better. A moment ago she was annoyed, she was insulted, she was tired of life and of living, and now... bliss. The warm inner kindling of bliss. "I think I am actually, literally starting to hate him."

"Don't do that, Yoko, you'll break up the band."

Missy laughs and flips her braid off one shoulder so it can hang down her back like a dead snake. She holds up a finger to the bar tender, ordering another refill.

"You don't need us, Darian. You like us around, but you don't need us for your music."

"Yeah, but I think I was going crazy as a solo act, I was way too inside my own head."

Missy reaches up and touches his head, pets it. She gets a lot more touchy when she drinks, and Darian knows this and tolerates it. It's nothing to do with him—Missy gloms onto Aaron too sometimes when she's drunk, she's just an affectionate lush. Darian doesn't hold it against her like he does with some girls who won't stop pestering him even after he tells them he's gay. He and Missy are like siblings at this point. Like, even if she were to get fully, embarrassingly naked and gyrate in his face, they'd still be friends tomorrow. They're like kids growing up in the same house, which Missy is happy to finally have. She was an only child, and sometimes wishes she hadn't been. But then Darian was only too, and so was Aaron, and so was... Natalie.

Missy can't tolerate the funk of the air in here anymore, it's like the whole place is one big shoe. She clangs her glass down on the bar, hands Darian her wallet so he can pay her tab. She's confident he won't steal from her because the band's profits belong to no one; Aaron keeps five hundred dollars untouchable in case the van needs an emergency fix, and he keeps gas money in reserve to get to the next gig, and after that, it's all the same pot. As long as no one's starving, money's for whatever you want and can get for money.

One nice thing about living in a van is that you're never far from home—every time they party with locals after a show they're always willing to stay out when everyone else has to square up to drive home. Who would choose such a lifestyle?

Missy gets out into the parking lot and tries to avoid it even as she walks through it. It's goddamn cold out here but she can still smell the sun that beats down on this place during the day, no trees to filter it through, nothing that shines for it to gleam over, just an empty oven. Missy shuts her eyes as often as she can, trying not to see the brown-sack-drinking men next to a downed tailgate, trying to ignore the cigarette butts that cushion her gravelly walk to the van.

171

She flings the door open, flumps inside, brings the door with her, and throws the lock behind her. Forget the world, forget it.

Missy hefts the mattress onto her shoulder, and it leans against her back like an overeager hookup. She feels her way to her vodka bottle, and a half-full jug of cranberry juice. She upends the neck of the vodka bottle into the large mouth of the juice bottle—this is mixology in the dark. Not knowing how much she's got and not particularly caring, Missy settles back against their bag of dirty clothes and gets down to the deliberate business of getting totally blotto.

"It's just too soon to be sober," Missy says to the things in the van. As the alcohol takes hold of her, she rolls her shoulders under her skin, she violins her legs together like a grasshopper, she curls and uncurls her toes like a kneading cat. "Maybe I'll sober up for Christmas," she says, and giggles even though nothing is funny.

Chapter Thirteen: Pretty Friendship

Lindsay is having a hard time marrying her little kid excitement for Christmas with her young adult apprehension for the upcoming holiday. Christmas has always been a favorite time, not just for the reasons everyone loves it—presents and candy and no school—but also because in Florida it's the only time of year where the weather is conducive to human habitation. The humidity leaves, the temperature drops enough for everyone to get out their one jacket, and kids start rolling up strips of notebook paper the size of cigarettes and pretending their visible breath in the air is smoke. It's the best time of the year.

"You're supposed to spend the holidays with your family," her mom says whenever she catches Lindsay looking happy towards the end of December. She'll look from one of her Life After Divorce self-help books and say, "Like you don't see Tristan enough every single day of your life. You know if he were any other boy I wouldn't allow it at all."

She means to say if she had any inkling of sex between them, she'd be needlessly prudish about it and chain Lindsay up under the stairs to guard her purity or something. Every time her mother brings it up, Lindsay thinks she's doing it, she's definitely going to have sex with Tristan. It doesn't matter if it hurts or if things get awkward for a while after, how great to have sex right under her mom's nose with the one boy she thought she didn't have to worry about? That'd teach her to have kids in the first place, wouldn't it?

But her mother has insisted: Christmas at home, and New Year's at Tristan's. Rita says she'll let them try real champagne instead of the sparkling grape juice of the kid's table, and Lindsay's going to stay the night, and... about that.

The day school lets out for the winter holiday, one of Lindsay's old friends hisses at her from behind a column. Amber is standing in the desiccated dirt of the butterfly garden. When it drops below seventy degrees in Florida, all the swamp flowers tend to dry up and shrivel.

"Do you want something?" Lindsay asks. She hasn't spoken to Amber since the last day of middle school. Lindsay had soured on Amber and Katie and Brittany around the time got kicked out of her house. They just seemed so juvenile to her, so petty. Not only had Lindsay matured a ton, she also met Tristan, who knew more hardship than nearly everyone Lindsay knew put together, so she just had no need for her old friends after that.

To be fair, they didn't want her around either; they didn't want to hear about her dad breaking her brother's arm, they wanted to talk about if they were cute, which boys they were cute enough for, and they just weren't speaking the same language as Lindsay anymore.

Except for Amber. She seemed to like Lindsay better than the other two in the group, and on the last day of middle school she stepped right into Lindsay's path as she headed towards the bus ramp and said, "It's been really nice to know you!"

She held out her hand for Lindsay to shake, which Lindsay did, wildly aware that Katie and Brittany were whispering about them a few feet away. Lindsay just assumed this was some kind of prank on her and that Amber had drawn the short straw. It just as easily might have been Amber being nice and genuine, and the other two whispering crap about *her*. Lindsay could believe that scenario now.

Amber has been crying. She still doesn't wear makeup (Katie and Brittany were all about makeup, Lindsay and Amber held out), so there are no mascara streaks, but her eyes are red and wincing, her nose is pink from being wiped forcefully, and her lip is quivering like she might start balling again at any moment.

"Amber?" Lindsay reaches out to touch her shoulder and finds herself enveloped in a breath-taking hug.

"I think I'm pregnant," Amber whispers to her, and then does start crying again, right on Lindsay's shoulder.

Lindsay's stunned for a moment. With Amber snuffling into her hair, she can see everything around her in surreal detail: leaves like wilted salad flap on her right, students gawk and speculate as to whether those two girls are lesbians or something on her right. She can't take being surrounded like this.

"Here, come with me for a second," Lindsay tells her.

"I'll miss my bus," Amber says.

"Well… whatever, my friend can give you a ride home," Lindsay tells Amber, and the girl nods and follows her like she used to do. It was hardly two years ago that Amber was their reluctant fourth member—Lindsay and Katie and Brit had known each other in elementary school. Amber got tagged on because she admired them so much. Lindsay always assumed that Amber would be the first to leave the group (she wasn't) and that she would be the last of the group that Lindsay would ever bond with (wrong again). She's got her arm around Amber's waist, her hand resting on Amber's hip, perilously close to where her maybe-baby might be.

Lindsay takes her to stand beneath a tree next to the senior parking lot. Tristan might already be sitting in his car, waiting for Lindsay to come meet him. She needs a few private moments beneath this skinny, young oak with Amber first.

"Tell me," she says.

"At my cousin's birthday party, there was this guy from his school that was really nice, and I… there weren't any condoms and he said he knew how to pull out and he did, but… that was like three weeks ago and I should have gotten my period by now!"

Everyone leaving the parking lot looks ecstatic to be out of school for the holidays. Amber looks like she's about to throw up from worry. Or it could be morning sickness. It doesn't always happen in the morning, that's what the textbook in health class said.

"Okay, assume the worst for a second. You're pregnant," Lindsay says, and Amber whimpers. "What do you want to do about it?"

Amber grabs her head and looks around like the sky is closing in on her. "I just want to go back in time and not do it! It wasn't even that great and it *so* wasn't worth this! Everything was fine and now everything is over."

Lindsay can't think of any words of confidence. The longer they stand over here the more people start to notice that Amber's distressed, doubled over, clutching what might be the biggest problem she'll ever have.

Lindsay supports her over to Tristan's car and puts her in the back seat.

"We need to give her a ride home. She lives right near me, I'll tell you when to turn."

Lindsay had been to Amber's once before, to film their middle school history project. She remembers there being static between Amber's mom and either Katie or Brittany's mom because one of them was rich, and showed up looking needlessly glitzy as if to shame the other women. At least that's what Lindsay's mom told her later, that no one ties a sweater over their shoulders and puts on a string of pearls unless they're trying to make a statement. That statement is usually: my husband has more money than yours.

Amber's house is a pock-marked white mobile home with dirty lattice covering the supports that hold it up. There's a tire swing hanging off a tree in the front yard, one that's bald from being driven around on first, and probably full of the standing water that births mosquitoes in warm weather. It looks like a miserable place to be a teenager, let alone a teenager's baby.

"Are you going to tell your mom?" Lindsay asks.

"Not until I know for sure," Amber murmurs, and gets out of the car with her eyes lidded, her face tilted down. She hurries into her house and shuts the door tight before Lindsay or Tristan can think of going with her.

Tristan reverses out of the packed dirt driveway and they leave in silence. These past twenty minutes with Amber have felt like a hurricane, and now she and Tristan are in the temporary peace of the eye.

Lindsay brings the wind back.

"She's probably pregnant," she says. She glances at Tristan only to see his lips pulling into his mouth, disappearing.

"It wouldn't be like that for us," he mumbles. "We'd use all the protection."

"I'm not going to do it," Lindsay tells him.

Tristan's expression wobbles underneath his skin, and instead of driving to Lindsay's house, he turns back the way they came. Lindsay watches quietly as he drives back to the park across from the middle school. There's a sewage treatment plant right next door, but there's no breeze today; the air is still and chilly, the sky a solid block of slate. Tristan parks and gets out, wandering towards the tennis courts through all the dried out, crispy palmetto fronds.

Lindsay heaves a deep sigh, and gets out of the car, very aware of how weird it is to deal with this.

Tristan isn't unsympathetic about that girl. He kept looking at her in his backseat, the blue-tinted light from the shade strip on his windshield falling right across her stomach, which she'd been holding with both arms as if she felt sick or ashamed.

But man, this just ruins everything.

Tristan walks over and grasps the chain link fence around the tennis courts and remembers the last time he was here, and how he didn't get laid then either.

"It's nothing against you, Tristan." Lindsay has come up behind him and stands back a ways.

"Of course not," Tristan says grimly. "How could it be, I'm irresistible."

"Wouldn't you rather spend Christmas break overdosing on chocolate and wearing ugly pajamas? I'm not really looking to have Amber's problems right now."

"Then why did you go out with that guy?" Tristan turns around with his arms crossed over his chest. "Clearly you want to start doing...

other stuff."

"Oh my God, will you get over that already?" Lindsay flips her hair out from underneath her hoodie. She's been huddled under there all cold since November, but seems plenty fiery now. She walks over to him and pushes his arms down. "He asked, I talked to him for like seven minutes before I realized he was as interesting as a soggy piece of bread, and you would have known that if you didn't quit talking to me."

"Yeah," Tristan says shiftily. "You know I'm sorry about that."

"You've always been sorry," she says, smiling sly, putting her hands up on either side of Tristan, trapping him against the fence. "But here's what you can do: you can give me my first kiss. How's that?"

"You've never kissed anyone?" Tristan looks right into her eyes, brown but quietly luminous, like a well-oiled baseball glove.

"Who would I have kissed? And don't bring up Jordan again, I never wanted to kiss him, there's always lunch in his teeth, he's gross."

"Should I, like, chew some gum or some—"

He's cut off by Lindsay's lips, coming up against his in a soft press. After that they're both smiling at each other, standing way too close, trying not to giggle.

"Do you feel how awkward this is?" Lindsay asks through her teeth.

"Yeah," Tristan says, and it's the truth. He kind of wants her a few steps away from him, but he doesn't want to touch her to move her. He feels like if he went to touch her shoulder he'd accidentally grope a tit, or end up with his fingers inside of her mouth, and then they wouldn't be able to look each other in the eyes for a month.

"So you're cool? We're not gonna do this?"

"No. I mean, fine, it would just be weird, but I still feel like I'm going to lose you. Rita doesn't talk to any of her old friends from high school. She barely has friends, she's just got me and the store."

"She's happy though," Lindsay says, frowning.

"Yeah, but I think she used to be a lot happier, or could have been if she'd had something like what we have, and what if she did and she lost it? Just, like, grew out of it, like the way you don't even talk to that pregnant girl anymore."

Lindsay shrugs and presents a deceptively simple solution. "I promise not to do that with you."

Tristan shrugs back at her, but it's harder for him, because his shoulders are heavy under a sense of doom. He loves Lindsay, but he can't tell if he pities or envies her for that naïve sense of optimism. Maybe it's just because she's younger than him.

He drives her home. They'll meet again later that evening, and every evening of the holiday break. Tristan has a stack of wrapped gifts for in his room, some movies she'll like, some cool hair clips, a big bucket of her favorite candy (Skittles), and a framed picture of the two of them that Rita snapped last summer of them both laughing, playing video games.

Tristan sits down on his bed and looks at the stack. Will that picture be all that reminds Lindsay of him someday? She'll be forty, and living in Jacksonville or Orlando with kids and that picture won't even be hung on a wall somewhere. Maybe she'll take the picture out and throw it in a shoe box so she can use the frame for a family photo. Maybe she'll skip the shoe box and put it directly into the trash. She'll have a thousand stupid pictures of her real family by then, and be too busy living a life with them to even assemble an album most of the time.

All of Tristan's baby pictures are still in the packets they came home from the pharmacy in. Rita keeps them in the crawl space above the garage. Says she'll get them down any time if Tristan wants to see them, but he never does.

"Why do you look like Christmas got canceled?"

Tristan startles, turns to see Rita leaning in his doorway with her sneakers crossed, her arms crossed over a bait shop T-shirt that says Master Bait & Tackle on it.

"Part of it sort of did," Tristan tells her.

"You know you can talk to me about anything, don't you?"

"I know," Tristan says, turning towards Rita and sitting back on his pillows so that she can come sit on the bed with him. "I just don't need to talk about anything. I get it, I'm just dealing with it."

Tristan knows he's being intensely cryptic, but Rita nods at him anyway, assuring him that his logic is sound.

"So for Christmas dinner I was thinking a ham," Rita tells him. "I know we'll want a ton of mashed potatoes, I've got a squash casserole that I'm sure you think sounds gross but trust me it's not, and I'm thinking instead of cranberry sauce that no one ever eats I'll try cranberry milkshakes for dessert, hmm?" She pokes his knee. "Sounds intriguing doesn't it? There will be pie too though. Apple, cherry, peach, strawberry, you just say which."

Tristan smiles at her. "Sounds good," he says, before launching at her and enveloping her in a hug. Her skin is warm and clammy under her thin shirt (she's had this one a while, it look gauzy whenever you pull it out of the wash), and she pats him back in surprise.

"What's that for?" she asks.

"Just felt like it," Tristan says, and is happy to see her so happy. A spontaneous hug from a teenager... with the way she acts so surprised, she might remember it her whole life.

"Okay, well, don't get too sad in here; no pouting and no crying around Christmas, you know the rules."

Tristan snorts as Rita leaves his room, and stretches out on his bed. He gazes out over his body, thinking about what it must look like to someone else, what it must feel like. It's not bad; he hates when his nipples stick out, but he's not too skinny, he doesn't have gross 70's chest hair or anything, and he washes thoroughly—he learned to do that in the boys' home because everyone else stank so bad. People have touched it before, they'll probably touch it again, just not Lindsay.

Tristan has a feeling like his heart is being slowly lashed by the realization that friendships don't last forever when he remembers something Marley said, some quote. The difference between a caprice and a life-long passion is that the caprice lasts longer. Tristan hopes that's true, that Lindsay might run through boyfriends, or husbands, or whatever, but never be rid of him. If he could just have that kind of friendship with one person he wouldn't ever need anything else.

Somebody's drunk ass forgets his phone when he goes to work the next day, and so Jesse is the one who hears it ringing when he's upstairs making his lunch. He uncovers it from their tangled bed sheet, which Marley used to shake out and tuck in every morning, and now leaves half knotted like they might need it to shimmy out a window. The glowing screen of the thing identifies the caller as **Missy XOXO**, and no telling who out of Marley and Missy typed it in like that, but either way, it's odd.

Jesse, after striking out with Rita and Mitch, holds the phone in his hand like a pulled grenade for at least two rings before deciding to answer it himself. It's time to make a try for his last, unlikeliest ally.

"Hey, Missy, it's Jesse, don't hang up," he tells the phone.

"Are you serious?" Aaron asks. "Do you always answer his phone? I was trying to call Marley, I thought this would work."

"He forgot to take it today."

"Oh. I got Missy's out from under her without even waking her up, and I figured I'd call Marley ask him to like, tell her to chill out with the drinking already, 'cause she won't listen to me."

"Oh, for fuck's sake," Jesse says, touching his head, and finding those dumb babyish curls Marley once liked so much. He yanks on them hard out of frustration. "They're probably enabling each other or whatever it's called."

"Why, what's Marley doing?"

"He hasn't been sober since you guys left, it's scary."

Aaron snorts. "Missy neither. Are they two peas in a pod or what?"

Jesse nods, oblivious to the fact that he can't be seen. He starts to strip their bed, since searching for the phone made him realize how bad it stinks. It's a cloying smell paired with a salty spice, like someone cut a fuck-hole in a warm cantaloupe and just left it in bed all day.

"It sounds like she's not helping me, and Marley's not helping you,"

Jesse says. He puts the sheets over by the washer in a wad, since Marley's the one who does laundry. It makes him feel like a bitch to do something so passive aggressive, it's something his mother might have done to his dad, but neither Jesse nor his father ever learned how to do laundry. Jesse would like to do it himself, but he doesn't know ass from elbow in this department. He simply gets their spare set down from the closet—the one so unused it retains its crease lines even after Jesse stretches it over the mattress.

Aaron sighs through the phone. "What's up with you outside of all that, anything?"

"No, what else would be going on?"

"I don't know, read any books or done anything lately? Even I managed to talk with a couple of college kids at a show the other night. They made me feel like a loser for not being in school, and so I've been thinking about that."

"Going back to school? I wouldn't do that if someone made it easy."

"Dude, don't worry, nobody's making it easy."

"Hmm," Jesse considers, sitting back down in the kitchen to finish his food (again unaware of how rude it is to chew right next to the mouthpiece of a phone). "I don't really do anything but work and hang out with Marley."

"Not even go see a movie?"

Jesse makes an incredulous face in his kitchen. "I haven't even watched TV in like three years, not since Colorado."

Aaron sighs again. "If all you do is hang out with Marley, how's that working out now that he's all weird or whatever."

"It's not," Jesse says. "That's why I picked up the phone to talk to Missy. I'm out of ideas."

"I've got an idea," Aaron says, a smile apparent in his voice. "Why don't you get a life?"

Jesse grins, and runs his tongue over his teeth to get all the food off. "You talk pretty big when you know I'm too far away to punch you."

Aaron laughs. "Well... shit. I mean I understand what's wrong with Missy, of course, this thing with her daughter dying, I just don't get why she isn't getting better yet. Like of course she'll still be sad, but I expected the drinking to taper off after we went to see the grave."

"You went to the grave?" Jesse asks. "You went to Loweville?"

"Yeah. It still completely blows, by the way. And apparently your cousin's gay now."

"Oh, no, he was gay before I left, trust me."

Silence and then, "Yeeeeeah, well, I thought that would be the thing she was building to, but she's still carrying on."

"We sure know how to pick 'em, don't we?"

"What option did we have? Trust me, Loweville's even smaller than you remember, we're lucky we found anyone."

"So what about now? Why are you still with Missy if you're not trapped anymore?"

"That's obvious, isn't it? At this point I love her too much to imagine being with anyone else."

"Oh," Jesse says. He cleans up the remnants of his lunch, wiping the crumbs right off the table because he doesn't see the point of using plates all the time. Crumbs just don't bother him like drunk sweat on his sheets, apparently.

"You know what I mean, right? It's like, I guess we're still young, but we've already been through so much together."

That Jesse does understand.

Hardly anything happened to Jesse before he met Marley. High school he left incomplete, Loweville he left in a hurry right after that, and the only person who'd had any serious impact on his childhood was his father, who seemed to do it from a world away. Marley's nearly the perfect opposite of his father, so aware of the world around him that he's a raw nerve all the time. Being with him makes Jesse notice things he never would have seen otherwise; it's like being pens and pencils, and then meeting someone who's sixty-four colors with a built-in sharpener.

"Oh, shit, she's waking up, I gotta go," Aaron tells him.

"No problem, I need to get back to work anyway," Jesse says before he realizes Aaron has hung up on him. Jesse looks at the phone for a moment and then tucks it into his own pocket. He'll just hold on to it until he sees Marley again.

The kid gets home right on time, but doesn't even spare Jesse a glance as he marches through the garage and straight upstairs, his footsteps humming through the metal as he goes. He doesn't do that swirling, dizzy ballerina thing when he turns onto the landing, so he's probably decently sober right now. Jesse finishes this oil change and goes upstairs to see him.

Marley is sorting through their dirty laundry, carefully shaking out each item before placing it into the washer. He starts to say, "Hey, Jesse, have you seen my..." but he stops when Jesse holds the phone under his nose. Marley takes it, lights it up looking for any notifications. Jesse wonders what kind of lie or half-truth he should have if Marley asks him why he answered the phone, but he doesn't ask. He puts the phone in his pocket and finishes loading the washing machine, and then walks straight into the kitchen to make himself a rum and something.

Jesse goes over too, fits his head over Marley's shoulder, and grasps the counter on either side of him.

"Can I help you?" Marley asks, setting down his jug of liquor hard. The back of the label has a pirate ship on it. The booze swills and swells around it like a stormy sea.

"The last drink I ever saw my father have, we were at the dinner table, which you didn't see when you were there, someone took it and the chairs, but it was in that niche past the refrigerator, the corner with all the windows?"

"Okay," Marley says. He pours soda into his glass—one part liquor, two parts cola, what Jesse's father would have called a girl's drink.

"It was the day after he had promised to stop drinking, but he was obviously gonna to use up his stash first, right? He wasn't just going to throw it out."

"Sure," Marley says, still now, his drink fizzing beneath both their faces like someone has dropped in an Alka-Seltzer tab.

"So my mom was pissed to see him drinking the day after he said he would stop, and when he tried to tell her what he was doing, she demanded he pour it down the sink, but instead he was like, 'Seems like a waste to me,' and he threw it in her face."

Jesse waits a moment to let that sink in, then continues.

"He just sat there calm after he did it. She ran into the bathroom and took a shower with her clothes on, like it was battery acid or something, like it was burning her."

Jesse dips his right index finger into Marley's glass, stirring the mixture and feeling the bubbles tickle pleasantly. Marley takes his hand and brings the intrusive finger to his lips, sucking it into his mouth. Jesse smiles, and very nearly laughs; the boy knows how to diffuse a tense situation.

Marley picks up his drink and turns around, and Jesse's arms come up to hold him instinctually.

"What did your father do after that?" Marley asks, then taking a sip.

"He looked over at me like he wanted to tell me to *do as I say, not as I do*, but then he just sighed and asked me to go look in the old tires out back for a bottle he hid in one."

"Did you find it?" Marley asks.

"Oh, yeah," Jesse says. "And I thought about telling him it wasn't out there and throwing it into the woods, but I think I liked him too much to take it away from him."

Jesse can't remember the last time he and Marley talked this close, fully engaged, eye-to-eye, and he tries to think of what happened differently today. Was it talking things out with Aaron? Was it talking about his past? The day Jesse just referred to, the one day he spent with Marley in his parents' old shuttered, abandoned house... he had talked a lot that day too. Maybe that's the trick.

Marley takes a long, quiet slurp of his drink and holds it out of the way delicately, like a Christmas ornament, as he comes up on his tiptoes for a kiss.

Jesse kisses back hard for a second but then breaks it so he can hold Marley against his body.

"Whoa," Marley says. "Somebody missed me."

"Does that mean you're back?" Jesse presses his lips against Marley's neck and feels him sigh. He never sighs when he's asleep, or passed out.

He's awake, and on his feet, and present with Jesse. It's excellent.

"Sure, but Jesse," and Marley pulls away and puts his empty hand between them, and he shakes the hand holding his drink. "Don't bother me about this. Don't roll your eyes behind my back about it, don't make any derisive noises about it, and for the love of god stop talking to my friends about it. If I want to talk about it, I'll bring it up, okay?"

"Fine, I don't care," Jesse says, and he doesn't. For a little while there he felt tolerant, and then stern, because he's older than Marley, and he knows better about some things, but now...

Jesse is so tired of his long, echoing days without Marley that he'll take him any way he can get him. What he's been doing so far hasn't made him content, and so he'll try something else, until that stops working, and on and on until he dies, probably.

Chapter Fourteen: Lovely Muck

Missy never would have pegged herself as becoming one of those teens who mope around cemeteries, but here she is in Alexandria, Louisiana, just moping her ass off.

She saw this place when they were coming in south on I-49. They went under another highway, popped out into the shabby daylight once again, and there it was sprawling on their left. She looked it up on Darian's computer once they stopped for food and facilities and found out they call it Garden of Memories. How could she resist another garden of graves?

They're headed to New Orleans tomorrow for a few gigs over New Year's, and since it's much cheaper to get a room in Alexandria, here's where they'll be taking their showers and getting a good night's sleep. Missy realized she had the rest of the day to blow, so she loaded vodka and cranberry juice into an old cough syrup bottle and took off. That's a trick some pro gave her at a bar—you can't get arrested for having a cough, and if you look a little red-faced and unsteady, it can be blamed on the cold. There's no cover at this cemetery, it's just a ramshackle little trailer and a couple of sparse trees, so she knew she'd need to be able to hide in plain sight.

Missy walks through the grave markers until she's out of sight of that caretaker's shack, cicadas screaming and grasshoppers trying to bounce up under her skirt the whole time, even in the middle of what's supposed to be winter. She's getting awfully sick of small, rural towns. What she wouldn't give to have a bullet train come roaring by right now, or to be in a place where paint isn't peeling off of everything.

She hears footsteps coming up behind her, hurriedly caps her 'medicine' and stuffs it into her bag, then puts on an innocent smile.

She turns around ready to lie and throw her boozy breath into the wind, but it's only Darian.

"Careful, Darian; if we hang out too much we might get sick of each other."

"I'm not about to let you have this kind of fun without me," he says, hopping up on a long slab of stone that says, among other things, *No one knows the day or the hour.* How comforting.

Missy gets up on the grave next to Darian, crosses her legs, and settles her skirt down modestly in her lap, out of respect for the dead.

"Hey, look," she says. "This guy was exactly sixty-three years and one month old when he died."

"Huh." Darian cranes his neck around to look at the stone he's resting his head on like a pillow. "I wonder at what hour."

"Right? Here, want a hit off of this?" Missy asks, getting out her bottle again. "I've got that little measuring cup in here somewhere if you want to do a shot."

"That's okay," Darian says, taking a wincing sip. "I'm happy to spare you the liver damage."

"You're a peach."

They get quiet for a while, which is something Missy really likes about Darian. Marley's a good friend for talking, and Aaron's good for nagging, but Darian's good for silence. He just sits basks in the sun beside her, a beautiful lizard on a rock.

After a spell, Darian asks, "You feeling any better?"

"I'm not interested in feeling anything," she says, finishing off her bottle. She pulls another one out of her bag, this one a water bottle of just pure vodka. Darian is surprised to see it, but he keeps his opinions to himself.

"I've never known someone who died," Darian tells her. "Even my grandparents are still alive."

Missy nods. That makes sense. Darian's a sunny guy, and a happy drunk, and there's just no faking that.

"What about your dad?" Missy asks. She's heard about a myriad of stepfathers but never about the real one.

"Don't know him. There isn't even a name on my birth certificate. I'm pretty sure he's the one guy my mother never married, and she's never made that mistake again."

Missy chuffs a laugh. "I like your mother more and more. Think she'd adopt me?"

"Oh, she already has. We've all got Christmas presents waiting for us in New Orleans, that means you're part of the family."

Missy accepts this with a nod and they lapse into silence again. No one's gotten her a Christmas present in like three years. It just hasn't been that kind of life.

"How long are you going to sit out here?" Darian asks. "If you're here past dark I'll come get you in the van, that overpass is spooky enough in the day time."

"Sounds good," Missy says. "I'll see you then."

Darian nods and leaves without another word. Missy takes his place on the grave stone, and finds it just a touch warmer where Darian had been. She closes her eyes, and even though the day starts to get overcast and a chilly wind starts to stroke her, she keeps taking sips of lightning, so she feels nice and toasty warm. She smiles to hear the wind whistling around her, and she feels... happy. Not real happiness, it's what Marley called Dutch happiness, like Dutch courage. That was funny, and a moment after Missy remembers it, she laughs.

She's getting sleepy. She pulls her braid out from under her, eyes closed the whole time, moving slow like she's under heavier gravity than Earth usually has. She pulls off her hair tie, undoes her braid, and splits her hair so that she can snuggle beneath it like a blanket.

She takes another big gulp of her vodka and realizes that she can't even taste it anymore, and chugs the rest of it so she can take herself a little nap. She thinks that it would be nice to fall asleep and not have to wake up all the time, and she falls asleep not knowing that her wish is about to be granted.

When Darian comes to get her after sundown, she's cold to the touch and impossible to wake up.

She looks like Ophelia plunged in the brook.

Marley calls her three times that day before he hears the news. The first time it's when he's coming home from work, excited about New Year's Eve. Jesse said he'd try some champagne with him at Kenny's house since they're having a little party, and he wanted to tell Missy that, and also have some company on the walk home. It's so much shorter if he's talking to Missy; the trucks are quieter, the sky is closer, his sweat is refreshing, and his feet don't hurt. Everything that bothers him gets so small he barely notices.

But he can't always get her on the phone in the daylight—she sleeps whenever she can and the band has no regular schedule. He tries her again later that night, during what he's come to think of as drunken brownouts, rather than blackouts. It's the difference between what a tropical storm does to the power, and what a hurricane will do—the lights dim, the ambient hum of things like the refrigerator and the air conditioning dip in time with that dim, but then come right back. Marley has come to recognize when he's having a brownout, when he's experiencing things he'll only remember the highlights of, but not forget entirely. He still doesn't know what he knows during a blackout though, for obvious reasons.

The third time he calls, it's late, and Jesse is in the bathroom brushing his teeth, readying for bed.

It's Aaron who answers with, "Hey, Marley, I didn't want to pick up until we knew for sure."

"Knew what for sure?" Marley asks, a cold plummet going through the center of him, sobering him emotionally in an instant.

"She's going to be okay, but earlier we... well, we couldn't wake Missy up. I don't know what it was that made her suddenly go to town today, but she got alcohol poisoning." He makes it sound like she caught the flu.

"So she's okay?"

"She *will be*," Aaron emphasizes. "After they get done replacing all the booze with water and vitamins or whatever."

"She's awake though?"

"Yeah, and in a horrible mood, but she can't talk because they had to pump her stomach, so her throat's raw."

"Oh," Marley says. He sighs and feels tears come to his eyes like a boot to the inside of his face. He finishes his drink in two huge swallows hoping to stave it off. He doesn't want to talk about this with Jesse if he can help it. In fact, before Jesse gets out of the bathroom...

Marley scrambles into the kitchen as Aaron is saying morosely, "I just figured you needed to know, since it looks like you guys talk a lot," and scribbles a note to Jesse that reads: *Not dead, don't worry.* He puts his giant bell jar of rum into his backpack along with a water bottle and half a bag of potato chips. He puts on his jacket, the third layer he has on his upper body, puts his childish little Velcro wallet and keys in one pocket, and (after stepping outside the door and saying goodbye to Aaron) his cell phone in the other. He's getting the hell out of here, that's for sure, and by the time he reaches the outside of the building, he figures out where he's headed next.

The cell phone comes back out and Marley calls Greg. Marley doesn't want to be alone, but he doesn't want to be with anyone who cares too much about him and will make him hash all this out and not just let him drink it away. If Missy's going to be okay, then okay, it's just a matter of passing the time between now and then. He doesn't have to feel any of the emotions he's got coming to him if he plays his cards right.

Greg says, "My boy, it's been a while!" And he says, "Of course I'll pick you up. I'll be there in about ten minutes, just hold tight."

Marley waits on the sidewalk about six feet from where he might be seen from the garage. His worry that anything might pop out at him from the dark fights with his desire to double-think away from what's happened to Missy. He really wants a drink or several, and scoffs as soon as he thinks it, bitterly aware of how fitting it would be if he poisoned himself along with her, out of some strange sympathy. Frank wouldn't let him do it, and Jesse wouldn't let him do it, but Greg will, and it's what he wants to do right now.

When Greg arrives, Marley gets in before the car has come to a complete stop. Greg looks good, jazzed even, smirking because Marley is probably giving him the wrong impression. He tries his hand at being honest.

"My best friend's in the hospital, but I don't want to talk about it."

"Fair enough," Greg says, turning his car around in the garage's driveway and speeding slightly back to his own house. Marley thinks, all things considered, he probably shouldn't get out the big hillbilly jug of rum in the car. In fact he should probably leave the jug where it is and let Greg make him a drink when they get to his place. That was their customary habit before, after all.

And so it is: before Marley can get comfortable in Greg's enveloping couch, he's got a rum and Coke in his hand, and then halfway down his throat. Greg's got a gentleman's portion of some amber liquid or other in his glass, and he throws it back in solidarity with Marley, and then gets them refills. He's a good guy, Marley decides.

"Oh, for a draught of vintage," Greg toasts.

Marley smiles, liking him better than ever because Greg has once again reminded him of Frank, and the way he used to quote poetry with Marley.

"For a beaker of the warm South," Marley rejoins, slowly, carefully, proud that he's finally practiced enough at drinking not to slur or spill.

Greg's face lights up and he's next to Marley in an instant. He removes the drinks to the coffee table, and he kisses Marley full and florid on the mouth. Marley's teeth are coated in a sugar film from all the drinks, and he introduces his tongue into Greg's mouth to lick his teeth, curious as to whether they will feel the same or different.

They are entangled thus when Greg starts to peel back Marley's jacket and overshirt. If he had gone for the pants, he might have accomplished something, but it takes a lot more alcohol for Marley to forget about the scars on his arm.

He locks his elbows down as Greg kisses his neck, and he spots their pale reflection in the sliding glass door, and doesn't like what he sees. Greg is trying to coax his clothes harder and harder down Marley's arms, and his resistance is nearing the place where it will have to become combative when the doorbell rings, and there are three sharp knocks at the front door.

Marley and Greg freeze, then separate.

"Get that," Marley tells him, with all the authority of necessity. He needs Greg to stop tugging at his shirts. It won't end well if he keeps that up.

Greg goes to the door. Marley is pulling on his clothes and buttoning himself up tight when Mitch walks in holding a thick stack of papers. Marley waves at him briefly before reaching for his drink again—he's starting to not feel right without a glass in his hand.

Mitch gets this insulted look slapped across his face. He turns to Greg, shakes his head, and tosses the manuscript off of his hands like it's time to play fifty-two pick up.

"Hey," Greg says in his own defense, "he called me, not the other way around."

"I don't want to hear it. He's leaving with me or I'm calling the cops, this is so inappropriate I can hardly believe it."

Marley turns his back on both of them, downs his drink before anyone can take it away from him, grabs his backpack up off the floor and—in swinging it onto his shoulders—nearly topples to the side. That one hit him fast, and no kidding.

"I'm jus' gonna take off," Marley squeezes out of his mouth. He wanted to be distracted from drama, not find a way to kick up more of it.

"Let me give you a ride home," Mitch offers, coming at him kindly.

Marley ducks his proffered hand and slips past him to the still-open front door.

"Not going home," he throws over his shoulder, and takes off running in case anyone feels like chasing him. Marley's half-jug jostles merrily in his bag as he hoofs it down the street, gangly as a fawn he knows, and suddenly violently aware that it's because he's still only eighteen.

"Nineteen in two months," he reminds himself aloud, with shallow puffs of breath in between. "I'm gettin' old."

He gets two blocks away before he realizes he's too drunk to be jogging—his muscles feel like they've been sucked completely dry—and the second he slows up to try and gain some composure, his blood pumps so hard into his head that it feels like his temples might blow out. He stops so abruptly the air seems to concuss against him, fore and aft, and his feet crisscross beneath him, and the best he can do as he falls is to aim for the sand and bramble of the ditch on his right, rather than fall over on the asphalt of the road.

Marley lands hard, his air knocked out, the things in his backpack unbroken but bruising the hell out of him. His first priority is to breathe, and his second is to check for a broken neck. His feet move, his hands. He can feel sandspurs in the back of his scalp, stuck in his hair. He can feel sand in his pants. He takes half a second to be grateful that he hasn't done anything he can't yet recover from, but in the next second he bursts into copious, irrational, probably very loud tears (though all Marley can hear is the inner ear roar of his blood—the same thing he's heard whenever he's listened to a conch shell). The stars above him revolve gently back and forth, a cosmic sashay. He can see the Big Dipper, which his mother used to tell him and his sisters poured good things on the roof of their house. What a lie that turned out to be.

He's lying in an undeveloped corner lot, not in anybody's front yard, but across the street from one that is neatly mown and even cut in around all their decorative rocks and driveway lights, features Marley's own father refused to install because of the pain in the ass they would be to maintain. Seeing that, and remembering the fights his parents used to have over petty shit like that—his mother screaming that it's such a small thing to do for someone his dad was supposed to love, and his dad coming back with, "If it's so small then quit busting my balls about it!" And Marley and his sisters hiding in the lower bunk of the girls' room, Marley telling them stories he'd read in books, trying to make them smile.

Marley hears himself for a moment, crying with a puppyish, deep-throated howl that he'd never thought he'd be capable of—he's usually too self-conscious to raise his voice above the rinse cycle of a washing machine. He only hopes no one pops out to see him do this, and ruin the private nowhere he's inhabiting where he can finally let loose some things that have always hurt him, but never been truly felt.

But naturally the moment can't last forever. A car comes crawling up from Marley's left, the headlights exposing him, picking him out like a reflector on the highway.

The car stops, and Marley surprises himself by snuffling up immediately, his tears gone behind some water-tight door, like the kind they had on the whatsie... the Titanic.

It's Mitch's car, with Mitch in it. He gets out and steps down into the ditch to haul Marley up by his arm. It's just the way Marley's father used to shove him around, and how he ended up with a broken arm last year. He struggles against Mitch, but without any organization, and hears his voice switch from the wailing keen it was a minute ago to an insulted whimper.

"Come on, into the car before someone calls the cops," Mitch says, brushing off the seat of Marley's pants and removing his backpack. He turns Marley around and urges him down onto the seat before returning to the driver's side. He obviously expects Marley to do the rest himself, and actually Marley does.

He's exhausted.

Mitch sincerely hopes he never sees Greg again. Mitch was being a good guy, he was ready to forgive and forget the dalliance with Marley, and he had even read and edited through Greg's latest novel just like in the old days.

The book was good. It's the final installment of his musical trilogy— the two guys fall in love in the end, just as they're about to go on tour in

Europe. It was funny and sweet and left Mitch feeling very satisfied; he literally had a smile on his face as he finished. It made him remember the best of Greg—his talent, his discipline, and all the stories he grows from daydreams into novels.

So he'd had a nice warm, fuzzy feeling as he left his house to surprise Greg with the manuscript, which was marked up with both red and green ink like a Christmas card, red for concerns, green for encouragement. He was expecting to sit down with some wine and talk it through with Greg, have one of those literary, cosmopolitan evenings that they used to pretend to have in college, drinking out of plastic cups and toothbrush holders, whatever was at hand.

But then what does he find at Gregory's? A drunk teenager struggling back into his clothes, and Greg wiping his mouth the way he always does after he's been making out with someone. Mitch used to see that gesture all the time when they were kids (kids, he might add, who were actually older than Marley is right now), and it used to fill him with pride, knowing that his friend had gotten some action. Now, however...

Mitch glances over at Marley, whose head is bobbling back and forth on his neck with the rhythm of the drive. They're on US 41 now, just a minute or two from getting him home. Mitch finally takes a break from being appalled at Greg to wonder what's going on with the boy.

"Did you really call Greg tonight?" Mitch says, speaking loud and slow. It doesn't make any difference in how disgusted Mitch is; even if Marley is the one who started this situation, Greg definitely should have been the one to end it.

"Yeah, I had to... get out of my own head. My best friend is... sick." He's speaking in a flat, careful monotone. He sounds like a sad machine.

"I'm sorry to hear that," Mitch says. "Does Jesse know where you are?"

"Nope, and he won't like to hear it either."

"But you'll tell him?"

"Sure. He won't like it, but he'll understand it. He knows how much I love Missy."

"He'll understand that your first impulse is to get drunk and kiss an older man?"

Marley snorts, and gets a joyless smile on his lips. "Well, when you put it that way it sounds pretty bad."

Mitch throws on his turn signal as he approaches the garage. He parks and waits for Marley to get himself in gear, but the boy only sits there, watching Mitch in between slow blinks.

"You look good without the beard," Marley says.

"You've seen me without it before, or don't you remember?"

"I do not. A lot of things lately have been politely excusing themselves from my memory."

Mitch sighs. He doesn't have any siblings, but the way he feels about Marley is the way he imagines he would feel for a nephew. It's more intense than the responsibility he feels for his students, that's for sure.

Marley inhales deeply and puts his hand over his face. "Sorry about you and Greg," he says, sitting up and gathering his things. "And for the sand in your car. And for making you do this whole chauffer thing again."

"You seem to be handling yourself a little bit better," Mitch says. "Everyone has to learn how to drink responsibly the hard way, you know. Moderation is a middle ground; you won't know where it is exactly until you've gone past it a few times."

"I'm not learning moderation, I'm just building up a tolerance," Marley says with another grim smile, his hand on the door lever. "Every time I try to knock it off for a day or two, I can't sleep. I used to always be able to sleep, it was the easiest thing to do all day."

"That's not a good sign, Marley."

"I know, and I bet it's bad that my hands shake sometimes too." He looks at the hand poised to let him out into the parking lot. It's perfectly still right now. "I'm hoping I'll be able to normal off with drinking though, because I don't want to go without it again."

"Why?" Mitch says, reaching out to touch Marley on the shoulder, his other arm across the top of his steering wheel. "What was so awful before?"

"Nothing, it was just the way I felt about it all."

Mitch is trying to figure out what to say to that, grasping for memories of his own teenage angst and ennui so that he doesn't start talking in meaningless platitudes. But before he can remember what it was like when even the most commonplace incident was profound in its tragic boredom, there's a knock on the roof of the car.

Mitch and Marley had been sitting in the little world illuminated by the overhead light, and they hadn't notice Jesse creep out of the building and come to stand directly next to the car, on Marley's side. Marley looks around, trying to find the button to roll down the window, and instead of watching him botch it four times, Mitch reaches across and does it for him. Marley touches his face with a *thanks, you're a doll* sort of gesture, and Jesse bends a knee so he can lean both hands into the car.

Jesse nods at Mitch, the kind of nod that belongs under a dusty old Stetson, and then he looks to Marley for an explanation.

"Sorry," Marley says.

Jesse shrugs.

"I knew you were wild when I married you, I guess," Jesse says with a smirk, and Marley warbles out a laugh.

Mitch smiles at them—it looks like whatever else might be wrong, they've made up and are on good terms again. Mitch resists the urge to scrub their heads and chuck their chins and pinch their cheeks. They're adorable. In fact, the only thing that feels sour about watching them interact is the knowledge of how flippantly Greg dismissed these two as a couple in a real relationship. Sure they're young, and when Greg and Mitch were this age they weren't serious about *anything*, but maybe the times have changed, or maybe these two are just a different set of boys.

"Hey," Mitch says, "you know I've got my own life, kids."

Marley starts laughing harder (Mitch can't help but keep grinning—that was the biggest lie he's told all month), and Jesse opens the passenger door. He even holds out a hand to Marley like a young gentleman, and when Marley sort of drunkenly pirouettes into his arms, Jesse catches his momentum and spins with him for another half turn.

"Help me get him upstairs, would ya, Mitch?"

"Yeah, bring my bag and stay for a drink," Marley adds, laughing still.

Finding him in a ditch isn't very attractive, but lord he does look like he's having a nice time right now. If drinking was nothing but ditches and hangovers, there wouldn't be any alcoholics; it's the good times that keep people coming back for more.

Screw it, Mitch thinks, and even feels a measure of satisfaction as he locks up his car and goes upstairs with Marley and Jesse. Greg *wishes* he could be doing this right now. This is some fun, immature behavior right here that he's not invited to at all.

Marley starts stripping off his dirty clothes as soon as he's upstairs and over the threshold of their boyish flophouse loft. Jesse has the presence of mind to take him into the bathroom to get him cleaned up, and while he's rolling the door shut, Marley yells, "Hey, make me a drink," and Jesse sticks his head out and bites his bottom lip for a second and adds, "Make three drinks, if you want, one for each of us."

Mitch gets the booze out of Marley's bag, finds ice and glasses in their unremarkable kitchen, all while listening to them laugh and fumble in the bathroom. An undercurrent of sweaty clothing stench seeps out from the closet behind their kitchen, and Mitch starts getting pleasurable yet violent memories of college. It was all liquor, and not enough quarters for laundry, and he and Greg making fun of each other for being smelly layabouts even as they exchanged panic breakdowns over whether they'd pass or graduate or make it in life.

Mitch starts to nurse his own drink, sitting at the table, when Jesse pops out of the bathroom trailing shower steam.

"Marley'll just be a few more minutes, he's getting dressed," Jesse says as he comes across his living/bed room and into the kitchen.

Mitch scopes him out in the harsh light of the florescent bulbs overhead. The dirty blonde curls on his head don't suit the rest of him—he's all cord and cut slab and ragged fingernails, which Mitch gets a good look at when Jesse twists his chosen glass around on the table before picking it up.

"I hate this shit," Jesse says, tossing half of it into his mouth and swallowing with a sneer.

"Why drink it then?" Mitch asks.

Jesse frowns at him like this is a dumb question, the answer obvious. "I'm trying to know him."

Mitch gets out a platitude at last, one he uses often on his students. "If he jumped off a bridge, would you do it too?"

Jesse snorts, sets his glass back down, and turns his inner arm towards Mitch. He points to a pale white cut across the fleshy part of his lower arm.

"I did that just to try and get why he did it."

Mitch nods uncomfortably as Jesse finishes his drink in another toss, and grips the table as it shudders through his body.

"Sit down if you're going drink like that," Mitch says.

Jesse obeys. Marley comes out of the bathroom a moment later, joins them at the table, and puts away the third drink like it's little more than a tart glass of juice.

Mitch feels like somebody's parents are out of town. When Jesse gets out a pack of cards, flips on the radio, and starts suggesting games, Mitch smiles to think that he has stolen this party away from Greg, and is having all his dirty fun without him.

"Hey, we should play Gin Rummy," Marley says with a small giggle.

"That's an old lady game, I don't know how to play it," Jesse says, shuffling the cards expertly.

"I do," Mitch says. It is an old lady game; it was his grandmother who taught him.

"Do you wanna teach us?" Marley asks.

Mitch considers his alternative—he's already fed Tasi so she's no excuse, and it's not a school night.

"Why not," Mitch says as he bends and shuffles the deck.

Marley refills all three glasses, and no one declines.

Chapter Fifteen: Livelier Liquor

For Tristan, getting a Valentine's Day gift for Lindsay this year is extra tricky. How to walk the line between saying 'you're my best friend' and 'I acknowledge that we almost had sex sort of'?

He started watching the other kids at school again, but this time with a lot more skepticism. He watched candy cause at least two meltdowns from girls on diets or insecure about being fat or whatever it was they were sniveling about. A combination of flowers and allergies happened once, and stuffed animals, though popular, seemed to be for the kind of girl who loses her mind over puppies or ponies. None of that traditional crap would do for Lindsay, and besides it's all really more girlfriend-boyfriend stuff. There is simply no Hallmark card for what Lindsay and Tristan have between them.

The school also decided they'd let the National Honor Society fund raise for charity by doing singing valentines on the 14th, which only sounds about ten times more embarrassing than having a restaurant staff sing you happy birthday.

He wanted a gift that was precious, but still unique. He wanted to give her maybe jewelry, but she doesn't often wear bracelets or even a watch, and rings are out of the question (way too symbolically loaded). He settled on a necklace, and a locket, because that would be the sort of special circumstance under which she might wear a piece of jewelry. Silver because Lindsay thinks gold is trashy; round instead of oval because he doesn't want her walking around with a huge egg on her chest.

Next question: the pictures. There are a ton of them, on his phone, on his computer transferred from her phone, on Rita's camera, so that's not the issue. Tiny faces seems a little too nineteenth century, and so he wonders: hands? Fingerprints? But while browsing his photos, he finds a few that they took up close of each other's eyes—that's perfect.

He buys special photo paper, he gets their irises the perfect size so that there's no white showing in the locket frames (it was easier with his own eyes—there's a black rim around his hazel-y eyes that Lindsay doesn't have). Once he finishes assembling the pictures, he closes it up. Now their eyes are in there, gazing at each other in the dark.

He's going to give it to her after school and after work, since it's a Friday and they'll have the whole rosy weekend ahead of them.

School is a slower agony than usual—half the student body won't stop writhing against the other half like hungry cats, and they are playing the sloppiest love songs they can find over the PA system between classes. He and Lindsay are so full of contempt through lunch that exchanging presents would have only been ruined. Their hatred crests when they spot Amber; she was absent from school for a week or two in January, and far from getting a baby bump, she seems to be getting thinner; she hardly eats at lunch, and she spends her time hardly eating alone. Tristan and Lindsay thought about trying to be friendly, but the one time she spotted them watching her in sympathy, she turned her back. Amber he has no bad feelings towards, but everyone else? The way they play around with the idea of love makes him ill; it's like watching someone light a bottle rocket they're still holding in one soft, intricate hand. They've got no concept of the kind of damage that can't be undone.

The end of the day can't come fast enough for either of them. They fling themselves into Tristan's car, and Lindsay finds a screaming metal rock station right away.

"I have to go home and punch my sister's stuffed animals for, like, hours before we can have our Valentine's, I'm so grossed out," she says.

They pass at least three cars that are decorated with balloons and have initials in hearts drawn on the windows.

"Yeah, I'm so thankful Rita isn't doing anything in the store for Valentine's Day. She thought about it, but seriously two women asked her out this week, and she just doesn't want to encourage that sort of thing. It's awkward trying to explain that she's straight to people, they don't believe her at all."

"Ooh, we should get flowers for Rita! Or figure out a way to replace her wine or something."

"Okay. Flowers sound good," Tristan says, wondering if he would have thought to do something nice for Rita on his own. Thankfully he's got Lindsay, and he doesn't have to know who he'd be without her.

They stop into a gas station, and Lindsay picks the flowers while Tristan tops off his tank. He comes in to get her, and they amuse the grizzly dude behind the register by splitting the cost of them, taking a few seconds each to dig exact change out of their wallets.

"Are these for your mom?" he guesses.

"Yeah," Tristan says, thinking there isn't even a reason to explain. The guy's as close to the truth as he can reasonably get.

"That's sweet of you kids, I'm sure she'll love 'em."

"Thanks!" Lindsay says.

They walk out feeling pretty satisfied with themselves. Tristan drops Lindsay off at home, drives himself over to the store, and decides to save the flowers for when he and Lindsay can give them to Rita together. He hides them in his trunk hoping they won't wilt or anything. The air isn't exactly hot, but it isn't wintry either—the whole world is room temperature today.

Tristan thought he was done looking at sloppy, lovey bullshit once the dismissal bell rang, but he forgot about Marley.

At some point in the last few months, he and Jesse reconciled, and they've been revolting about it ever since. Marley hasn't quit drinking, though he's gotten better at covering for it, and Jesse still doesn't like it, because Tristan's seen him wrinkle his nose when he goes to kiss Marley, smelling the booze on his breath. And yet... Jesse's in the store today during his break, leaning across the counter with Marley, being exactly as disgusting as everybody else.

Tristan gives them a wide perimeter as he comes around the counter. Marley knows how to ignore him, but Jesse doesn't.

"Tristan," he says with a nod.

"Jesse," Tristan says back unwillingly.

"Get anything good for Valentine's day?"

"Not yet." Tristan notices a red box of candy under the counter. "I guess you got him candy," Tristan says, as if Marley isn't right next to him.

"Yep," Jesse says.

"Bourbon balls, right?"

Marley tsks and starts to frown. Jesse just shows his teeth in his weird, unnatural smile. Tristan has never been more enthusiastic to start stocking in his life; he stows his bag and goes straight to the back.

He doesn't see Lindsay until she comes over to Rita's later that night. She's changed her clothes. She has the smallest touch of makeup on her lips, and around her eyes. Rita almost cries when they give her the flowers they got her, even though they were the cheapest ones. Tristan gets his gift (a book she hollowed out so he could hide stuff in it), and then he gets out the little draw-string bag with her necklace in it.

She loves it.

"Oh my God, this is so weird and cool! These are ours, right?"

Tristan nods. Mission to get her an awesome present: accomplished.

"Eeeeh, put it on me!"

Lindsay sweeps up her hair and turns around so Tristan can drape the chain around her neck and secure the clasp. She hops up and goes to the mirror hanging inside his closet door.

"Excellent," she declares.

Tristan smiles and knows that watching Lindsay turn in his mirror is going to be one of those life-long memories. In truth, the realization makes him feel a tightening sense of doom. He'll be a senior next year, and after that there's just no telling how many different kinds of crap will start flying at him. Rita wants him to go to college, a real college, not the community college that Tristan's partially considering since it wouldn't take him away from Lindsay. Maybe he could wait a year and start school with Lindsay—they'd have to apply to all the same places and both get in to at least one. The chances of that plan not working out are first-class. There's an absolutely splendid likelihood that life will tear them apart.

"You look cheerful," Lindsay says sarcastically when she shuts the closet again. "Come on, I want to ruin my dinner with candy, let's go."

Tristan shakes off his mood and follows her. If their time is short, then he can't waste a moment of it.

Missy's brief stay in the hospital for alcohol poisoning—an incident that she and the band now refer to as the 'Louisiana accident'—did at least curb her miserable little bender. No one had to sit her down for a serious talk about it either; when Missy wakes up with her stomach pumped and a swollen bag of fluids dripping into her arm, you can cancel the intervention, she gets it.

"Every worst day of my life is spent in a damn hospital," she told Darian as he handed her a bag of her things. She got out her hairbrush first because her braid had started turning into one huge, long gingery dread, then dug for some chapstick and a stick of gum—her lips were the friggin' Gobi, and the inside of her mouth tasted like the gunk that collects on the backside of her wisdom teeth when she doesn't brush well enough.

"Oh, not every hospital stay is bad," said a youngish blonde nurse who had just walked in with more fluids. "Think about the birth of your first child!"

"I was thinking about that," Missy told her venomously. "It really dicked up my summer vacation, to tell you the truth."

The nurse scowled and didn't linger any longer than necessary. Just because Missy makes a ton of mistakes doesn't mean she wants to be reminded of them.

"Being nasty to the nurses isn't going to make your stay any more pleasant, Missy," Aaron told her.

Missy didn't respond to that. In fact she's gotten pretty good at not even looking at Aaron since her discharge, mostly speaking to him indirectly when she absolutely must, through Darian. It isn't easy to do when they're in the same ten feet of space most of the time, but Missy's willing to make the effort. Aaron hasn't done a single thing in months that hasn't bugged the shit out of her; she's tired of even acknowledging he exists.

So the hospital took a few days. They missed the gigs in New Orleans, but they picked up their Christmas presents on their way through town after her release. Darian cracked open the box in the temperate post office parking lot and distributed their presents quietly. Nobody really had the Christmas spirit anymore.

Miriam got them each an item with the band's name engraved on it, The Homo Superiors in fancy script. Darian got a silver guitar pick on a charm bracelet. Aaron got a multi-tool folding knife with a holster he can clip onto his pants. Missy opened her gift last, and it made Darian go, "Hmm."

Missy's gift was a slim, slightly curved, ladylike flask.

She's been keeping it strapped to her inner thigh, empty. Missy's no quitter, she'll fill it up someday, and she wants to get comfortable wearing it. But just right now she's rather lost her taste for alcohol.

Best part about quitting for a while though: she still keeps getting drunk dials from Marley. After the initial serious call in the hospital, that is. That one was a downer.

"So are you really okay?" he asked her after exchanging a couple of stiff hellos.

"That's what I'm told. It was just an accident." The silence on the phone was louder than the person down the hall with some kind of back injury that hadn't stopped moaning to Jesus since she came in. "I'm sorry, Marley."

"You don't have to be sorry, you just have to not die."

Missy smiled. "For how long?"

"You can die as soon as I do, after that I promise not to complain."

"Well, how come you get to die first? What am I supposed to do without you?"

"Oh, don't worry, dude," Marley said, a glass of booze audible in the background. "I'll be with you in spirits."

He's a funny kid when he drinks—somewhere between two glasses and slurring there's a magic window of clever puns and bravery and honesty. That's why Missy refuses to stop drinking all together, which is what Aaron wants her to do. It's poison sure, but it's also wit, and sex, and solace, and fun.

"If anything happened to you, that would be totally heart rendering," Marley told her. "Or heart rending. Or actually, sort of both work I think. Heart rendering is good, I should write that down."

"I'll do it for you, babe, it sounds like a song title if I ever heard one."

"Ooh, you should write me a song!"

"I'm already writing you a song. I'm going to record it with Darian this year."

The New Orleans gigs were going to be their last for a while, so it wasn't the biggest tragedy to miss them. After Louisiana they headed back to Florida, where Darian had been ordering microphones and software, stockpiling for when they had an album's worth of original songs. Most of them will be his, but Missy will be represented too. Maybe this latest one will have a spot, if she can finish it on time. So far it's called "Substance." Half of Marley's weird drunken insights are already scribbled on the page of a notebook where Missy's been tinkering with them.

They got out of Louisiana. The first week in January drove them along the gulf coast all the way south to Sarasota. Marley begged her to come see him, but first of all they had work to do, and second of all she wanted to be able to drink with the boy, and she wasn't ready for that yet. Instead she kept Marley in her loop by calling him while she knew he was at work, and leaving snippets of his song as messages.

Darian does all the hard work of the recording. Aaron and Missy sing and play for maybe two hours a day, and Darian spends the rest of the time locked up tweaking every layer of noise. Aaron is trying to figure out the best way to build them a website. Missy mostly hangs out with Miriam, learning how to cook, which might come in handy if she ever finds herself living the kind of lifestyle that includes a kitchen.

"How would you like to garden?" Miriam asks her one day, after about two weeks of mostly passing the time baking.

"I don't think I've ever gardened," she says. Pulling summer weeds out of the driveway as a kid probably doesn't count.

Miriam beckons her with a thick-gloved hand, already in clothes much plainer than she normally wears, grass-stained gardening pants and a big goofy hat. She has a caddy full of little shovels and claws, the sort of implements Missy used to have in plastic for the sand box.

Miriam puts another big hat on Missy's head. "I don't have extra gloves, but I have plenty of hats—you never want to burn."

Miriam keeps the kind of flowers in her front garden that Missy's mother would have found hideously gaudy. They're Florida flowers growing against her pale pink stucco house: red and fuchsia hibiscus with huge, fuzzy stamen sticking out of them; heavily perfumed night-blooming jasmine growing up a trellis between her front windows so she can smell something sweet if it's ever cool enough to open them up; instead of a plain shrub, the giant pink-stained leaves of a Caladium breaks up the bed like bloodied green hearts; and all along are dotted tiny red and yellow Butterfly Weed flowers, which Miriam shows Missy how to pick and suckle. There's also a single blushing orchid growing out of a pot which hangs from a stand by the front door, and a couple of trees lining the side of the yard with pink groupings of flowers on them, called Starbursts.

Missy is quiet while Miriam takes her through each one. Miriam picks out weeds and Missy follows behind her, misting the beds with the water hose, smelling or tasting or touching whenever instructed to do so. She's especially quiet because no more than a minute into gardening it occurs to Missy that she should have brought flowers to her kid's grave. That would have been so, so much nicer than what she actually left there.

After no more than half an hour, Miriam stands up and takes off her gloves.

"That's about all this takes," she tells Missy.

"Cool. I'll go turn off the water."

"Thank you, dear."

Missy collects the hose as she goes. She wanted this job because it's very private on the side of the house, shady and still, crowded by Starbursts. She re-hangs the hose and turns off the water (reminding herself: righty tighty, lefty loosey), and then puts her back against the wall and starts to cry as quietly as possible.

This pain is just a part of her now. She'll probably spend the rest of her life occasionally sneaking away to let it burble up out of her, like water from an eternal spring.

She hears someone coming. She prays it's a neighbor, just some stranger she'll never have to see again, or at least Darian, who would leave her alone. This isn't the kind of crying she can stop, all she can picture is what never happened: visiting Natalie's grave with dignity and propping a little spray of flowers there, with petals as pink as she used to be, and a ribbon around them like the corsage she'll never get old enough to wear. This is why Missy doesn't like to even start crying, why it was so easy to hold off until she decided to let it go; once she gets started it's like trying to stop a pee, it's total bodily function override.

And so naturally it's Aaron who's found her, and who comes sidling up under the trees, his plain brown hair picking up ornaments of dead leaves and flower stalks as he goes.

Even with tears streaming down her face and her nose all snotted up, Missy's pretty sure she'll try to hit Aaron as soon as he opens his mouth.

Except that this time he doesn't open his mouth. For the first time in what feels like forever he doesn't have any canned advice or simplistic wisdom, he just puts his arm around her shoulders, and after a moment of silence, Missy sighs and rests her head on his chest.

Her crying runs down in its own time as they stand like this, and once it's over she turns the hose back on for a second to rinse her face. Then they file out of the dim little grove alley and into the clear sunlight without speaking a word about it.

And as long as they live, neither one of them ever will.

Marley started prepping to see Missy again as soon as she arrived back in Florida. She warned him that she might not be free to come see him for weeks or months, depending on how the recording was going, but the state of anticipation was sweet to him. Plus, he kind of hadn't been keeping the apartment clean lately—any reason seemed like a good one to spruce it up and keep it tidy.

There was a weird, persistent stickiness near the bedside table from all the spilled cups, some of which Marley remembers, most of which he suspects he does not. When he finally went to clean the toilet again, there were some hidden puke splatters under the rim that he scrubbed off. He found they were missing a few bowls, broken in attempts to drunk-eat. He thought about throwing away or even burning his stack of drunken notes, but instead tucked them into his copy of *On The Road*, since he doubts he'll ever read it again, and he doesn't want those notes popping out at him on accident.

He kept drinking even though Missy had stopped. Before, when he felt like one of Those People who have a Problem, he would remind himself that Missy still drank. Every time he called her she was as toasted as he was, without fail. And Missy wasn't a mess; Missy was way more capable than he was. Imagine being the kind of person who could live in constant motion, who could perform on a stage, who could hook up with strangers? Everybody wants to be like that, so it must be okay to be like Missy. Missy was living the dream.

His bookshelves were dusty, but he only ever cleaned those by blowing on them anyway, and with the apartment clean, and Marley learning when and how were the best ways to drink (switch from regular soda to diet, sneak a little water in there when he was past the point of tasting it anyway, try to start drinking long and slow after work so he isn't bombed in an instant, but instead comfortably buzzed and functional for the longest period of time possible), things were finally returning to normal.

It gets especially normal once Jesse starts sleeping upstairs again. Marley was sort of aware that Jesse didn't always sleep next to him when he passed out, but apparently it was a lot more significant than that. The couch in the office stayed permanently made up as a bed, which means even Kenny knew something was wrong before Marley did, and Kenny barely knows which side of noon the clock is pointing to if he can't see the sky.

"Don't think just because your friend's around you have to overdo it," Jesse says, plopping his pillow unceremoniously back onto the bed.

"You sound like a parent when you call her my friend."

"Whatever," Jesse says, dragging Marley onto the bed with him.

Marley allows himself to be kissed on for a while, before bringing up an idea.

"Hey, how about if Missy doesn't come here before my birthday, my present can be us driving up to see her?"

"Which day is your birthday again?" Jesse asks with a smirk, though he actually probably doesn't know. It's always just written on the calendar, why should he bother remembering?

"It's February twenty-sixth, and you're the worst."

"Of course," Jesse says. "It's your birthday, we can do whatever you want."

"Cool," Marley says as the kissing resumes, but the trip turns out not to be necessary.

A few days later Missy calls to say Aaron will be dropping her down in East Arrow that weekend since her voice is no longer necessary, and the boys are the ones who will tweak the songs.

"That means I'm all yours," she told him. "Let Jesse know he's headed back to the couch."

Marley is actually relieved. Not that he would have hated a short road trip, and it would have been like a second honeymoon of sorts for him and Jesse—they've always been their best on the road—but in all honesty the thought of leaving his books untended and having to deal with gas stations again makes his heart squirm. It's better this way.

Saturday, the third week in February, she comes in blazing and happy, and pulls Marley into a hug so fierce it makes Jesse leave the room.

"I'm so glad you're not dead," he tells her.

"Oh honey, all the boys say that to me." She steps back and beams around the room. "God you guys could use a couch, I forgot how much this place looks like a prison library."

They plunk down on the bed and are still telling stories half an hour later when Jesse returns with grocery bags on one arm and cases of soda in the other.

Marley and Missy go quiet as Jesse unpacks a jug of Marley's preferred rum and a bottle of vodka for Missy onto the table. He found a blonde guy's ID dropped in the shop, and even though the picture barely looks like him, Jesse lied to the dude when he came looking for it, so that he could do this chore for Marley sometimes. He gets carded way less anyway, he says. Jesse looks like a man already, and a man's allowed to drink without anyone asking him a bunch of damn fool questions.

"Thanks, Jesse," he calls across the room.

"Yeah, thanks," adds Missy. Otherwise it's just the sound of the grocery bags for a bit.

When finished Jesse says, "Aaron and I are going to get some dinner or something before he heads back. I'll be home later."

He leaves, but the silence he brought in with him hangs around.

"Thirsty?" Marley asks.

"*Parched*, let's do this already."

Marley gets glasses and juice out of the kitchen, but he doesn't try to be bartender. Surely Missy knows her own limits better than he does.

"You're okay to drink, right?" he double checks.

"I haven't had one since *the incident*, so that must be a long enough break to heal, don't you think?"

"Don't ask me, I haven't taken a break yet."

Marley pours his liquor in first. At some point over these past six months, the sound of it hitting the glass has become sweet music to him.

Missy lets out an appreciative (or at least Marley thinks) sigh.

"Hey, you'll like this," she says, hiking up her bright, lily-patterned dress to about mid-thigh, revealing a virginally white garter about two inches high, to which is strapped a small flask under crisscrossing elastic.

"Hot," he tells her with an earnestness that surprises him.

Missy snorts. "It's just a little four-ouncer, don't go falling in love," she says, popping it out and handing it to Marley. It's warm, engraved, and beautiful.

"What do you keep in it?" Marley asks, unscrewing the cap.

"Nothing yet." Missy takes it back and starts trying to fill it, but quickly realizes how tricky that's going to be. "Don't suppose you have a funnel?"

"Why in the hell would I have a funnel?"

"I know, right? I'll have to get one especially for this purpose, which I'm sure isn't alcoholic at all. What about a piece of paper you don't need back?"

Missy carefully maneuvers the liquor into her flask and re-secures it to her leg. She picks up her vodka and orange juice.

"Is there a place we can drink these where I won't feel like I'm on suicide watch? Like a room with a window or a roof or something?"

Marley, already half a drink in, beckons her with two fingers, and leads her outside without a word.

He's taking her to the modest junk yard out back. There's an old truck with the seat still in it (though the leather's pretty ragged). It's a nice place to sit and watch the sun set over the back fence.

It's a pretty one today. A pink and purple fade with yellow clouds decorating it like piping on a little girl's birthday cake. They've got no radio and it's already warm enough for the cab of this truck to feel stuffy, even without its doors, but Missy kicks off her shoes and lays her legs out on the dash, and Marley takes off his over-shirt, and they just mellow like that for a spell.

Halfway through her drink, Missy refills from her flask.

"You want a hit of this?" she asks.

"Just pour some in here," Marley says, extending the dregs of his drink.

"That's gonna taste like ass," Missy warns him.

"I know, it doesn't matter."

Missy raises her eyebrows and pours some in. It goes across Marley's tongue like peroxide, but he doesn't even flinch.

"You know you don't have to impress me right? Like, it's a long life, you should really pace yourself with the way you drink."

"I know *you're* not going to start in on me about it. I just got Jesse to lay off, I figured I wouldn't have to explain it to you."

Missy makes a face like she's about to choose her words very carefully.

"I'm only an occasional drinker, you know. I just happen to've had a lot of occasions recently. Most of the time I only drink when we've got shows and the booze is comped for the band. I was just going through a rough spot with, you know, the kid dying and everything."

"So why do you drink then? Are you trying to be happy or sad?"

"It depends," Missy says, looking out at the sky and stroking her finger along the rim of her glass. "Usually I drink because it's easier to sing and be social. But then just now I was using it to... I guess feel sad, like you said. Why do you do it? Do you know yet?"

"Oh yeah," Marley says, nodding. It's the way it makes the jellied quiver of constant apprehension in his chest go away, and when that goes away, Marley feels like he finally has access to his whole life. Roads, relationships, the rolling spread of a wide world that's his to interact with if only he has a little liquid courage. "I drink to feel right. It makes me feel like I think I'm supposed to feel." It's the way he deserves to feel, to be totally honest; everyone else comes to it so much easier, but it belongs to Marley as well.

"I mean," Missy says with a plaintive look, "be careful with that kind of attitude, that's how people get a problem with booze. Just don't become an alcoholic, okay?"

"It's probably too late for that already," he says after a beat. He looks out from under his hair at Missy, wary of her reaction. He's been thinking it for weeks, for months, since the very beginning. The more regular people explained what drinking does to them, the more evidence he had that he was one of Those Other People, the ones who can't seem to help themselves. This substance does something special for Marley, something different than what it does for most everyone else.

"If you really believe that, then just stop right now," Missy tells him, her eyes a little wider, her buzz probably gone.

"I'm not going to," he tells her.

Another silence gathers around them. The sky is deepening into a rich navy and the golden clouds are turning gray.

Maybe she'll roll her eyes. Maybe she's thinking, *Here's someone who thinks he's so special and damaged or whatever*, when she's the one all the really bad things have happened to. It's at last too dark to read her reaction.

Even with the alcohol in his system Marley is starting to feel the hot, crawling sensation of shame and anxiety, but it ends when Missy reaches across the murky space between them, and takes his hand. Their fingers lace, and she brings his hand to her mouth, to kiss the back of it.

The sun disappears.

"Come on, let's get the hell out of the dark," Missy says.

Marley is happy to follow her; to get out of the dark is all he's ever really wanted.